About the author

John Latham has won awards both as a scientist and a poet. Born near Liverpool in 1937, he studied at London University and was chair of the University of Manchester's Physics Department (UMIST) between 1978 and 1988, before moving partially to the US, where he is presently a Senior Research Fellow at the National Centre for Atmospheric Research in Colorado. His literary work includes several plays and stories broadcast on BBC Radio 4, and his collections of poetry are *Unpacking Mr Jones, From the Other Side of the Street, All Clear* and *The Unbearable Weight of Mercury* (all published by Peterloo Poets). His fifth collection, *Sailor Boy*, is expected to appear next year. This is his first novel.

ditch-crawl

JOHN LATHAM

First published in Great Britain in 2004 by Comma Press
4th Floor, Alliance House, 30 Cross Street, Manchester M2 7AQ
www.commapress.co.uk
Distributed by Carcanet Press
www.carcanet.co.uk

A CIP catalogue record of this book is available from the British Library

ISBN 1 85754 768 3
Comma Press gratefully acknowledges assistance from the Arts Council of
England North West, and the Regional Arts Lottery Programme.

Set by XL Publishing Services, Tiverton
Printed and bound in England by SRP Ltd, Exeter

*For Ruth Mary and John William of
Hillside Road*

one

In the darkest corridor, amid a maze of boxes, the lids that would never quite fit slide away.

And out they come, blinking, stumbling, nervous, cursing into the shadowed light, those occupants of the boxes who could not be pigeon-holed, a miscellany of citizens whose only common bond is that they dwell in deep recesses in the unsorted sub-structure of me, a region no-one has yet found his way out of, a region I must bite my lip to enter – my blood-blister the next day as ripe as Will Tarporley's – but it is always worth the trip. And now, on this special day, they spill or clamber from the boxes onto the granite flagstones of the thirteenth corridor, the drums begin to roll, the cobwebbed ceiling is festooned with coloured bladders, the candles gutter but never quite go out, the gathering commences, under the horn-rimmed whiplash of ancient Nellie Preece, who's painted the great wart wobbling on her chin phosphorescent pink. I watch it fade and swell, as she welcomes everyone, her thin-lipped smile more frightening than her customary fury.

Some boxes open easily, others burst apart, some flex and shake but do not open. Most hold a single occupant, a few yield two or three. All seem bewildered, unsure of where they are. They mill around each other, uncertainly, or sit on boxes, taking stock. Some wander down the corridor in search of solitude, a few engage in desultory chat, and in some I sense a growing puzzlement.

I spy on the arrivals from behind my velvet curtains, which separate a small chamber from the corridor. I'm not ready for them yet. It will take great effort, after all these years, to join them. I've always preferred the role of observer or voyeur to that of participant.

My gaze moves steadily from person to person, identifying each one. I marvel at how little most of them have changed:

Mrs Campion, even larger than she was in life, her ancient parrot wading through her hair, smelling like an oven whose residues are black with camomile and cinnamon, plucking on the threads of wool with which her harp is strung, its silent music soaring.

Mr Campion, unpeeled from the steam-roller that squashed him flat, unsteady on his feet, nodding almost to the ground each time Nellie pours him champagne. He spots his wife, raises his glass to her.

Alex, naked except for bullrush kneepads and a peacock feather in her tangled hair, crawling patiently round scattered objects in a shady region of the corridor, her face uplifted, the mouth that has coaxed and scolded every part of me open to the harp-notes, drinking each one in, assuaging for a while the thirst that keeps her with me in the ditchways, and will not let her rest or stop her dreaming. She knows she would find comfort in the feather lining of Mrs Campion's bosom, but she fears she'd lose her way in the old lady's mists of lavender.

Lionel, on a stretcher straddling two boxes, still burning peacefully. No smell of frizzling hair or scorching flesh, just a coil of scarlet smoke that spins and thins around a barley-sugar pole that Mr Campion hangs on to, to save himself from toppling over.

Someone whose face is hidden behind a tent of hair is rocking my mother in arms she never knew, rocking her until smiles come, until she sails, until she sheds the skins of eighty-two years, they're incinerated in the flames of Lionel's burning, and she's pink and new – big rooms with high ceilings do not frighten her. She can at last be naughty.

My father is a boy riding a red tricycle with yellow seat. It is old and somewhat battered but he's very proud of it, and likes most of all to ring its silver bell as he weaves between boxes strewn along the corridor. He has a bandage round his leg, tied in a bow. I am his father, and each time he falls off, I put him on my knee and cuddle him. He keeps falling off on purpose.

Mr Maddock, grunting as he lifts the last fork-full of compost from his steaming pile, sitting down heavily on a crate, taking out his lunch from a chipped cream-coloured tin: his sandwiches thick, smelling powerfully of cheese, as he and Mr Trolley sit companionably munching.

A little girl with yellow ribbons sits demurely on a box nearby, fingers dangling into a bowl, making arches and caverns through which tadpoles glide. She has no face, just a pale oval, yet I know she's Wendy Eva, who was in my class at school, but was never there because she was ill, her name called out by Miss Hutton each morning and afternoon, along with all the others in the register, each time greeted with silence until, three weeks into term, Old Shelley, the headmaster, announced in assembly that she'd died and gone to Heaven, we all sang *Jesus Loves Me*, Shelley thrashed Ernest Moon for not knowing the words and Josie Whitworth wet her pants because she didn't know them either, a pool steaming slowly at her feet. Johnnie Greenway knelt to dip his finger in, pretended to suck it, pulling diabolical faces. Shelley leapt from the piano, cuffed Ernest round the head for laughing.

**

My mother's hat is green, floppy, though at the same time stiff. A corrugated pancake perched above her auburn hair.

I know it's auburn because they said it was, because my memory doesn't reject the idea, because any other colour I try seems false.

But all I remember is the hat and her smile, geometrically joined, linked by elastic, the hat always higher than the smile, the green twisted one way if the lipstick curled the other, the distance between them always changing. Sometimes the lips push forwards and the hat retreats, a pallid pimple on the edge of vision. Sometimes the smile is a pale ghost below an emerald sky.

They're both behind thick glass at the far end of a tunnel which is my only route to home. The glass blocking my end is impervious to pressure, dulled by the blunt moisture of my nose. A tapered space full of denial.

I want her. I want to curl into her, dissolve into her warmth. I want to be forgotten, assimilated. I want cushions on all sides of me. I want the sound of her voice – the words don't matter at all.

It's not just a visual blockade. I'm cut off from all those sounds and smells that make me real. Poker raking ash, cup chattering in its saucer, crackle of bacon wafting up the stairs; softening my mouth.

What use is her smile if all it does is tease me, promise me what it can no longer deliver? What use are her lips if they can't brush against my skin, if I can't taste them before I sink to sleep?

It's not your fault, Mummy, but I hate you. You've let me down. You've always saved me, from falling and bad dreams. But now you're out of earshot, however hard I scream.

It's your fault, Mummy. Scarlet fever, that's why they've brought me here. Scarlet fever from those strawberries you gave me, my first ever strawberries, just before the ambulance came.

So I won't come to the tunnel to see you all distorted, and not touch. I don't listen to Nurse Cora's coaxing, I struggle when she tries to carry me.

I've come to the tunnel, but I won't smile at you. I won't wave back as your fingers flutter below your nodding hat. See, I stick my tongue out at you. I make the most horrific face since time began. I drool my hatred down the glass. Why don't you wince, pull back? Why do you keep on smiling, as if you'll never go away?

Isolation hospital, that's what they say. *Isolation*. A white word. Not whitewashed – there's no texture – but the white that has no shadows, can't be touched.

I'm frightened of those white words, like isolation, which pluck me out of warmth, drop me, naked, on a frozen lake. *Desolation* is another one, *lonely, polio*. They all have O's the shape of howls, the shape of my mouth at the entrance to the tunnel at the other end of which, beyond thick glass, your green felt hat is weeping.

**

In this deepest region of a long-neglected ditch I find a spot where the mud has three colours. It gives me an idea: I'll make a jug for fellow-travellers to drink from.

The brown slithers easily through my fingers,

splashes as it plops onto my foot. It is too thin for my purpose. The green, on the other hand, which is warm, as if some exothermic reaction is going on inside it, is too thick.

The grey is perfect, with the consistency of dough my mother used to knead. I feel happy as I squeeze and pummel it, press it flat between two old boards, knuckle it to shape, mould a florid handle, use two fingers to depress part of the rim for pouring. I inspect it from all angles, admire its imperfections, dismember it for the simple pleasure of starting again.

Finally, after the fourth version, no better or worse than its predecessors, though somewhat more ornate, I set it on the grass in a pool of sunlight. I press my nose to it, inhale an aroma of prehistoric ovens.

**

Not guilty, rules Mr Maddock.

He thumps his gavel onto the bench in front of him, on which Miss Capper, passing through a few minutes earlier, has left a paper bag containing the set of best false teeth she shares with Mrs Bickerstaff, her sister, thinking they're the humbugs she's bought specially from Alick's, a gift to Mr Maddock who, seventy years ago, winked at her from the boys' side of the room, in scripture, since when she's been trying to pluck up the courage to respond.

The teeth crack, splinter, fly in all directions. One fragment swoops, glinting, into the flames licking round Lionel's forehead, causing Miss Atkins to see an arrow from God, a sign from the Almighty that she would not be damned for looking at the burning man's nakedness, and so she does, secretly biting her dry old lips as she watches the play of dancing light around his testicles.

Another fragment lands on Uncle Harry's knee. He lifts it up, inspects it, looks perturbed.

I'm falling to bloody pieces, he grunts.

He pushes it swiftly into his mouth, moving it around with his thumb until he finds a cavity into which it seems to fit.

A third fragment pings against an unplucked string of Mrs Campion's harp, producing a sound that only Ernest and Wendy Eva can hear, its pitch precisely that of the sorrow in Wendy's missing eyes, causing tears to well out of her forehead, and Ernest to remember his father's shoulders more clearly than ever before.

A fourth piece trips the mechanism controlling the scroll that is the flattened Mr Campion, causing him to wind up suddenly and Miss Atkins, distracted for a second from the burning man, to wonder who it is who's been called so peremptorily into the presence of the Lord.

I appeal against the verdigris, screams Aunt Lil.

Appeal sustained, thunders Shelley, who's taken Mr Maddock's chair.

He turns to Ernest, who's trying to will Wendy to stop crying.

I sentence you to be stitched inside the blood-blister on Will Tarporley's lip.

But I won't be able to see Germany, wails Ernest.

I'll come with you, I mouth to him.

No-one else hears me, but he looks pleased.

**

Not far from Wendy, in the lilac fragrance of Lionel's gentle burning, my Uncle Harry and Professor Abdul Alam are sitting cross-legged on a square of tattered carpet, playing chess by the light of an oil-lamp hanging from a chain. They have a regular board but no chess pieces, instead of which they're using eggs, which are all identical, so the players need to remember not only which eggs correspond to which pieces, but also whose are whose.

Professor Alam, who is a man of peace, and would prefer to lose this game rather than win, is intrigued by this challenge to his memory, and has devised a matrix of partial differential equations which he solves in his head to keep tabs on all the pieces. His mind is filled with mathematics, which he addresses without conscious thought. He is perfectly content, smiling sweetly at my mother who has just spilled tea on the bishop he's moved to king's knight 4.

Uncle Harry, eighty-eight, house-painter all his life, has not played chess before, and doesn't know the rules. He finds it easy, just moving an egg from one place on the board to another, occasionally removing one and stacking it with those already by his knee. He confides to Professor Alam that the game is rather like sorting out his old brushes before he starts on a new job.

Uncle Harry likes this gentle brown-skinned man he's playing with. No-one has told him that the professor is a Nobel Laureate, and if they had he would not have understood. All the sums that mattered could be done on the fingers of one hand, counting aloud if they were hard. He's never before met anyone with a dark skin, and he wonders if a white man would ever take so long to move an egg.

Suddenly Hitler goose-steps from behind a pile of boxes, and halts. Everything about him is polished – his boots, his leggings, the swastika on his chest, his moustache, his pallid face, the saliva that spurts out whenever he screams orders. He stands in the centre of the corridor, swishing his cane, waiting for silence, obeisance. But nothing changes, the harp music plays on, only my mother notices him, pours him a cup of tea, walks towards him smiling, offers it.

D'you take sugar, Mr Hitler?

His cane swipes it from her hand. It shatters on the stone flags.

Oh dear, never mind.

She kneels, picks up the shards, stows them in her apron, swabs the floor. A few spots of tea have landed on his boot. She polishes it until it's as flawless as before. He lifts his foot, inspects the boot, kicks her in the throat.

Her head turns a half-circle, stays locked in its new position. She struggles to her feet, walks backwards to the teapot, pours him another cup, backs towards him, smiles up into his face. Her voice is a pale croak.

D'you take sugar, Mr Hitler?

He lifts his foot to kick her, but something in her face has shamed or frightened him. He lowers his foot, accepts the tea, mutters his thanks inaudibly, hangs his head.

That's how it was, isn't it, Mum, when I was little, you were you, I was Hitler sometimes, I needed to explode, smash things with my stick, needed to vent that anger boiling inside me, a healthy need, so I could breath out again, slow down, feel calm.

But you wouldn't let me. You took me on your knee, folded me in; into your breasts, your cotton frock, the tent of auburn hair that spilled down over me, sealing all the exits, imprisoning my rage, so that it seethed and festered, lost its focus, simmered, bided its time, turned slowly rancid.

**

Time and space are more entangled here in the ditch, perhaps because there's no sky, no views into the distance. You can measure them both in heartbeats; it would be wrong to carry a watch. This world is always changing, every part of it – the foliage I crawl through, mud's coolness on my knees, shadows cast by filaments of sunshine that break through the canopy, the colours of my sleeping dreams, the fragrance of my waking ones. Simplistic to think of journeys in terms of miles or days. They're passages towards the future, and when anything is registered it belongs already to the past.

So I don't care how long or far I've been travelling when I round a bend and see a grassy knoll, overhung with willow, on the edge of the ditch where its depth is low, so that the cow sleeping at its centre is lying in part of my new world.

I didn't know cows could smile, but this one is definitely smiling in its sleep: a smile of reconciliation more than happiness.

She senses my presence, inches to the side to give me space to lie next to her. As soon as I do so, nuzzle her aroma, I relax to the slow thump of her heart and fall asleep.

My dreams are brown. Elinor is in them, but she's running away, barefoot, skirts hitched up, trying to outdistance the wings that cruise behind her, their warm feathers ready to descend.

The cow is grazing when I wake, the leaves of the willow shimmering with trapped sunlight.

**

For the first time since we've returned from Easter camp, it isn't raining. We are climbing to the top of the hill to look for Germany. Miss Ryder told us, in

Geography, that when it rains, dust in the air that stops us seeing far is washed away. And Johnnie says there's been so much rain this week we can look right round the world from the edge of Windy Rock. In particular, we can see Germany, and Hitler. Johnnie fishes from his pocket his old fob watch on a silver chain, that once belonged to Marco Polo. He snaps it open. We peer down at its blank face. He rotates it slowly until his hand quivers and the motion stops.

Magnetic North, he declares dramatically.

He swings round, points his finger straight above the cows we can see below us, grazing on the banks of the canal.

Germany, he announces.

Ernest shivers with excitement.

We stand on tiptoes, straining. Johnnie doubts if we'll see it immediately but if we concentrate, our gaze will intensify and eventually drill the air like searchlights. Then we should see Hitler.

I don't really believe him. And when he says curly-haired people see best, and I look again at those tight black whorls I always want to stroke, I'm sure he's making it up. But I don't mind. It is a new game: and Dirk, Legger and Pardy are happy to accept it, too. As for Ernest, he believes completely, as always.

He's on one knee, concentrating fiercely, though his gaze is slightly angled to the cows. Johnnie moves to him, adjusts his shoulders roughly.

That's not the right direction, you idiot!

Ernest smiles apologetically, but turns back to his original position. He speaks gently but obstinately:

I don't want to see Hitler. I want to see my dad. He's in Germany too, but he's not with Hitler. He's been away soldiering for six years now, and I can't remember all his face.

Everyone else, children and adults, including Mrs

Moon, is certain that her husband is dead, but Ernest is convinced he'll come home.

Johnnie moves away from him, stares above the cows. Ernest resumes his concentration.

There's Hitler! shouts Johnnie, pointing.

We stare along the line of his arm.

He's on a horse. Can you see him? A white horse dangling from a barrage balloon!

Yes! shouts Dirk. *I can see his moustache.*

He's Heil Hitlering, I yell.

I can see his crucifix! shouts Legger.

His swastika, you fool! scoffs Johnnie.

No, says Legger, firmly. *His crucifix.*

We can see him clearly now, Himmler and Goebbels, too, in the square far below him, goose-stepping, strutting, clicking their heels. But after a while they just look silly. The game is beginning to pall.

Ernest is oblivious, motionless, staring hard above the canal. Johnnie goes up to him, rests his hand gently on his shoulder.

Can you see your dad, yet?

Ernest shakes his head.

That's because your hair's not curly! Keep trying. I'm sure you'll see him before long.

Ernest smiles and keeps on staring.

It starts to spot with rain, large slow drops, so Johnnie suggests we shelter in Tom Thumb's Hole.

I'm staying here, says Ernest. *I think I'll see him soon.*

You mustn't move, says Johnnie.

He winks at us.

You'll spoil it if you move. Don't even blink!

Ernest smiles and tries to nod without moving his head. We leave him kneeling and hurry away. The rain is coming down hard.

It becomes torrential just as we climb into the

cave. Raindrops bombard the leaves of the oak-tree at the entrance. Its branches are shaking, though I can't feel any wind. Johnnie angles a flat rock so that drops splash from it into the cave. Some reach us even at the back. Dirk catches one in his mouth. The rain lessens, becomes steadier. The roar of the leaves subsides into a busy hiss. We start scratching initials in the sandstone with broken glass.

The rain clears after a while. We clamber down the rock-face, meander up the short stretch of path to Windy Rock. Ernest, utterly sodden, hair plastered to his forehead, hasn't moved. He is concentrating so fiercely he doesn't hear us, and jumps when Johnnie grips his shoulder.

Have you seen him yet?

Ernest shakes his head, miserably.

Let me try, says Johnnie.

He kneels beside Ernest, stares hard in the same direction, his hand shielding his eyes from the sun, which has reappeared. He scans left and right, slowly. For a minute or two there is no sound and scarcely any motion – just the scanning, and occasional drops falling from trees alongside Windy Rock.

Suddenly Johnnie stiffens.

I can see him now. Can you?

He turns eagerly to Ernest, whose face lights up. He strains even harder, blinks and slowly shakes his head.

Here! snaps Johnnie. *Look!*

He crouches behind Ernest, takes his arm and points it far over the water.

You must see him now! He's ever so plain!

Ernest, trembling, stares along the line of Johnnie's arm. As the seconds tick away, his joy turns to uncertainty, then to wretchedness. He swallows, but can't trust himself to speak.

Keep trying! urges Johnnie. *It's hard because your hair's straight.*

How do you know it's my dad?

Johnnie stays quiet for a moment, then speaks without taking his eyes off the horizon.

Is he tall? he asks, his stretched finger quivering.

Yes! cries Ernest, desperately trying to follow Johnnie's gaze.

Is he handsome?

Yes!

I remember the awkward-looking man in the photograph Ernest showed me. Ernest's eyes are shining.

Has he got a silver medal on his uniform?

Yes! Yes!

Ernest is alight, drooling a little onto Johnnie's sleeve.

It's my dad! He's there! Show me!

He clutches Johnnie's arm, as though it is connected by a thread to his father, and he's trying to draw him in, to land him.

Johnnie raises his voice.

He's wearing a gas mask. He's by a tree. There's a silver sword...

He hesitates. Ernest swells with pride.

There's a silver sword. Right through his heart!

As he speaks the final word Johnnie nudges Ernest, topples him off the edge of Windy Rock. We rush to watch. He tumbles over and over in the wet bracken, finishing sprawled, head lower than his legs, which are badly scratched. He lies without moving. We laugh and stamp, but I can tell from the way Dirk's eyes are following mine that he's uneasy, too.

Slowly Ernest gathers himself together. He clambers to his feet, through the bracken, up the rock. His face is sad, not angry. He ignores the rest of us, walks up to Johnnie, looks into his face. Johnnie shifts his eyes away.

You're a fidget, Johnnie, he says quietly.

He turns away, starts to descend the track for home. Legger runs after him and catches him up. We watch them disappear.

I thought he was going to thump you, says Dirk.

Pah! retorts Johnnie. *As if he dare!*

He pauses.

How about a game of outlaws?

I'm going home, says Dirk.

So am I, says Pardy.

Johnnie turns to me, holds me in his gaze. He smiles, mockingly.

C'mon then, Zack.

I'd not realised quite how small he is.

I shake my head.

The three of us troop off, leaving Johnnie on the rock.

**

I take off my kneepads, don my rush-weave sandals, replace the stub of candle with a full-length one, grasp the upper rung of the rope ladder, swing my body through the hatch, lower it back into place, and stand, swirling slowly round, as much at the summit of a world as someone on top of Everest.

I can't tell how far the ladder stretches below me, but I suspect that if I dropped a stone I'd never hear it land.

I have a choice to make. Keep my candle lit and see what a camera might see; blow it out and see what a camera could not. I decide to keep it lit for the first part of my descent. It seems right to move gradually into this new experience, insinuate myself into this atmosphere, rather than plunge in cold.

The throbbing, though still quiet, is more pronounced, the beating of a drum from far below, each roll echoing round the cavern, reverberating, climbing up its sides, the sound slipping away before the next one comes, the interval of silence filled less with absence than anticipation.

Thoom, thoom, thoom: the deep slow heartbeat of the world.

**

Do it now, express it while your stomach's clamouring for food, searching to assuage that emptiness so present for the last few months. Emptiness surrounded by an arch of aching, dull but inflamed even so.

Express it. Yes, shit into the toilet bowl a coil of healthy, early morning turds, orange brown with a large yellow seed I can't place. One turd is broken in two places, but all remain quite firm as I spoon them in turn into the yoghurt carton, add a little tainted water from the bowl. Over to the kitchen sink, run steamingly hot water until the turds are covered, stab them with the spoon until the soup, though lumpy, has no major structure, gives off an aroma which I find quite pleasant. Wash the spoon, put the lid on the carton, seal it inside a plastic bag, place it on the window-sill outside in the sun with the vague idea that the heat will add richness to the smell.

I've not found my full anger yet. There's some, cold rage and desperation too, but most of all I feel a sadness to which my stomach-ache, now building, testifies.

I've been abandoned, unfeelingly and with contempt. I've been shat on and I want to shit on you. I love you. I want you and I can't have you. I know you're right – it couldn't work – yet I've only to close my eyes, reach out into my fantasy, and you're in my arms again. It's early morning, I've been watching you in sleep, I've been patient and impatient. You sigh, raise an arm up to the sky, hold it, fingers flexing, lower it slowly, curl it round me.

That was so lovely. I'm as ready for it now as ever, but you won't share it with me any more.

So I'm ripening this carton of liquid shit, my shit, substance my body has discarded, flushed out of me just as you've flushed me away, and somehow I'm going to feed it back to you. You'll eat my shit, though you won't know you're doing so. You punched me in the groin, watched without compassion as I writhed. I won't punch you. I perhaps won't ever know what effect my hatred had on you. Possibly there'll be none at all, and if not it won't matter, I'll still know I poured shit into your shoes, behind your fridge, underneath one of your rugs. So I'll be able to hate myself, hate myself instead of you, which is better because I'll be able to feel my hatred, fist its mass around my stomach: whereas I can't grasp your contempt, or worse your indifference.

But the idea that you might sense it makes me smile. The effect on you, I think, will be subtle, on the margin of detection, something slightly out of kilter, a heaviness in the air, a suggestion of a headache, but too diffuse and subdued to be clearly registered. No major harm, just a few hours slightly sullied.

But for me, in the last analysis, it will be awful. Self-disgust, stripping away of self-respect, and what's worse, perhaps, the possibility that I'll keep doing this, smiling the smile that is the shape of wretchedness, doing it until some cataclysm occurs. Digging deeper into abomination: becoming dangerous.

**

two

Less than a moon-cycle since I started ditch-crawling, yet I feel I've been doing it all my life.

The equipment's quite heavy, but more comfortable than it looks. Wellies, with a clever waterproof seal onto the oilskin suit, a helmet with large goggles and a variable intensity lamp fastened on top, pliable gloves built into the suit and – most important of all – thick knee-pads which in the Middle Ages were made of matted straw, but are now something like canvas stuffed with foam.

But though it's comfortable, I usually prefer to be without most of the equipment, wearing just the kneepads, like in the old days.

Ditch-crawling has no rules, just aesthetic principles.

The most important one is to travel lightly, leaving no legacies. If you need to move a coil of briar or rusty barbed wire in order to crawl through, note its position, the tension it is storing, and restore it to exactly how it was. If your passage causes leaves floating on a puddle to sink, stretch up into the grasses on the borders of the ditch to find replacements.

Try to make no sound at all. It amazes me how, with that in mind, I've learned so swiftly how to gauge my pace and pressure to extinguish sucking noises as my palms and knees rise out of the mud. I'm even able to sponge out the pounding of my heart. Only then, with my own sounds expunged, can I hear the subtle traffic of the ditch: the bubblings, chitterings, chuckles, gasps, groans, farts, slow drownings, surfacings. If I tape-recorded these sounds, all I'd hear is silence. But here in the ditch I'm overwhelmed by them.

It's best, I think, to meet no-one at all. Ditch-crawling is true communion, but not with other people. If you do meet someone coming the other way, try to flow through each other without touching, like ripples from a pair of stones tossed into a pond. Though at times it will feel good to linger.

I'd never have guessed that there are more than seventeen hundred miles of roadside ditch in Shropshire, and that most of them are over three hundred years old.

I find it impossible to predict how people will react when they first go ditch-crawling. Some will be bored or fulfilled after ten minutes, others will crawl throughout the night or season. When I started I was feeling sceptical, imagining that ten minutes would probably be my limit. I couldn't have been more wrong, and now I doubt if I'll ever be able to leave the ditches.

The one I've just been exploring is deep and narrow, scarcely wider than my body, shoulder-high if I stand up. It is long-neglected, and in many places grasses, brambles and rushes have grown across the gap at the top, or left only an occasional sliver of sky. I'm in a tunnel located in some nether region between the surface of the earth and underground.

If I'd have been asked to guess the colour of the light here in the ditch I'd have said green or possibly violet, but in fact it's red, from the soil I suppose, a kind of mellow rustiness that makes the space rich, cavernous and welcoming. It feels primitive, ageless. If words are spoken here they'll be in a language long-forgotten.

I've often been in places where I've felt overwhelmed by the abundance of life – at football matches, in the depths of a jungle in Costa Rica, sitting on a pine-stump in Colorado by a seething ant-hill bigger than an ox. I've also been in places pervaded by aridity or death – a petrified forest in Arizona, Pompeii, or the lunescapes of several mountain-tops. But I've never been anywhere where the senses of growth and decay are simultaneously so strongly present. Not just present either, but intertwined, almost indistinguishable.

When I started crawling, discovered the magic of the ditch, its primeval qualities, I half-expected to make some spectacular discoveries – buried treasure, a dead tramp, a hand-carved canoe, birds' nests in the spokes of an old wheel. And it's true that some things I find are amazing. But what has struck me most strongly is the extraordinary nature of ordinary things. In part, I think, that comes out of being in a tunnel with little direct illumination, just a diffuse light that makes its way to me by dodging round, squeezing through or bouncing off roots of trees or bracken, trailing vines and branches, long-abandoned buckets, lichen-covered stones, rotted boots and fence-posts, cobwebs so thick and strong a cat could trampoline on them; light that has been filtered, nibbled, diced and sliced; so sieved, worked over that though it's often clear enough to read by, it casts no shadows, permits no reflections, not even when I peer down into puddles. This absence of light and shade gives all objects an aura – not a halo, not external to it, but a kind of glow from within, scarlet in the ruby light.

I've been there before, I know I have, but it

wasn't in this lifetime. It was long ago, when the Earth's air was fresh, when the stratosphere was filled with ash from great volcanoes, when rocks were soft enough to crumble in one's fist, red enough to blend into the sunsets.

The ditch is a legacy of primal times, a link with our origins, our innocence.

I'm learning that the deep earth sings. Or maybe hums is a better word. I'll crawl quietly for a while, taking in the little businesses I mentioned before, and then halt, remove my helmet, cradle my head on my arm and press my ear to the soil where the side of the ditch meets the bottom.

I hear nothing at first, except once light breathing when some creature slithers through my hair and down my neck. But after a few minutes of concentrating hard and making my heart slow down, I hear a deep tone, continuous but with slowly varying pitch. A kind of dirge, yet it's not sad music. I sense harmony, reconciliation, forgiveness, and I feel that the song is at the same time both for the whole world and for me: an emanation from ditches everywhere, a distillation of everything that has happened under the cover of the earth.

**

Clickety clack, clickety clack, clickety clack.

But for some reason, this afternoon, the train-wheels don't signify the bleeding away of time, but rather the opposite – some kind of obstinate affirmation of the continuance of life. Today I can hear it, without old Tewkesbury around.

Just the two of us in the carriage. First time ever. As the months have passed by, I've almost stopped noticing her, tucked into a corner, scribbling, never looking up, while that buffoon maunders on and I feign interest. How does she manage to evade him?

Hard to put an age to her. Late twenties, perhaps, early thirties. A fine smile, though I've only seen it once, when those kids waved to us from the viaduct. I imagine her voice to be soft, but with an edge if she feels invaded. Self-reliant, probably lives by herself, likes silences. She looks good in that white blouse. Does she usually wear white?

Scribbling's the wrong word. True, her pen's always raised, but it rarely comes down onto the page. It's as if she's composing something. She looks like a musician. If I had to guess an instrument it'd be the cello.

Whatever she's creating, she's absorbed in it. I'm sure she's not noticed me squinting at her from time to time.

It's a good silence. I don't want to break it. In fact, I think I'll write, too. To Elinor.

Clickety clack, my notepaper. *Clickety clack*, my pencil.

**

Elinor is sitting in the bay window, gazing down into the valley, where night has reduced the village to a scattering of rectangles, yellow and orange, and an amorphous patch of grey stamped on the blackness of the wood. She doesn't turn as I walk up to her, touch her lightly on the shoulder.

I'd like it if you'd read this.

I hold a sheet of paper in front of her. She doesn't take it.

What is it?

It's a poem. It says what I feel better than I've been able to explain to you. Please.

She takes it from me, places it on the cushion beside her.

I'd be grateful if you'd read it now.

She grimaces, holds it up to the light. I can sense her tension as I squint over her shoulder to read it myself. She shrugs me away. I don't mind. She wants to focus on it, to understand why I've been so erratic. When she finds in it no anger or reproach, just bewilderment, she'll open to me again, and this time I'll be more sensitive. We both will.

She puts it down, looks out across the valley again.

I picture her hand sneaking across the cushions towards mine. I imagine its touch, tentative at first, growing stronger.

Well. What d'you think?

Her hand starts the journey, meets the poem, lifts it onto her lap. She grasps it tightly as her other hand rips it down the middle. She places the two pieces neatly together, tears them in the perpendicular direction. She flicks the pieces away, swivels, sweeps past me, stalks into the bedroom, shuts the door.

I have a violent urge to race in there after her, confront her, but I know that what little might be left of her goodwill towards our marriage couldn't stand another invasion of that kind.

I kneel on the floor, pick up the torn paper, notice that the word *journey* is torn in half. I sit in the bay window. In the valley a yellow light flicks on then off, winking at me with a touch of mockery.

I tell myself to keep calm, think things out slowly, but anger keeps interrupting my thoughts. I try to breathe calmly to suppress the pounding of my heart. I decide to sleep the night in the bay, and stretch out with a cushion for my pillow. The starlit sky is enormous, beautiful and bleak.

When I wake I'm shivering and my neck is stiff. I pad quietly to the bedroom, undress in the dark, slip in beside her. She wriggles her buttocks into my stomach. I curl around her warmth, feel hopeful and loving. Bodies are much better indicators of the truth than words. From now onwards I'll not write poems for her, I'll not talk to her about our stresses and strains. We'll communicate, express our love by touch.

I lower my hand gently onto her shoulder. She shakes it off violently, lunges so far away that not only are we not touching, but I can't feel her heat or hear her breathing.

I must escape from this humiliation, this insanity.

**

D'you feel lonely?

Of course I do, whoever has floated this question to me. Though it feels less like a question than a statement from someone who knows me. How can it be she, the silent woman, the scribbler in the corner of the carriage?

That's a strange question.

I don't think so. The man you always talk to isn't here this afternoon. It's as simple as that.

I doubt if I've ever felt lonelier than when I was chatting with old Tewkesbury.

What d'you mean?

For me being lonely is feeling so out of place I can't recognise myself.

So why do you talk to him?

Because he's chronically lonely, and no-one else bothers with him.

Then you must despise me for ignoring him, getting on with my poetry.

On the contrary. I admire you for having the

courage of your convictions. You see, I don't do him any good. He knows I'm not interested. I know he knows. It's all a charade.

She smiles at me, lowers her eyes, picks up her notepad. I wonder if I've been too pompous. On the other hand, we've made contact, and the silence as we rattle through the Cheshire countryside feels companionable. Not just companionable, I realise, as I glance at her bowed head. It's exciting.

I pick up my pen, but I can't concentrate on my letter.

**

When Corporal died, in the field behind the hedge at the top of our long garden, it took a couple of days for Ernest and me to realise he'd passed on. He'd always been so placid, so slow to move, it seemed natural for him to sleep all day in the shade of the twin oaks we harvested for acorns every year. When, yesterday, we finally went to him, his huge belly felt warm, and when we pressed our ears to it – though we couldn't sense his heart – we heard water trickling down a hillside, splashing into a pool. We decided he was neither dead nor alive, he was in passage to where old horses go, so we garlanded his head with bluebells, draped daisy-chains around his hooves. He seemed grateful, perfectly at peace.

But this morning his eyes have disappeared. They've been replaced by two vortices of buzzing flies, fighting to burrow deep, lifting off then plunging down again. The fragrance of our flowers is smothered by a khaki smell that wasn't there yesterday.

The flies are as huge and black as those always present in Mr Gregory's butcher's shop, the most disturbing place I know. There they cover, in a seething mass, each monstrous joint of meat hanging from iron hooks in his window. He swats them away with a rag, lifts down half a lamb and with his bloodstained carver slices a piece off for my mother. While he wraps them in the pages of the *Daily Herald* she's brought with her, the flies are steadily regrouping.

It all fits together. Eyes, flies, meat, feet, jackboots, Germans. Germs, worms, blind eyes, blistered feet. Meat, heat, flies, pies, rotten meat. Yes, it all fits perfectly together.

As Ernest and I stare shocked at Corporal's transformation, his hand slips into mine, and I am glad.

**

I blink awake, feeling groggy, stare out of the carriage window at a crow circling a group of grazing cows, men in overalls wandering to and fro. Only then do I recognise what my unconscious mind has known for a while – that the train has stopped, its engines are turned off. There's no railway station, no houses within view.

The silence and stillness intensify my awareness of the woman in the corner of the carriage. She and I are alone, the only living, breathing creatures in a static world – except for the white butterfly resting on the rack above her head.

She's still absorbed in her writing. I'd like to continue our conversation, but it felt concluded and I'm nervous of destroying her concentration. I try to walk a tightrope between not staring at her and being fascinated at the way she keeps biting her lip, just on one side of her mouth, as she searches for the right word or for balance. I can feel the dull pain, I think I know how she controls it to heighten her awareness without being distracted. She's allowing me in, even though she's probably forgotten I'm here.

I wait until her eyes turn from the paper to the fields.

I bet we've been stuck here half-an-hour already.

She jumps a little, peers out of the window, presses her face to the glass to look behind us. She sits back, turns to me and laughs.

You know, I can see my place from here.

I move over to her and she points acutely back towards a wooded hillside.

There. I'm only half a mile from home.

I can't think what to say. I feel sad because she'll be leaving shortly and I fear that however often we share the same carriage in the future, we'll never make such contact again.

She puts her pen and paper away, sits restlessly for a while, then suddenly stands up, opens the window, reaches through it for the door handle.

Are you getting out now?

Yes. Why not?

She flashes a smile at me.

You coming?

The sun bursts through the clouds. I'm about to embark on an adventure.

I grab my shoulder-bag, stand up. Just then the engines fire, the train starts to lurch forwards. I look at her. We don't need to speak.

She turns the handle, the door swings ponderously back, she leaps into space.

Aieeeh!

I follow her within a second, making the same wild cry,.

Aieeeh!

I leap more powerfully than she did, deliberately angling back a little, so that I tumble into her just as she's rising to her feet, my momentum taking us both rolling over and over to the bottom of the bank. We lie there, laughing, in deep grass, our heads almost touching.

Her face, upside-down, is beautiful. I feel a surge of attraction for her, raise my head, lean across to kiss her. She waits until my lips are on the verge of touching hers, then rolls lithely away and in the same movement gets up, holds out a hand to me. I grasp it and she tugs me to my feet. Her eyes challenge me.

Race you across the field.

She whirls round, kicks off her shoes, grabs them, sets off running. I follow. She's fleet, but I could catch her if I wanted to. I don't. I want to soak her in, enjoy her exuberance, the tilt of her shoulders, the way she flails her arms to maintain her balance.

She flops down in some ferns at the top end of the field. I join her, and for a while we lie together on our sides, breathing heavily, recovering our breath.

After a while she sits up, turns to me.

You can kiss me now if you like.

I move towards her, but she raises an admonitory finger.

Just once. A friendship kiss.

Her lips are cool. Their touch is delicate. At that moment I feel I wouldn't have swapped that kiss for any of the thousands of purple, bruising ones Elinor and I shared at the height of our passion, before the rot set in.

**

It's beginning to grow dark as we reach her cottage, which as far as I can tell can only be approached along the narrow footpath we've been following. She lifts the latch and we walk in.

She switches on a table-lamp that gives weak, golden light, which she supplements with a couple of candles. She kneels to the old wood-stove, opens its doors, applies a match to some twists of paper. As the fire takes hold the mica windows of the stove shimmer and radiate. She swings aside the nickel-plated trophy capping the stove, revealing a circular flat surface onto which she lifts a blackened pan.

Soup?

I nod enthusiastically. Already, it seems, I can smell the spices mingling with the scents of sage and mint that washed me as I came into the room. I'm hungry.

She motions me to sit with her on the floor, festooned with rugs and cushions, in front of the fire.

What d'you most want? she asks.

Ordinarily such a question would both irritate and floor me, but in this strange and increasingly heady atmosphere it seems natural.

To travel, I answer, without thinking.

Alone?

I'd like to travel with someone when I can, but I think most journeys are solitary.

She nods: *Where to?*

It takes a while to frame my response.

I'd like to journey forwards to some new, fresh place, but I think I can't do that until I've been back to some old territory.

I'm feeling sad now, unsettled. She squeezes my hand, sits up, rests her chin on her knees, rocks gently from side to side. Her voice is low.

I think I need to make a similar journey.

I'm beginning to feel excited. The soup is bubbling, so she gets up, slides the pan to the side, sits down again. My mouth dries a little as I speak.

Shall we travel together for a while?

We could try.

We sit quietly, listening to flute music. She ladles soup into a couple of bowls, hands one to me. It is full-bodied and delicious.

I ask to use the bathroom and as I flick on the light I notice the arm of a doll sticking out from under the belly of the claw-footed tub. I pull it out.

It's female. Its legs are splayed so far outwards they're sandwiching her head, to which they're fastened with black electrician's tape. It would be hard to imagine a more powerful image of helplessness and vulnerability.

I walk slowly back into the living room. She looks up at me, quizzically.

I sit down beside her, pull the doll from behind my back, hand it to her. She takes it, places it on the floor.

I wait for her to speak, but she doesn't.

Will you tell me about it?

One day, perhaps. Not now.

There is another period of silence, which this time she breaks.

D'you still want to travel with me?

I hesitate, not because I don't know my answer, but because I need to assimilate the experiences of these last few hours. I feel exhausted, yet alive and hungry for more.

Of course I do.

We listen to the end of the tape, then she rises, takes my hand, and after switching off the light, snuffing the candles, she guides me to her bedroom.

We sit on opposite sides of the bed, undress and slip between the sheets. We move to each other and hug.

She takes my face between her hands, kisses me as chastely as before.

Goodnight friend, she says.

She turns away. I'm vaguely disappointed, yet at the same time I feel the evening has been perfect.

I'm slipping into sleep when her voice comes to me.

Zack.

Yes.

My name's Alex.

**

It swoops again into view, a jug, bone china, white with a glistening blue filigree ringing its lip. It's old, I can tell, but it has a newness, a kind of gullibility that makes me want to catch it, warm it in my hands.

I reach out into the laden darkness, but once again I'm too slow, it swoops between my arms just as they're closing. Its handle grazes my wrist, I feel a thread of chill that sets my teeth on edge.

It doesn't want to escape. It just doesn't believe anyone can catch it.

This time I don't sink back so far, I sense it earlier, my arms make a cradle into which it swirls. It settles.

I have it, I hold it close, and I realise that the jug is her voice, swooping out of dream or nightmare, each journey carrying only a few words across the chasm that separates her pillow from mine.

Don't make me!

And now I've netted that one message I find others, in a tangled heap. I separate them gently, one by one.

It tickles, Big Bear. I don't want to be tickled. Tickle me.

Why are you crying, Daddy?

I'm too little to be eaten.

Are you better, now? Please be better now.

Don't go, Big Bear. I love you.

I raise myself carefully, lean over her.

In the filtered moonlight she looks pale as porcelain. She's on her side, turned away from me. Her thumb is in her mouth, and from time to time she sucks it.

She turns onto her back, raises both her arms, and I pull back a little as she makes slow sweeping movements as if she's trying to brush away a swarm of flies or fend off some heavy weight pressing down on her.

She looks tiny, three years old.

Don't stitch me in the curtains.

Her face is puckered. She's biting her lip.

I want to hold her, swab her fears away. But I'm afraid to invade her. I settle back onto my pillow, and before sleep engulfs me the jug swoops in again. It swirls and loops, stays far out of my reach.

**

I must have been about ten years old when I found the extraordinarily long hair on my left leg, just on the inside of my shin. It was fine and very fair, so it was often difficult to locate. It was at least four inches long.

The best place to extend it was in bed, especially early on a summer morning when the sun made it translucent – except for a golden filament running down the centre, over almost its whole length – and sometimes, though I could never work out the necessary angle, splayed a nest of rainbows, slightly displaced from the surface, onto my leg. I'd be very gentle when I stretched it, since I knew I would die if it came off. The tautening formed a cone around the root, which was always whiter than the skin surrounding it, so it looked hurt, humiliated. When I let go, it recoiled sharply into a wavy spiral that seemed still to have a lot of tension in it. But if I stretched it in the bath, the loops when I released it were much wider. Its energy had been dissolved or drowned.

I only revealed it to two people. Alan Wadcock, in the changing room, grinned, then lunged for it, and chased me – terrified of dying – several times between the rows of showers before he gave up, drenched.

Several years later I showed it to Helen, my first girlfriend, whom I'd known since we were small. We were resting on the grass after a few sets of tennis in the park when I found it. I parted my knees so she could see it better, stretched it in the sun and gestured to it. She looked puzzled at first and then flushed:

Laddo! I can see right up your shorts.

Today, fifty years on, naked but for kneepads in an ancient Shropshire ditch, examining a scratch I've just sustained, I find the hair again. It's just as long as before, though not so springy. It's gone grey. It's opaque, no golden filament, and despite all my efforts – for more than an hour in dazzling sun – I've not been able to make rainbows.

**

My face is on fire. I daren't open my eyes. The blackness is shafted with scarlet arrows. I've been beaten and I don't know why.

At the same time I've been swallowed. I'm enveloped in warm flesh, whose smell is fresh yet ancient as any world I know. And I'm safe, completely safe.

I've not felt such freedom from fear since my mother held me to her breasts. Which is where I am now, in this moist and beating cavern that tastes of milk, I feel a nipple hard and soft against my cheek, I turn my face, search with my lips until I find it, pull it in, suck on it, fierce at first then gently, until it simply lies there and I stroke it with my tongue.

It's alright now, Zack. It's alright.

The words are liquid, from far away, taken in with the milk I know is there even though I can't taste it. They are a song that swells into the cavern I never want to leave. But it's unsettled me, and I suck on the nipple for a while.

Come on, Zack. It's time.

Now I can't assimilate the words into my safety. I blink open into dawn-light and I'm curled in Alex's arms, her face above me, her red hair tenting me, her nipple quiet in my mouth.

She withdraws herself and we lie on our pillows facing each other.

Oh, Alex. I didn't want to come back.

She strokes my head.

Wait here.

She leaves the bedroom and I touch myself gingerly, all over my face. I'm very sore.

She returns carrying a bowl of water, a towel and a swab of cotton wool.

Sit up.

I do, and she attends to my wounded face carefully, her tongue sneaking out in concentration. It feels good.

She finishes, puts the bowl beside the bed, strokes my forehead.

That's so much better, Alex. What happened?

I woke from a dream filled with heavy drumming, and I found you kneeling on your pillow, eyes closed, bashing your face into the wall. So I took you in. I felt that's what you needed.

You were right.

We lie quietly for a while, our faces almost touching. Her whisper is urgent.

Answer quickly. Who comes first to mind?

My mother. And you?

Her voice is small.

My father.

She whirls over me, grabs my hand, tugs me out of bed.

Time to go swimming.

Her face is alive with exuberance. It's contagious. We dress quickly, grab a couple of towels and set off running, stumbling over roots, along the track between the oaks.

**

And so it's moved into a second phase, a smaller jar of diluted shit, from a separate defecation, two end-pieces of turd carefully spooned into a screw-top jar, mixed with hot water until the jar's half-full, lid screwed on tightly, then shaken hard until the structure is demolished and the liquid looks like heavy sediment, with flakes and shiny globules, an occasional seed.

I tuck the jar into a plastic bag, fasten it tight, hide it away to bloom and germinate until the opportunity arises.

Knowing she'll arrive soon and will probably accept my home-made chai, I choose two mugs, repeating to myself *the one with flowers is hers* so often it becomes a mantra. I pour chai into both, and then into hers some liquid from the jar. The chai is a strong brew and the liquid in her mug looks and smells no different from that in mine.

Elinor arrives, we hug, she accepts my offer, chooses warm rather than cold, I go into the kitchen, take the mugs out of the fridge, pour milk into both, put them in the microwave, watch them circulate, the flowers and the regal face.

We sit in the bay, sipping, chatting about the day. Before I make the meal I wash out her empty mug with scalding water.

I chop and cook while she chats to me. She's tired, a little irritable, but as the evening proceeds, the meal's a success, I give her a massage, she relaxes more and more, and is loving when she leaves, thanking me for a fine evening.

Early the following day I call on her to collect the dog. She seems fine, her apartment looks tidy, smells immaculate. All my planning, my deviousness, my guilt-ridden sleepless night has had no affect on her at all. I feel a mixture of relief and anger.

Late that evening she swings by to pick up the dog. She looks exhausted and is anxious to leave, get to bed. She says she's been feeling nauseous all day. I feel no pleasure at this news, but even so I have a sense of power, control.

Another night of restless wretchedness.

Why did I deliberately omit one part of the story? That when I walked with her in darkness, along my driveway, at the end of our evening, I tipped the remainder of the liquid shit onto the thick coat of our dog, so that if her apartment smelled she'd think it was because he'd rolled in shit. I left that out because it's the part I'm most ashamed of. He's a sweet dog, I love him. He's done me no harm.

**

three

I feel more at home in the ditch's environment than in any other I've known. I think this is largely because of the moisture. As I crawl along, mud sucks against my kneepads, dribbles through my toes, squirts through my spread-eagled fingers. My chin ploughs through it as I wriggle underneath great hoops of brambles, too fierce to push aside. A pillow made of fisted mud is as comfortable as any stuffed with feathers. The damp earth of the ditch's sides drains fear from my forehead more smoothly than any medication. It is somewhat cooler, yes, but the mud has the viscosity of blood. The darkness in its deepest parts, its moanings, lappings, sighings, return me to the time before my eyes had opened. Crawling along ditches is a journey through myself: my ancestry.

While crawling, my most intimate contact is with the ditch's floor, so my perceptions come mainly from below; and since they're muted by my kneepads, they enter my body largely through the palms of my hands. This is why, in the old days, crawlers sensitised their palms by massaging into them a lotion made from honey and malt vinegar. I always use it. It is just as effective as modern creams, and its smell seems more in keeping with the ditch.

Hands prepared in this way are amazingly effective antennae. They can detect the slow upwelling of geothermal heat when the finest of thermometers cannot. When my palms are resting on the ditch-floor's mud I can hear the deep earth's throbbing, yet if I lift them from the floor the sounds immediately cease. My fingers trace the damp soil's scars and lesions, constructing a topographical map. Not just a map, but a history of the ditch's life and deaths, from the day of its digging until now: feather-patterns from a resting bird; indentations made by hailstones from a sudden summer storm; shallow craters formed by the bursting of air bubbles which have risen through the slurry from a soup of decomposing leaves; scratch-marks made by infant voles in play; labyrinths of flow-lines etched into the soil in regions where the floor is not quite flat. So many journeys, completed long ago, stories which enter my consciousness through my palms. I've no need to learn their details. It is sufficient to know that they exist: that they occupy a place in history's continuum, to which the strivings of the ditch-crawlers, ineffectual or not, are added.

**

When we arrive, the lake is swathed in thin mist so I can't see the far side, though I judge from the curvature of the water's edge close to us that it's about a couple of hundred yards across.

It's chilly, so I decide to keep active. I start to undress then notice that Alex is sitting on a patch of grass, fumbling with a small pipe and the contents of a jar she's just unscrewed. She beckons me to sit beside her.

She strikes a match, holds it over the pipe, eyes

closed, inhaling deeply. She blinks open, offers the pipe to me. I suck slowly, deeply, and almost immediately I feel a sense of dreamy well-being. I start to laugh, though I'm not sure why.

I feel happy with her. She's allowing me in, she seems to want to know me. Such stark contrast with how it's been with Elinor for so long now.

I no longer feel cold or energetic. I want to lie down and stretch into the haze that surrounds me.

But Alex is on her feet, tugging me to mine, her eyes wonderfully alive.

Race you to the island.

She points. The mist has thinned and I can faintly see a grassy knoll in the centre of the lake.

I'm a lousy swimmer. I've never swum that far. But I want to do it, I know I can, I feel safe with her.

I tear off my clothes more swiftly than Alex, wade in. The water's cold but I don't mind. I lunge forward, turn onto my back.

Waieeeh!

I hear her laugh from the shoreline. I start my stolid side-stroke, right hand stretching each time for the island, which doesn't seem so far away.

I hear a splash behind me. She's taken to the water, and a few seconds later she catches up with me, swimming lithely. She slows.

OK?

I give her the thumbs-up sign.

She blows me a kiss and surges ahead, and all I can see as she zooms towards the island is the rise and fall of her arms, the occasional flick of her heels.

I settle into a routine, a rhythm easier than I've ever felt before in water. I dovetail each stroke with my breathing, each movement of my limbs taking me perceptibly forwards. I feel so relaxed that I close my eyes, glide on.

I don't know whether I let my head drop, or something sent a wave across the lake. Whatever it was I've swallowed water, I'm choking, flailing my arms. I force myself to relative calmness, try to quench the retching. I open my eyes, stare around.

I see nothing familiar. No Alex, no island, no shore. The fog has closed in again, thicker than before, and all I can see is a patch of placid water, featureless, biding its time.

I start to laugh but gulp water, panic again, beat the lake with my fists. But I don't rise above it, dominate it, as I always do in the dream I've had since childhood.

The sun appears, a pale yellow disc hanging in the fog. I start to swim towards it, try to work out – since it rises in the East – which direction the shore must be, but I grow confused until I realise with delight that all I need to do is keep aiming for it because there's shore in all directions. I immediately feel stronger.

Thank you, sun, I breath into the fog.

I begin to swim with all my power. I'm enjoying the effort, the excitement. I'm in control again.

I see it coming, a whorl of thicker fog that rears out of the lake, curls over the sun and blots it out. I pray for it to reappear, but it doesn't.

I'm exhausted and cold. My teeth begin to chatter, I'm frightened. I can't go on much longer. It doesn't occur to me to cry for help.

Halloo! Zack!

I feel too tired to respond. Anyway, she'll find me now and I'll be safe.

Halloo! Zack!

Her voice is from further away. Somehow I lift myself out of my torpor.

I'm here!

Then I swallow water, panic in earnest, thrash around, choke and vomit.

All I can remember of my rescue is an image or two. But they'll stay with me forever:-

Alex surging out of the mist, droplets spraying from her chin.

Crimson streaks of pain screeching through my head as she slaps me twice across the face.

Her nimble savagery as she quells my flailing, yanks my arm over her shoulders.

A feeling of great peace and helplessness as I'm tugged and cajoled, seemingly weightless, to the shore.

Lying on thick, cool grass, Alex astride me, weeping onto me, shaking my shoulders to try to stop my laughter.

Back inside her house, drinking camomile tea, both of us draped in blankets, the stove pumping out heat, finally sober, I begin to shake. She holds me.

I'm sorry, Alex.

She twists my shoulders roughly, makes me look into her eyes.

For God's sake, Zack! Stop apologising. It's you I want to know, you not some sanitised, tight-arsed effigy of you.

She takes out the pipe again, fills it, inhales, but doesn't offer it to me. She breathes out, and as the fragrance washes over me, she shakes her head, speaks dreamily.

I wish I'd known this stuff doesn't suit you.

I don't need to reply, and the period of silence that follows, punctuated only by the crackling of logs, is lovely. I'm almost asleep when she breaks it.

Don't ever lie to me. I couldn't stand it. OK?

I'll try.

She starts to shiver. I want to put my arms around

her, I feel she wants me to, but all I can do is reach out for her hand.

I think she wants to talk, but the time doesn't seem quite right.

So I stroke her hand, start to learn its geography, until the kettle on the woodstove splutters and boils over.

**

Odd to be alone in the house in early morning, still an hour before I leave to catch my train, Elinor already on hers, headed for London.

A good feeling, though. I can expand into the house's emptiness, this unexpected window of ruminative time. I need it, too, after the stresses of the past few weeks.

I sit naked on the edge of the bed, forcing nothing, allowing images and thoughts to flow through me. I feel happy.

Those stresses, suspicions vanished in one wild hour yesterday evening. I finger the soreness of my lower lip, limp cock, and smile. How ridiculous of me to have felt nervous of her trip, her night away. The sun shafts through the window, sucks the smells of our love-making out of my stomach-hair. I breathe them in.

I look down at the tangled linen sheet, the rumpled pillow-cases. I'll wash them for her return. There's no feeling more satisfying, full of promise, than stretching into an expanse of cool, clean sheets.

I find the laundry basket, gather up the bed-linen, pile it in. Its rough warmth in my arms brings last night's passion flooding back. I sit down on the bed again and close my eyes.

She'd seemed excited when she came in late

from work, her eyes bright, provocative, in huge contrast to the coldness and reserve of the preceding weeks, which had given me that constant dull ache in my stomach. Before I'd time to take in this new atmosphere she'd drawn my head down, her tongue had stabbed into me, we'd pulled each other into the bedroom and were tearing off each other's clothes.

A mixed pleasure of our recent, less frequent love-making has been the increased slowness with which she's reached arousal. I've enjoyed the challenge of it, the time it allows for me to attend to her, languorously, in whatever way I choose; the almost imperceptible signals of the breaking down of her passivity, her softening, emergent excitement. On the other hand, until I've sensed these indications, I've been worried that she wouldn't respond, and sometimes she hasn't and has turned away from me. I've also wanted her to show interest in my body, in the ways she used to that so thrilled me, and still does when I conjure them. But nowadays she's almost completely inactive, and I feel unattractive, undesired.

So it was marvellous yesterday to be overwhelmed by her lust. Her body was completely ready for me as soon as we fell into bed. I felt shocked by her violence, my tension exploded as we came, together. We didn't get up again, didn't eat. We simply tugged the duvet over us and lay hand in hand, until she drifted into sleep. Then I rested on my elbow, watched her in the faint light from the window, listened to her night-noises, feeling so easy now my stomach-ache had disappeared.

I decide to wash our cast-off clothes at the same time as the bed-linen, so I pad round the room picking them up.

I press my face into her shirt, breath in the smell of her, nuzzle it before dropping it into the basket. I think I've gathered everything, then notice a crumpled twist of black, her pants caught on a handle of the chest of drawers.

I lift them up carefully, walk over to the basket by the window, twirl them on one finger into a shaft of sunlight. They dazzle. I do it again. I'm almost blinded by the brilliant whiteness of the reflection.

Pain begins to gnaw as I open them out, half-guessing what I'll find. Yes. An archipelago of stains, whose chalkiness I recognise. Semen.

Not mine. It couldn't be. She's not worn them since before we made love. My stomach-ache intensifies then suddenly leaps as I realise that her excitement, her body's readiness, was nothing to do with me. She must have come straight home from her lover.

**

There must be a colour I can thin into a rope and swarm up into sunshine. That I can weave into a hammock, fasten to the upper branches of a giant oak and swing with the soft wings. That I can bake into dry soil in which I'll sit, sieve it through my fingers, watch it glint, wink at me as it spirals down to make a castle fit for any king or queen. That can condense into a small child's secret smile, bursting into view, pulled back once again into a mouth already curling at the sides, while I feign puzzlement, and she fists her stomach to hold her laughter in. That can suck out of the pine needles scattered over the ground a fragrance that makes me take the deepest breaths I can, that allows me to forgive myself for everything, to be released again.

I think it's orange. I think it's the orange of the coals quietly burning in the kitchen range, the cat dreaming on its iron shelf, my mother's rice pudding slow-cooking in the oven to the side, in a brown earthenware jar up to the rim of which the golden cream has risen, old potatoes baking in their skins below, no sound at all except, from time to time, an exhausted coal slipping down below its livelier companions, the cat purring in a rich part of its sleep. No movement, but a sudden spurt of multi-coloured flame, the cat's claws gently flexing, a lazy churning of the milk inside the jar, an ash-fleck meandering the heat above the coals, then surging up, through the chimney to the sky.

I'm in the safest world I know. It engages all my senses. I open the oven door, stroke the roughness of a potato's hardening skin, smell the browning of its underside, watch its plumpness wrinkle in a friendly way, salivate at my knowledge of its taste sprinkled with salt, listen to its heart as it eases through its final journey.

All the better for knowing that the swirling snow outside is beginning to stick. That my mittens are warming by the cat. That my mother is close by, with mop or brush or duster, that she'll bring a mug of cocoa fairly soon, and when she tips coal from the scuttle, a million sparks will whirl into the air.

The duster stuffed into the pocket of her apron smells of polish. Its colour is the orange of the coals.

**

The rain stops, the sun comes out, I'm bored with staying at home, so I climb over the fence at the end of our garden, into Mr Maddock's field. No-one is around. I walk at random, past the horse-trough, the giant oaks, the bluebell grove, until I come to the damson tree I've always wanted to climb, but whose smooth trunk has so far foiled me. This time, for reasons I can't comprehend, it's easy. I climb into the upper branches without a hitch. When I look down, the grass is obscured by leaves. The tree is higher than I thought.

I inch along a branch, its rough bark scuffing my calves and thighs. Near the end of it, I see a nest containing several blue eggs. I stretch as far forwards as I can. My finger touches them, counts five. I can also feel a piece of folded paper. I ease it from the nest, draw it to me, sit up and open it. It is torn from a notebook, faintly lined, rather like the pages in my ledger. The words are in large capitals:

ZACK. DO NOT TAKE THESE.

I'm not surprised. I know God has written it. But I'm cross with him for forbidding me to steal the eggs.

I rip the note into little pieces, slither down the trunk onto the ground.

**

She's been somewhere else for a while, possibly meditating or working in her garden, and I'm glad. Her cottage already feels like a sanctuary to me, but I don't yet know its shapes and shadows, its smells, books, herbs, knots in floorboards, flaws in the old glass of the windows, its quiet spots, cobwebs, unsettled places, prejudices, its potential for secrets, its scars and stains, the traffic of its roof. All these I can learn better when she's not with me, when I'm not dazzled by her presence and the rooms can't hide behind her.

So I'm settling in, savouring the cottage both for its own sake and because it's hers, and I feel disrupted, disappointed when she returns, carrying a few carrots and a bunch of thyme.

Zack. Will you do something for me?
Only if you'll let me stay here forever.
I'd like you to come with me to see my father.
Bit quick isn't it?
What d'you mean?
And if I'm going to be offered for inspection, shouldn't your mother see me, too?

I smile at her, then realise she's upset.

My mother's long-dead. If you want to fool around, just forget it.
Alex! What's wrong?

I can see her trying to regain control, forcing herself to speak quietly.

I'm sorry. There's no way you could have known how difficult it was to ask you to come with me.
I'll be happy to. When?
When I've had a cup of camomile tea and my blood pressure's back to normal.
Does he live close by?
Just round the corner. He's in hospital. He's dying.

**

The ditch has been pristine for hours and hours: liquidity and suction, mud and green life in cool shade. And now I'm in a region where someone's dumped their rubbish, cleared out their attic, it seems to me. I sift through it.

Junk, that's all it is. But sometimes junk's exciting. It tells good stories if I can only work them out. This particular collection, though, doesn't seem promising. Three rolls of floral wallpaper, a suitcase with a broken back. A tennis racket so warped it's like a black hole – if the ball got into it, it could never escape. Catgut still strong, though. I'm surprised the dampness hasn't snapped it. A ship in a bottle. A rusty stirrup pump. And, damaged and discoloured in a sodden cardboard box, a hand-carved cuckoo-clock: the workmanship superb.

What's this, wrapped in plastic, red under its dust? An umbrella. I wonder if it works. Yes. That click as it latches, one of the most satisfying sounds I know. In good shape. Spokes intact, tight as a button. Hard to manoevre if the ditch is overgrown.

I open it again, press my nose to it, loll against the damp ditch-wall, breathe in. Yes, it was hers, and I'm a child again. I cover my face with its material, breathe in again, even more deeply. I want to lose consciousness, to find her.

**

We're not in a regular visiting period, and the communal wards we walk through en route to her father are quiet, the loudest sound coming from a distant vacuum cleaner. Most patients are sleeping or sitting by their beds reading newspapers. No-one seems to notice us except for an old man with a ravaged face who stretches out his arms to us without speaking, beseeching us to take him away.

The wards are festooned with flowers which – perhaps because they're so lovely – make me angry. It seems wrong that they've been snipped out of their life to feed a fantasy that can't possibly work. How could anyone surrounded by flowers cut off in their prime derive hope and comfort from their presence? Much better surely to bring gifts which symbolise hope, or at least a natural process: acorns perhaps, turnips, twigs.

He's in a small room by himself, propped up on pillows, head tilted to one side, mouth open, asleep.

Despite the wrinkles, loss of hair, discolorations of his skin he looks quite beautiful, like many people who are very old or frail. Transparent plastic tubes run from bottles suspended from a rack beside his bed, to somewhere underneath the sheet that covers him. A thinner tube, taped to his chin, passes up his left nostril.

Alex looks as if she's in shock. I squeeze her hand. She grimaces. She leans to him and whispers:

Dad!

The old man makes no response. She speaks more loudly, and when there's no reaction she claps her hands next to his ear. Nothing.

She turns to me.

No point in staying. Let's go.

But Alex...

She grabs my arm, steers me towards the door. I'm shocked, but it's her father, not mine.

At the door she halts, whispers to me that she won't be a second, and goes back into the room. I feel relieved, imagining that she's going to give him some message of love she'd been too embarrassed to speak in front of me.

I don't want to intrude, but my wish to feel better about the encounter is strong, so I move back a couple of steps, peer round the door-jamb.

She's bending to him, whispering in his ear. Her voice is sibilant, as though she's hissing at him, and the one word I'm able to almost register sounds like *vile*. But then she caresses his forehead, straightens his pillow and I know I've misunderstood. She stands up quickly and I duck out of sight.

**

Dear Mum,

You were gentle and we cremated you. I imagined that your ashes would lie lightly on our memories, keeping them warm; that they'd stir at the passage of chance breezes, slip off, grain by grain, as years passed by, but never wholly vanish.

But you're lying heavy, I feel oppressed, I can't sleep. I set out to write a poem about your fine white ash, and what comes out is violence.

Why, Mum? Why does this viciousness, this filth emerge when I'm thinking of you? There was never any violence between us. Or you and Dad, I feel sure.

I took photographs of you over your last few days, though Tony's diffidence restrained me while you were still warm in your hospital bed, just after you had died. You change, as I look at them in sequence, from a half-smiling old lady in a pretty night-gown, chin-in-hand, to a battered, swollen figure on the verge of extinction. Yet each one is clearly you, reveals the strength you kept hidden, strength that enabled you to die without a fuss.

But I can't find you at all in the final two photos, taken a few days later, dressed in white, in your coffin, in Madelaine's Chapel of Rest. In those, the face is hard and cruel, filled with a bitterness and disapproval I never glimpsed in the 57 years of life on earth we shared.

My explosion of ferocity when I sit down to think of you. Your unprecedented harshness after death. Why these, when what I need and seek is a state of peace in which you take your place within my history? I have nothing but good feelings about you. It should be easy.

Am I wracked because I still can't grieve? Because of things unregistered I didn't do or say? Am I held back because I'm angry that in these last few months of stress my wife has taken a lover and pulled away from me? Night after night, I slide a carving knife into his back while she lies below him, looking up at me, wondering if I'll take it out and slip it into her?

I, for that moment, that moment only, have total power; and will probably decide at random.

**

four

We're the only customers in the cafe at the hospital. Alex has just returned from speaking with the doctor in charge of her father's case. She looks shaky, so I suggest she has a drink before talking.

She sips slowly, abstractedly, her finger making spirals in the pool of tea she's slopped from her cup onto the table-top.

They give him a week at most.

I'm sorry. Is there no hope?

She shakes her head, takes a gulp of tea, and as she puts her cup down it rattles in the saucer.

I don't want him to die.

It's hard to think of words of solace.

D'you love him a lot?

Her voice hisses, just like in his room.

I hate him. I hope he rots in hell.

I don't want to believe what I'm hearing.

If you hate him, why don't you want him to die?

She glares at me. Her face is contorted, its expression vicious.

Because I want him to suffer. I want him to know how much I loath him.

But Alex, I saw you tidying him up, straightening his pillow.

The more comfortable he is, the longer he'll be in pain.

I have an urge to throw my tea in her face and walk away. I've never heard such violent words spoken about a parent, never felt such anger as she's displaying now. I've just seen the man, the milk of death in his unfocused eyes that once or twice crept open and just as slowly closed again. She's demeaning herself to hate someone so far gone.

But I can also sense the pain that is ravaging her as the knuckles of the hand holding her cup grow white. I struggle for understanding. Perhaps she needs to hate him because she loves him too much to let him go. I want to help her. We've known each other for less than a day, but already I feel more intimate with her than I ever felt with Elinor: or with anyone, in fact. I want this journey. And if I'm close to her, I'll be less likely to engage in activities that disgust me.

Well?

She's looking at me, quizzically, but there's no lightness in her eyes. She knows what I've been deliberating about, I've no need to express it.

I'm with you, Alex.

I feel her tension ease. I take her hand.

I'm wondering if you're speaking so harshly out of love.

She almost comes out with a swift rebuttal, but she swallows it and smiles.

Perhaps.

Her voice rises, she jumps to her feet.

Let's get out of here. I want to go the forest. I want to run until I drop.

I pick up on her excitement, leap up from my chair. We race out of the hospital.

**

When we ran across the fields after leaping from the train I'd felt the stronger runner, fast though she was. But now it's different. She's running like someone inspired. Her energy seems boundless, so it doesn't matter that she wastes so much by swirling, laughing, jumping extravagantly high over tussocks and clumps of bracken, twirling round to beckon me on as I puff and pant behind her, towards the trees.

As far as I can tell we're the only moving objects in the forest, and the trees that give us shade as they mark our passage seem tolerant, protective, mildly stuffy.

I catch my second wind, find an easy rhythm, run more easily from within myself, but it's still as much as I can do to keep within striking distance of her. I imagine that each stride she takes brings her nearer to acceptance of her father's death. I want to cheer her on, shout *It's happening, Alex: It doesn't matter, love,* but I don't because the silence is so gorgeous, and can help her heal more than any words from me.

I'm level with her now, and we keep turning to each other, flashing smiles, pulling faces. She's tousled, dripping sweat. There's an arc of crimson across one cheek, probably from brambles she's dived through. She looks beautiful, her eyes amazingly alive.

As we enter a clearing surrounded by oaks, a few butterflies rise from a bush in front of us. She leaps for one, tumbles to the grass. I pole-axe to the ground beside her. We lie for a while panting, unable to speak. As it slows, our breathing is in synchronism, remaining so until we've calmed.

She opens her hand, and the butterfly stutters away. The sky is a canopy of shifting green. She points to it.

That's where we should sleep tonight.

I turn to her, take out my handkerchief, drop a gob of saliva onto it and carefully clean her bramble-scratch. Even when I've done so, and the crimson beads have been smoothed away, the scratch looks angry. She watches me, wincing once or twice. A lock of hair is matted to her forehead. I ease it free.

My voice seems to well out of the depths of the green.

I'd like to make love with you.

She bites her lip, picks up my handkerchief, presses her face into its crimson stains. Her eyes above the crumpled linen are huge.

You've just made love with me as completely as anyone could. Don't ask for more.

She kisses me on the forehead and we lie quietly. I drift into sleep, feeling happy and astonished.

**

The fissure is almost wholly overgrown. I'm sure we'd both have assumed it was simply a small indentation, an irregularity in the line of the ditch if, as we'd crawled past it, we hadn't felt a pull: mild but insistent, like an undertow or the almost imperceptible tug before the river funnels, and the flow towards the waterfall gains speed.

So we push our way through ferns and bramble-loops, nudge our shoulders through overhanging turf, until we're wholly in this tributary ditch, weaving slowly through filtered light. In two or three places our path is almost blocked by immensely thick roots from trees long-since fallen and decomposed. This is an ancient ditch.

The pull seems somewhat stronger. We don't speak. We haven't spoken all day. There's no need to.

The ditch ends suddenly, broadening out into a

shallow hollow, studded with gorse and broom, bracken and springy turf. We are below the level of the surrounding fields. There is no longer any pull.

We had been crawling in the direction of a fairly stiff breeze, which is probably why we'd not smelled burning. Now, however, there is a heady smell, slightly sweet, though not unpleasant.

We notice faint white smoke rising from behind a patch of gorse. We edge our way towards it, trying not to add to the scratches we've already sustained. It helps that the ground is almost perfectly flat.

A carefully arranged log fire is burning slowly below an iron grille on which a dead man is lying, naked. His underside is smoking, charred, but his face, chest, folded arms, genitals and thighs seem unaffected by the flames. His eyes are closed and his face portrays something like amusement.

I feel clear that we should leave, and I can tell Alex thinks the same. We stand alongside him for a final few seconds. A flame sneaks out from behind his head and we hear hair crackle as it burns. Alex bites her lip and splashes a little water from her flask onto his face. I turn away. She follows me.

Again we crawl in silence, halting only when we reach the main ditch. We sit on a bank of turf, backs against a tree. She begins to shiver. I take her hand.

Did you see his name? she asks.

What name? No.

On a piece of board behind the fire.

What was it?

She swallows. *It was Lionel. My father's name.*

I reach out to touch her, but she pulls away.

Keep crawling, Zack, she says.

**

...bluebirds over
    The white cliffs of Dover,
        Tomorrow...

She smiles down at me as I lie in my bouncing chair, lifts the galvanised iron lid off the boiler. Steam surges up, bounces in billows on the dark roof of the shed, slithers down its walls, engulfs me once again. She disappears, except for her song, which now is from far away. She's above the clouds and might float off. I need her. I bat the steam with my arms until I've whirled it all away, and she's back with me, full-skirted, sandalled.

She takes more sheets and shirts out of the linen basket, plunges them in the boiler, places the lid back on. It's quiet for a while, then lifts a little at one point, releases a kiss of steam. Quiet again, another kiss, the intervals diminishing until once again it's chuntering, expelling puffs around its rim.

She grabs the steaming laundry, takes two steps, plonks it down on the floor next to me, ruffles my hair. The green, wrought-iron mangle towers above me. Drops hanging from its handle fall past me, splash onto the tiles. I dip my finger in the shallow pool, trace mazy patterns.

I can tell from her song that bluebirds make people happy, but there's something in the melody that makes me want to cry.

She plucks a rumpled, soggy sheet off the floor. It unfolds slightly and although it's still steaming, the skin that clings to my face feels cold. Before I've time to claw it off she's slid it up, beyond me, started to feed it into the mangle's grinning mouth.

It's not a kind grin. In fact, it's cruel. The wooden rollers wouldn't be grinning at all if decades of mangling hadn't worn them in the centre, making a thin grin, like the one Tibby wore throughout the afternoon he was playing with the mouse.

She turns the handle. The sheet is pinioned, drawn in. It emerges from the far side of the roller looking white as shock, while water cascades into the drainage bucket.

The boiler is going berserk, grumbling and hissing, spurting steam from all parts of its rim. The shed is filling with steam, once again I can't see her, except her brawny arms when they lunge to take another sheet. And once again, without a view of her, I can't tell where her voice is coming from.

Another sheet slides over my face, almost sucks me out of my chair. I try to cry out, but even I can't hear my voice above the thirsty bluebirds.

The pile of washing is much larger than I am -she wouldn't notice me, wound into a sheet, even if the steam abated.

She's so strong it would be easy to feed me in feet-first. I'd try to stretch out to her but the wet linen would pinion me. I'd see her hazel eyes but she wouldn't notice mine. I'd see her smile and for the first time in my life would doubt it. My legs might pass through with just heavy bruising, but my ribs would crack one by one. And as for my skull...

She picks me up. I close my eyes.

**

I took three photos of her, in the last week of her life.

Alex is sitting up in bed, hugging her knees. She's wearing a white cotton nightdress studded with tiny red stars. She's excited, rocking from side to side. She looks about ten years old. I'm lying next to her, beginning to become absorbed in the conversation she's nudged and steered me into.

I'd sparked off the discussion when we were talking about anger, hers and her father's, and I'd said I don't think my mother was ever angry in her life. Alex flatly refused to believe it. She forced me to think back, and I finally acknowledge that I once saw her angry, though not in her life.

Keep talking, Alex says.

**

In the first one she's smiling in her sleep, and since the smile is the one I've seen so often, for decades, it's easy to retrieve her broad Cheshire burr as, a few hours earlier, she'd asked Rosie how she'd done in her exams, me if I was sure it was alright to keep taking time from work, Tony if her cat was being fed three times a day, a nurse if she'd please bring her a glass of water:

But only if you get time, love.

Shy and awkward though she was, her face's presence fills up the photograph, and I think few people would spot that she's in hospital. I think they'd see simply an old lady in a floral nightgown in pleasant sleep. No intimation at all that she's ravaged with cancer, two days from death, on heavy and increasing doses of morphine, which can't prevent her sometimes from crying out in sleep; though never when awake.

In the second photo she's in her final day. Her face is bruised and blotched, her unseeing half-open eyes are wild. She's deep in coma, from which she'll return just for a minute. Not to speak – her tongue and bloodied gums are too swollen for that. Not to see – her eyes are already milked over – but to raise one finger for her year-old grandchild, who's been placed beside her, to play with. She's battered beyond redemption, but not beyond recognition. She's palpably, in spirit though not in face, the mother, grandmother, great-grandmother who's filled a warm niche in the lives of all those people who've visited her these past few weeks.

In the final photo she's one day dead, lying in her purple-shrouded coffin, in Madelaine's Chapel of Rest. Only her face and hands are visible, and the third finger of her left hand is naked. As she'd grown plumper over the years her gold ring had sunk deeper into her flesh, but always at least a glint was visible. Now it has gone.

But the shock was that I didn't recognise her face. I truly felt I'd gone into the wrong room.

It's large, hard, cruel. Her nose has become a heavily curved beak, her mouth an arc of disapproval. All these qualities conspire to make a total effect of fury. She's railing at something; or someone. Her face is tight with concentrated anger. My mother isn't present at all.

I tried to convince myself later that her expression was simply a result of natural changes that accompany death and the beginning of decomposition, but I couldn't. The anger seemed alive. I couldn't relate it to, but it emanated from her, I felt sure.

**

So there you are, Alex. Posthumous anger. What d'you make of that?

She continues to hug her knees and rock, and for a moment I think she hasn't heard me. She's biting her lip, as always when she's working something out.

I'd like to hold you, but not just yet. There's more I need to know.

She speaks carefully, with some pauses.

I don't doubt that her face in the coffin told the truth. That she was angry. She could hide it all her life if she was skillful enough, if she was sufficiently scared or protective, if she perhaps didn't even realise it was there. But she couldn't hide it when she was dead.

So out it came, in all its bottled fury.

That makes sense to me, Zack, and the fact that she didn't show it suggests to me that it was deep and very strong, too strong for her to acknowledge and at the same time function. I suspect it was old, perhaps from her childhood. Was there anything in her early life that could have caused such anger?

I hesitate, then open the gate, let out in a flood the story I'd never told in full to anyone, the story my mother never knew I knew. She'd have been riven with shame if she'd known that my father had quietly told it one rainy Saturday afternoon when she was out shopping. Told my brother Tony and me, with fierce injunctions never to let her know we'd heard it.

She was abandoned, Alex, in the first week of her life. Her father never acknowledged her, and her mother was shipped off to America to start a new life. She never saw her mother again. She never had the chance to be a daughter. She was the village illegitimate, brought up by kind and well-meaning grandparents who felt it vital that she'd never be willful like their daughter. Throughout her childhood she was taught to be good and compliant, never to question why. She was filled with shame at her illegitimacy, and she brought that shame to her marriage and her motherhood.

I'm feeling bleak. I close my eyes and her face comes to me, the one from the first photograph. Alex squeezes my shoulder, speaks gently.

Can't you see where that anger comes from?

She strokes my forehead.

I think her anger was bound to overspill on you, so you imbibed it, that dreadful, festering trapped anger that sometimes comes out in sneaky, vicious ways.

I never saw that in her.

I'm talking about you, not your mother.

I know she's right. I'm flooded with images of punctured tyres, bottled excrement, burnt photographs, stolen letters. I know I need to take this issue on, and that Alex is someone who could help me.

But not now. At the moment I'm ground down and could easily sink into despair.

Alex, can we discuss it some other time?

For a moment she seems irritated, then she looks into my face, slips down into the bed, puts her arms round me.

**

She's just left, and the trembling I've been fighting to suppress takes over, the mug I have to scour for my own safety clatters on the stainless steel, the jar that holds the evidence that could condemn me is triple-wrapped and hidden in my car, to be driven away and stashed in some dark place where it will never be found. Though even now, when I need not just to wash, but to scour my hands to rawness to blot out every trace, even now I feel a frisson of pleasure as I picture someone finding this parcel, a safe distance from now, unwrapping it slowly, perhaps growing excited, and finding human excrement that once was me.

I was too cocky, it's as simple as that. Cocky and angry that when I saw her this morning she was short with me, but said she felt fine. She looked it, too –

fresh, alluring. I caught a whiff of perfume, which she never wore when we were together. She seemed not to remember yesterday's nausea, then surmised that she'd eaten something bad for lunch. Her kiss as she drove away was distracted, condescending. After all my efforts, all my guilt and hot sweats in the night, the dose I'd slipped into her drink had no effect at all.

Who is she seeing in town? I conjure her in the spiced heat of my bed, make her pull me down to her. I spin out our love-making until I yell her name and the dog comes in to see if I'm in trouble. I subside, eased for a while. But the stomach-ache comes slowly back and with it the fury.

**

So the brew I make this morning is stronger. Yellower than before with a few flecks of red pepper and some globules of fat that bob up to the surface, threads of colour slowly draining from them. I shake the jar hard to homogenise the mixture. A little sneaks out onto my sleeve.

She's cheerful when she calls by in the late afternoon. Yes, she'd like a mug of chai. As I look at her, bowled over once more by her beauty, I see no indication that she's been making love. But then I never did.

I'm flustered in the kitchen, as she sits in the bay, talking to the dog, waiting to be served. She's early, so I've not added the pollution in advance. I tip some in quickly, clumsily, and a piece of pepper and a greyish lump of fat circle the chocolate-coloured surface of the chai. I carry it over to the sink, spill some on my trousers, rapidly spoon the tell-tale signs away.

Her voice floats from the other room.

Lousy service in this restaurant.

Coming!

I take the mugs out of the microwave. A huge glob of fat glistens on the surface of hers. I spoon it away, hurry to her with the chai.

She chats for a while, as I hold in my impatience, then takes a sip. I watch her face, which gives no signal. The same with the next sip, but she senses my scrutiny, looks at me guardedly.

Something wrong?

I force a smile, shake my head.

We resume our conversation but it's now somewhat strained, and I wonder if she's suspicious.

She takes a larger sip, puts the mug down heavily, wrinkles her nose.

It smells of shit.

I feel myself flushing. My body wants to tremble but I can't allow it to. At the same time I feel like laughing. I'm scared, too. My throat has gone dry.

You mean the chai?

Yes. Shit.

She seems disturbed but not angry. I sniff my mug ostentatiously.

Smells alright to me.

I hold my mug out to her. She takes it somewhat reluctantly, lowers her nose to it.

That seems OK. But mine definitely smells of shit.

I'm sorry.

I pick hers up, carry it into the kitchen, tip it down the sink, flush it thoroughly, walk back to the bay.

She waves her hand as if she's forgotten it already. I know I should leave the issue there, but I can't.

I bet Jen washed your mug in the same water as the dog bowl.

Jen, who comes to clean for three hours each week, and had been that afternoon, wasn't perfect, but would never be so sloppy. I feel guilty at my insinuation.

She looks sceptical.

Sholto doesn't shit in his bowl.

I'm confused now, somewhat desperate, but I still can't let go.

He could have had some on his fur, perhaps.

She's irritated by my persistence.

Can't you drop it? Anyway, it smelled like human shit to me.

I drop it. The conversation picks up. She accepts my invitation to dinner. The hug she gives me when she's about to leave is intimate and loving.

I like being cosseted.

I want her so much.

You could stay the night and I'll cosset you more.

She laughs, but at the same time steps back a little.

I'd rather have you as a father than a lover.

I smile and see her off.

And then it comes. Trembling mixed with fury. Scouring of her mug and the jar that held the shit. A long, long night of stomach-ache and fever, snatches of sleep from which I wake covered in sweat, half-conscious dreams in which she dies of poisoning, and all our friends turn their backs on me; in which before they hang me I tell the truth, and one small clear voice I don't recognise says: *It doesn't matter, now.*

I must stop, throw away the mug with flowers on it. I can't protect her if I don't protect myself, so I must stop seeking her out, trying to hold on to her. I must wean myself from her, wish her well, accept each new lover when he comes.

The madness has to end. I don't want to be her father. I don't want to be swept up in an avalanche.

**

five

The Shropshire ditches down which I crawl are so old that in most places their sides are covered by vegetation, or encrusted with dried mud which has trickled down from the fields. The soil exposed by the labourers' spades at the time the ditches were dug can't be seen. But in a few places, where clay is not conducive to plant-growth, or canopies of grass have protected the sides, the original cuts are still visible. In these locations, if I use my magnifying glass, I can discern faint striations in the soil, roughly horizontal, which make me think of tree-rings without curvature. The ditch-sides are soft fossils, whose temporal ranges precede the ditches and extend over many centuries at least. Each layer is a skin through which water, air and nutrients slowly percolate, exchange occurring at all levels. As gently as I can, I run my finger downwards, across the strata, season by season, year by year, back into history. I feel at one with the soil, and in some vague way with the Gaian idea of the Earth as a single living, breathing, organism. I close my eyes and travel through cycles of drought, flood, blizzard, beating sun.

The extent to which, as I'm crawling, the ditch conveys its knowledge to my palms and outstretched fingers varies hugely as I move along its length. My sensitivity to its history and traffic depends on many factors: my emotional state, the distraction of the sky, the melodies of birdsong, the distortions of shadows cast onto the walls, the aromas and viscosity of the mud. But more powerful than all these is my degree of closeness to the ditch's nodes and anti-nodes.

At certain places in the ditch its activity is intense. These are the anti-nodes. All my senses are engaged and the impressions I receive are mainly from below. Their flux is huge, sometimes overwhelming. It's as if a line of great magnifying glasses, widely spaced, lying deep, underneath the ditch, gathers up all radiation, of every wavelength and beams it up to some focal point on the ditch floor. The individual components of the flux are neither uniquely discrete and identifiable, nor fully subsumed into the totality. They are somewhere in between, with features I can recognise, but only partially, distorted from the original but not wholly: as if I'm floating in a featureless ocean whose surface, here and there, is broken with jagged rocks whose shapes are somewhat familiar.

By contrast, the nodes, spaced evenly between the anti-nodes, are places of utter silence. Nothing moves. There are no aromas. Insects are not present and the light is subdued, even on the brightest day.

It seems logical to me that the places in the ditch where I'd feel most responsive to its atmosphere, most at home in fact, would be at the anti-nodes, where its emanations and clamour are the greatest. But my intuition is wrong. In reality, I most feel these connections – and am most swept up in them – in the total stillness of the nodes.

I've found that to experience their full power, the nodes are best visited in darkness. I take my time as I approach them, savour the stealthy muting of my sensory impressions, the shrinking of light and sound, dissolving of fragrances, softening of touch and taste. When I arrive at a node, I can't discern my breathing, I don't want to move.

I sit on the ditch floor, and wait until all dross has slipped away and I feel purged. When I reach this stage I hold on to it, but only lightly. Then I can start to inhale the air of non-existence. I breathe it in until my lungs are full. This is the point where I become aware of my total isolation in this world, not in all respects but where it matters most – at the very nub of me, which not even Alex can approach. This recognition always makes me sad though not afraid. I can't know if other people, arriving at a node, will feel the same: but I'm convinced that those who do are the ones with whom I can achieve the greatest degree of intimacy. Intimacy emanating from a mutual recognition of our solitude. Once I thought that concept inconsistent, but now it seems completely natural.

**

Why d'you do that? It makes me nervous.

I can't help it, Alex. It just happens.

I'm sorry. I don't want to be like this. I want to be normal.

Then let's tackle this together. Little by little. There's no hurry.

We lie quietly together for a while. A soft breeze through the window makes the candle-flame flicker, and as we drift our fingers through its light, faint shadows flit chaotically around the whitewashed walls.

She lowers her head onto my chest, slips slowly down the bed and starts to play with me. I force myself to stillness, I want the pace to be hers, I mustn't frighten her again.

You're so hot. I could hold you, feel your pulse all night.

I couldn't last the night, love. Not even for you.

She laughs and drops a kiss on me, then another. My excitement is almost uncontrollable. I feel happy. This is working well.

The sudden touch of her tongue is excruciatingly wonderful. I gasp and my body jerks, involuntarily. She recoils.

Don't make me. I can't bear it!

Alex, please come back!

**

So I'm lying alone in Alex's bed, on fire, feeling hurt, bewildered, clumsy. I think she's in the bathroom, though she might well be racing barefoot through the fields.

I need to understand, but first I have to release. It seems wrong to conjure Alex so I choose Elinor, who – in that one respect – is far more reliable and gifted. She gives me what I want, I come quickly, lie panting, feeling guilty because I've made love with her in Alex's chaste bed.

But the earlier guilt is beginning to consume me. I'd no intention of subjecting Alex to pressure. I simply wanted to try to help her ease out of some pit of fear which she's been in for a long time, perhaps always. I'd wanted her at all times to feel able to pull out, but at the time she called *Don't make me!* I was willing her to continue, to satisfy my lust. I imagine she could tell, and that had frightened her.

And of course it's true that right from the beginning I wanted to make love with her. Was everything I'd done simply part of a plot to induce her to have sex with me? Is it possible simultaneously to harbour good motives and bad? I feel confused and the guilt won't go away.

The door opens quietly and she slips into bed with me. I lie still, not wanting to make the first move.

Her hand slips into mine, and the lightness in my stomach lessens immediately.

I'm sorry, Zack. You'd been so patient with me.

I'm sorry I frightened you.

That wasn't your fault. It was bound to happen. I've been carrying this problem since I was a little girl.

Your father?

Yes.

Is that why you hissed at him as you were leaving the hospital today?

Yes. But let's not talk about it now. I want to do something for you.

Her hand slides down my stomach, finds me limp, curled, damp and tiny. She gives a gasp of surprise.

I had to, Alex. I'd have exploded otherwise.

She smiles rather wanly.

Well, at least you got to make love with me fully, without my neuroses getting in the way.

I smile back, but I can't speak. I can neither tell the truth nor lie to her.

She senses this.

Or were you with someone else?

I had to, Alex. I couldn't violate you.

She's quiet for a while, then snuggles into me.

Complicated business, isn't it?

I feel very tired, and though my guilt is still nagging at me, the need for sleep overwhelms it. I'm almost gone when her voice drifts to me.

If you'll bear with me, I want to keep trying. I'm twenty-eight. It's time for me to have a lover. A full lover.

I wake up a little.
Can I volunteer?
Yes, if you'll continue to be patient.
I'll try. If you'll let me get some sleep.

**

We've had coffee, the morning sun is slanting through the window onto our pillows, making them dazzlingly white, and we're lingering in bed. We've had a lot of physical contact since she freaked out and fled from me to the bathroom, but it's been of a simple, not sexual kind. I'm fidgety, excited, wondering if we can try again. On the other hand, I'd do anything to avoid distressing her again. She reads my mind, as she's done several times before.

I think it's time, Zack. But I'm nervous. I'd like you to take charge.

Are you sure you want to try? We have lovely times as things are. And pain comes with sex, as you know better than I.

Yes, but so does ecstasy. That's what I want to taste, with you.

She moves to me and this time I'm the explorer in a slow and easy journey round her body, with ample pauses for her to pull away. She doesn't, though I think I feel her tense sometimes.

She lets me touch and savour her in every way I choose. She's quiet, passive but not unresponsive. For much of the time her hand is stroking the bones at the back of my neck, and as time passes the movement of her hand grows faster, more erratic.

I raise my head and look between her small, taut breasts at her face. Her eyes are closed, but she knows I'm watching her.

I think we're making progress, Zack?

Oh, yes.

She smiles. I pull forward, hold myself above her. She nods, a small movement but a definite one. I close my eyes, guide myself into her, move slowly deeper.

Alex. I'm so happy.

She doesn't answer. I open my eyes, look down at her. Every part of her is quivering with tension. Her fists are clenched, her eyes squeezed shut, her mouth a thin line of wretchedness. I feel desperately sorry for her. I feel myself wilting and slip out of her.

Thank God!

I know she doesn't mean to hurt me, that her words were involuntary, the truth, and nothing to do with me.

But I can't not take it personally. I feel humiliated, teased.

For Christ's sake, Alex!

She crumples into tears but I ignore her, whirl out of bed, grab my clothes, storm out of the room.

I dress quickly, and when my shoelace snags on something I yank on it so hard it breaks. Hours later I find my sweater's back-to-front.

I know I'm behaving badly, that she tried her best and made good progress with a horrendous problem, that she's lying in the bedroom crying, feeling inadequate, that if I went to her now I could make her feel better.

But I need to rage and be impossible. I need to be alone, burn up some energy. I know that if I go to her, tell her I need space for a few hours, she'll understand, she'll feel much better than she does at the moment. But I won't do it. I'm not consciously wanting to punish her, but I'm not going to do anything that will make her feel good while I'm so confused and frustrated.

I leave, stomp through the forest, but as the exercise calms me and I breathe the fresh air I begin to feel better, I'm sorry for my violence, I want to hold her, be held by her. I realise how important she's become to me.

I start to run back to her cottage, fall into rage when I get lost. I'm filled with joy when I stumble on the right path, and am sprinting when I reach her gate.

I race up to the door, try to turn the handle. It won't move. The door is locked.

I'm surprised, in despair. I can't have been gone for more than an hour. It's possible that she's got up and gone shopping, but then I remember she told me she never locks her door when she goes out. So she's in there, hiding from me. I bang on the door, shout her name through the letter-box. There is no answer.

I try to tell myself that it's she who needs space now, that if I come back in a few hours time she'll let me in and we can talk. But I don't believe it. I think I've hurt her more than she can bear. I don't think she'll let me in again.

I walk back towards the forest, not knowing what to do. A ladybird settles on my wrist. I swipe it with my other hand and all that remains is a red blotch on my skin.

I'm sorry, I say. *I'm very sorry.*

I walk on slowly, sucking my wrist.

**

For a few days it ceases. As before, she comes for the dog after work, stays for chai, a meal, sometimes a massage. She's pleasant but untouchable, leaves with thanks and a hug, but never having washed up, never having brought a contribution to our evening. Once more I feel I'm eating shit, and though I know it's a self-inflicted condition, my anger grows, I doctor the chai again, this time more carefully. I carry jars of diluted excrement to her apartment while she's at work, let myself in with the key I copied from one she briefly loaned me, tip the shit in various places: in one of her winter boots; inside a sweater folded in her closet; in the workings of her vacuum cleaner; under the carpet near the toilet bowl, and always pour the remainder behind the cooker, an inaccessible place. I wait for a response, don't get one, carry on. I piss into her milk carton, flip the circuit breaker that controls the fridge. I stuff fistfuls of tissues into the toilet. It overflows, the shit under the carpet is revealed – a hideous mess which she can't deal with. So I play Sir Galahad, cut out the carpet for her. It has to be destroyed.

At about that time the accumulation of shit behind the cooker starts to smell. Badly. She's distraught, rows with her landlady who threatens eviction, eventually can't tolerate the stench any longer, accepts my invitation to move in temporarily with me.

She's very grateful, calls me her rock, her salvation. We get along fine, I cosset her, but I'm still unsettled and I continue doctoring the chai. And since nothing has harmed her I look for a new dimension. I consider grinding up pellets of rat poison to add to her drink. I plan it in detail, in the full knowledge that everything I've considered so far, I've subsequently done.

I'm hooked now, terrified, excited.

**

I force myself to keep away from Alex's cottage for three whole hours.

At first the time passes terribly slowly. I walk into the village, look around the church, which makes me feel cold, and the graveyard, which makes me feel sad. I try the small library and am amazed to find that though I regard myself as an avid reader, there are only two books out of the entire collection of fiction – *Silas Marner* and *Great Expectations* – that I've read. I feel peckish, go into the almost deserted local pub and have a ploughman's lunch and a pint of cider, during which period I play a solitary game of darts. I'm pleased that though it's years since I threw the arrows, I seem as proficient now as I was then.

I glance at the old clock ticking in the corner. Quarter of an hour to go. Just enough time for a brisk stroll through the oaks.

I walk up to the bar to pay, then discover I've no money. I've left it at Alex's.

I splutter out my story to the publican, who seems much less genial than earlier. He hears me out, though I don't think he's listening.

I'll be in this evening with the money. OK?

Don't bother. Regard this as my treat.

But I want to pay you.

And I don't want to have to think about you after you've gone through that door. Good day.

His nod as he turns away is neither friendly nor unpleasant. At any other time I'd have wanted to sort it out with him, part on amicable terms. Also, I'd like to know him better. There was something impressive in his capacity just to snap his fingers and expunge from his life any concern over whether he'd been cheated. If only I could do that, my life over the past few years would have been much happier; and I'd like myself much better than I do.

But this isn't the time to address that issue. Now I want to be with Alex, and I'm late. I run all the way back and am only a couple of minutes over the schedule I'd set myself when I arrive at the cottage, rap on the door. There is no answer.

I knock a few times but don't shout, as I think that would annoy her. I've no doubt she's in there, waiting for me to go away.

I walk into her garden, snap off the largest rhubarb leaf I can find, and leaning against her door, with a flint I carry in my pocket, carve into the leaf the words:

I'm sorry. I love you. Please let me in.

I push it through the letter-box, rap once on the knocker and walk back into the trees.

I sit for half an hour then walk back. The rhubarb leaf is pinned to the door, with new words on it, written in viscous white, probably toothpaste.

You should have tried the handle. Come in, if only for your wallet.

I race into the cottage, find her in the kitchen, open my arms to her. She steps back, shakes her head.

Take it easy, Zack. Sit down. We need to talk. I've made a pot of tea.

We sit opposite each other, just as in the hospital. She pours the tea, settles herself to speak. I wait.

I don't want to threaten you, Zack, but you need to understand that I can't deal with how you were this morning. If it happens again, I won't continue with our journey.

You mean my swearing at you?

Of course I don't mean that. That was natural. I think it's happened every time I've reached that cul-de-sac. No, it was the way you abandoned me.

I needed space, Alex. Space to wind down.

I know. And you know I'd have given you that space. But you left without a word. That was cruel.

I start to marshal arguments against her, then I

look into her eyes and stop. She's so transparently honest, I want to be the same.

You're right. I felt so churned up I didn't want to try to make you feel better.

Her voice takes on a gentler note.

Thank you. Though I'd put it differently. You had power over me. You could give me happiness or withhold it. You chose the latter. I think it's almost always the wrong decision.

I'll do better next time.

Good.

We hold hands for a while across the table. I feel eased and happy. Her face tells me she feels the same. There's much to discuss, but not now.

As we peel and chop the vegetables for our evening meal, I ask her a question that's been nagging at me.

You said you'd been down that cul-de-sac many times before. D'you mean...

Are you asking if other men have come inside me, and we've had the same debacle as today?

I suppose I am.

I'm not a nun, Zack. I'm just screwed up about sex, that's all.

For a moment I feel jealous, upset that I wasn't the first to try to help her through this problem. Then I realise how ludicrous I'm being.

I'm glad you let me back in, Alex.

And I'm glad it's not winter.

What d'you mean?

It was the rhubarb leaf that made the difference. I'd washed my hands of you. I've always done that. Always. If you'd left me a note on an ordinary piece of paper I'd not have responded. But there was something so crazy about writing on a rhubarb leaf that I wanted more of you.

I know she's speaking the truth. I know also that if I'd had pencil and paper I'd have used them.

I've been lucky. At least I think I have. I look at her. Her eyes are wild and shining. I know that the one quality our journey won't have is boredom.

Let's wrestle, I say, out of nowhere.

Why not?

She pushes back her chair and leaps on me.

**

six

In my early weeks of crawling I'd have missed the side-branch. The grass and creepers covering the entrance look no different from those to either side of it. The only clue is a slight shiver of the hairs on my left forearm, as the faintest of breezes percolates through the foliage.

I burrow through, into total darkness. This narrow section of the ditch has been so long neglected that turf along the edges has grown across the gap, transforming it into a tunnel. I fumble in my oilskin, unwrap my stash of matches, light a stub of candle, wedge it in the sheath tied to my hat. Only then do I allow myself to look.

The tunnel extends beyond the candlelight into a tube of blackness so pure I know it has never been seen before. Its walls are dry, and in some way I can't fathom they've become concave, so the tunnel is a cylinder, its floor cushioned by leaves dropped by centuries of autumns. They crackle into powder as I crawl over them.

The tunnel is horizontal, shrubs or grass above me, deep earth below, yet it doesn't seem strange that the air grows warmer as I crawl on. It doesn't seem strange either that the tunnel ends at a massive sandstone rock; or that when I rummage through the dead leaves covering my knees, I should find an iron ring wider than my fist; or that when I twist and tug it a trapdoor should creak open; or that the air – as I lower my face into the perfect dark – should be spiced with the scent of animals; or that somewhere deep below me, at the audible threshold, is a throbbing.

I feel sure this cavern is filled with shapes and images that can only be perceived in total darkness. I want to go there, but I'm not quite ready yet. Neither are they.

I take off my kneepads, don my rush-weave sandals, replace the stub of candle with a full-length one, grasp the upper rung of the rope ladder, swing my body through the hatch, lower it back into place, and stand, swirling slowly round, as much at the summit of a world as someone standing on top of Everest.

I can't tell how far the ladder stretches below me, but I suspect that if I dropped a stone I'd never hear it land.

I have a choice to make. Keep my candle lit and see what a camera might see; blow it out and see what a camera cannot. I decide to keep it lit for the first part of my descent. It seems right to move gradually into this new experience, insinuate myself into this atmosphere, rather than plunge in cold.

The throbbing, though still quiet, is more pronounced, the beating of a drum from far below, each roll echoing round the cavern, reverberating, climbing up its sides, the sound slipping away before the next one comes, the interval of silence filled less with absence than anticipation.

Thoom, thoom, thoom: the deep, slow heartbeat of the world.

Thoom: the sound that was there at the

beginning. There and everywhere before the beginning, the sound that ushered in all life.

It comes from far below, and the invisible straight line that links its source to me, swaying at the top of the rope ladder, is as true an arrow to the centre of the Earth, as gravity's vector, which would have plummeted the stone I hadn't needed to let go.

Each stumbled step from rung to lower rung is a step into my history, into all history, a step en route to my first home.

Jerfal.

The word passes through my consciousness, but I don't hear it.

I have many shapes as I descend. All are distorted, all ephemeral. A twisted, stunted runt of me, projected on the escarpment of a granite shoulder rearing from the night. A stretched chin flung onto a pillar stubbled by dry moss. A wild arm thinned into a jagged pencil line inching up a cliffside as my head drops down.

Jerfal.

This time it registers. It thrills me as it always does. I know she's here, is always here.

Gribnocks.

She laughs when she hears me, a wraith of pleasure that leaves me standing on a hempen rung, my arms outstretched towards her, the idea of her. She's somewhere in the cavern, on a similar rope-ladder, but I don't know where.

No matter. We have our game to play.

Yatterfail.

Dinch.

Millimangie.

Lesserwings.

Aridater.

Fooze.

And so, as we descend towards the seat of the deep throbbing, we dip into our reservoirs of words that might have been, tie them in pale ribbon, float them though darkness to each other. On arrival they wallow in their welcome, hesitate, spawn their successor, slip away.

Litterwinkles.
Mersery.
Glipponightshale.
Pote.

The communion between us as we float words across the thickening blackness to each other is the communion of play, in which our tongues are simply vehicles, our intellects irrelevant. It is the interplay of Alex's subconscious with mine, light, unloaded, a pure exchange, unsullied, confirming the feeling I've always had that play – not competition, but reinforcement, in which we simultaneously dance across each other's keyboards, in which we lead and follow each other along unknown paths – this kind of play, transcending gender, race and species, is the holiest of contacts between two breathing creatures; and as such might save the world.

The communion between us in the long intervals between the spates of words is very different. It is the communion of mutual uncertainty, of risk and fear, amazement and loss. Its essence is its ephemerality. I daren't stretch to it, embrace it, because in so doing I would change it. So I hold it without power, without breathing. I revel in it. Alex and I are both inside this cavern, but this time we're alone, and our physical closeness accentuates our separation. This is not a communion that can save the world. It is one that can destroy it unless we learn to accept its presence as the price of life. If we can find the courage to do that, force ourselves to experience the associated pain and terror, then perhaps we'll also retract our claws, find joy.

The candlelight is weak, and as we descend it becomes even less effectual. This is in part because there is little within its range to illuminate. If I look up I see five or six rungs of my ladder, each one the ghost of its predecessor. If I look down I see only the shadow of my sandals, silhouetted against the seething dark. If I use Alex's voice to pinpoint her direction I can sometimes see a faint aura that flickers now and then. But I don't see her, except once when her wrist and hand glide into focus and swiftly out again.

Sometimes she's to the left of me, sometimes to the right. Sometimes she's in front, sometimes behind. I've no way of telling if these changes of position are because my ladder is slowly spinning, or if one of us is somehow circling the other.

Mellawrinkles.

Harthrough.

Kraptin.

Froo.

The light is changing below me, with spurts of greyish-white, shifting mounds of intense blackness. The deep throbbing remains, my heart in synchronism with it, but now – superimposed on it – is lighter drumming, complex, variable, exciting. The air is warmer, smells of sulphur and a spice I can't identify whose fragrance I've met just once before, when I was little and my Auntie Maisie sliced a huge, dark cake she'd lifted from a tin embossed with purple flowers.

My foot, probing the darkness for the next rung down, hits rock instead. I disengage from the ladder and when, a moment later, I feel round for it, it has gone. I blink to help my eyes accustom to the greenish dark, lower myself onto a patch of fine sand. I sift it as I stretch behind me, find Alex's hand reaching out for

mine. We clasp for a moment and leave go. It is sufficient to know we're in the same theatre. We'll come
together, if we care to, later, after the show.

The show. I'm not sure where those words come
from. True, the air seems fidgety, with an underwelling
of stored energy straining to get out; just like at the
theatre before the curtain rises. True also that now
we've extinguished our candles we can see that the air
is populated with faint shapes, more shadow than
substance, large and slow, imbued with a kind of
benign gravitas; and this makes me think of actors,
invisible, off-stage, before the performance starts,
breathing deeply, gathering themselves.

But the feeling I have isn't simply an indication,
it's an absolute knowledge that the show is about to
begin; a level of certainty I scarcely ever feel, except
with Alex. I settle back in the warm sand.

You must be respectful of the heavy creatures.

She's whispering in my ear.

*They've been wounded, Zack. By us, I mean by
people. They've no cause to let us see them, but
they're trusting us. After all the damage they're still
able to trust. Respect that.*

I will, Alex. I do.

As we've been talking there's been a subtle
change in the drumming. The deepest throbbing,
which I now realise is the heartbeat of the world, is of
course unchanged, but the other, lighter drumming is
no longer random, it has taken on a structure, faint
but real, through which runs a vein of urgency,
excitement.

Suddenly it stops. The darkness is profound.

Give yourself, she whispers: Let everything go. I'll
be with you, though you mustn't try to touch me.

I wait for the curtain to rise.

**

I've taken the day off, to think. The situation seems desperate, Elinor is on the verge of leaving. Such a prospect is unbearable. I get up early, without waking her, drive to the edge of the moors, put my boots on and start hiking.

The weather is exactly as it should be up here, the mist patchy, whirling, so that sometimes I can't see at all, while at others I can, though I seem always on the edge of a clearing, not within it. It's drizzling and when wind gusts, cold raindrops smash into my forehead. Already, I can feel my mind growing clear.

I'm lost immediately, as I need to be, and for the next few hours I see no-one – just an occasional sheep, hugging the lee-side of a dry-stone wall. Although my boots are heavy and mud sucks at every stride, I seem to gain strength and lightness. The elements are scouring all the dross away. I sit with a sheep in the shelter of a wall and eat beef-and-mustard sandwiches, thick and cool, moistened with water dripping from my hair. They are perfect. My apple cleaves with a crack that makes the sheep turn round. Its sharp juices cleanse my mouth. I hurl the core far past the pallid sun and decide to go home. I've been neurotic and stupid. Now, everything is simple.

When I pull into the drive, a few hours early, his car is there. That doesn't matter. I've been jumping to ridiculous conclusions, and he's probably just called by for a few minutes. But I don't want to meet him, not today, so I slip into the cellar, planning to wait until he's gone.

I sit in the workshop, rather cold and damp but still exhilarated. I hear them talking in the kitchen, but the words are blurred.

There are some shavings on the bench, from

when I'd planed the doors to the kitchen cabinets. They are tightly coiled, and I wonder if their shapes are like the eddies that lashed me throughout the afternoon. I take one by its tail and flick it high towards the light. It falls awkwardly.

The conversation in the kitchen seems about to cease, but then picks up again. I plug in the electric fire, undress and hang my damp clothes from hooks screwed to the wall, I sit in front of it, on an upturned box, spreading my legs to dry my thighs. It feels good to be naked and warm.

The label on the can says: *Stir thoroughly, do not thin.* Threads of paint have dribbled down the outside and dried, obliterating some of the letters. At the end of each trail the paint is thicker, blistered, as though it tried to gather its resources for a further journey, but failed.

I remember the paint-shop in my Uncle Jack's back-yard – a low brick building, smelling wonderfully of turpentine and putty. For thirty years, at the end of every day, he and my Uncle Harry had cleaned their brushes on the inside wall. All colours were there, with more pinks and yellows than I'd have expected. Whenever the sun shafted through the latticed windows the whole room would glow, and I felt sure the light in Heaven was the same. The accumulated coatings were enormously thick, and I wondered if my uncles would build me a shelter out of them, if I asked. I'd make holes through the walls, but if the sun didn't show me all the different colours I'd install a small mirror, or a prism, so they'd be reflected into the room, and I could lie in my bed as they bathed my outstretched arms.

There is less laughter from above. Their conversation seems more intimate, the silences longer. The message on the tin is mocking me.

I take my blunt chisel and pry off the lid. A thick skin droops across the tin's width, rather like a trampoline. I nick it with the chisel and the tear extends nearly all the way across. The folds of skin sink into the paint. The green is deeper than on the outside of the can. I suppose this is the paint I used for our new gates, a year or two ago. I stir it slowly with the chisel. Now I know what I will do there is no hurry.

After a while the skin stops surfacing, and when I lift the chisel out a stream of paint flows smoothly from it, thinning, spiralling onto the featureless green disc, like syrup onto porridge. It is fully mixed.

There are two brushes in the drawer; a worn four-inch one I use for varnishing, and a slightly smaller one, still in its cellophane wrapper. I choose the latter.

I shiver as the first stroke stripes me from my groin up to my neck. In the light reflected from my stomach I can see my pores, black against the green. The tingling is quite pleasant. A large drop wells out of my navel, tickles as it slides towards my thighs. I'm swift but calm, with little overlapping of the stripes – as economical as mowing a lawn. I can't be certain that my back is fully covered, so when all I can see is painted green I stoop and tip the can onto my shoulders. There's more paint left than I'd imagined and I can feel the skin-flaps sliding, slower than the rest.

I find a smaller tin of paint – maroon gloss – and use it on my nose and chin, my nipples, navel, private parts. I no longer care about the droning from the kitchen. All that matters is that I finish before he leaves. I daub maroon paint on my kneecaps, pour the rest into my hair. I am ready.

I tiptoe up the cellar stairs, the concrete cold

against my feet, which I realise I've not painted. Each hand-print on the rail is fainter than the one before – like the lipstick mouths on my Aunt Lil's paper handkerchiefs.

Elinor is sitting on the bench. He's standing over her, one foot resting on the stool Aunt Lil gave us for a wedding present. No words had been spoken since I started climbing up the stairs. I enter slowly, crab-wise – more stooped than on the moors – and have almost reached them when she spots me and screams. He spins round. A smile seems to flit across his face.

I spring, higher than I thought I could, wind my arms and legs around his face. For a moment we balance, and I can see the label on the inside of his jacket collar.

Christ! he exclaims, in a muffled kind of way.

He sinks slowly to his knees, rolls backwards to the floor. I ride with him, finishing astride his face; his nose – green and maroon – poking plaintively from between my legs, his spectacles snapped, the broken stem pressing hard into my thigh. Paint is dripping from my lower stomach onto his hair. The green shows up more clearly than the red. His eyes are open but they don't seem in focus. He's not moving.

You bloody fool! she shouts.

I kiss him fiercely on the lips, rise, drop her a curtsey, crab hurriedly away.

**

My heart is no longer confined within my body. It ranges free, beats with the pulse of a hundred other hearts, a thousand, loosely packed into this coarse-weave sack, its uniqueness subsumed into a common slow-pace throb, that spreads into my chest and into Alex's, across the flickering dark into the heavy creatures, waiting in the wings. And now I understand that I can't join them until our hearts are one: and that Alex and I, however thin and tenuous the thread that loops its ends around our belts, however savagely we slash and burn it, scrape it over jagged glass, drown it in the sea, will never fully disentangle from it, and it will from time to time contract, tug us without our knowledge into the same place, a charged and strange one. Like now.

I am growing bigger. I am flowing out into a different shape. I and we can no longer be distinguished.

**

I've always thought that the faster the dance, the more exciting, joyous and abandoned it would be. I now know that I'm wrong, that the spaces and silences of slow-pace dancing permit these qualities to reach a greater level of intensity.

The first object that enters into view is part of a rock-face, extending into blackness above and to each side of us. It is virtually sheer, and though quite smooth is not plane, having a range of protuberances and declivities. It is flooded with a roughly circular patch of bright scarlet light which appears to come from somewhere below and behind us. A stunted bush somehow clinging to the granite face above me looks black.

I don't see the heavy creatures appear. They are suddenly present, four of them, in front of us, facing the cliff, their shadows on the rock distorted by its curvature and stretched by the angle of the light.

The drumming, without changing beat or volume, becomes conspicuous, fuelling the heavy creatures' dancing.

Each of the four dances is very different, yet all are in sympathy with the drum music.

They are slow, grave and smiling: at the same time wild and full of tears.

They are solitary, snatches of lone journeys. At the same time they support and reflect each other.

Joy and despair are strongly present; and indistinguishable.

What the dances express is from deep within each dancer, yet the reservoir of riches from which they draw their spirit is common.

The shadows magnify the dancers' movements, so that when a heavy creature engages in a slight twist of its shoulders, a mild twirling of its arm, its shadow sweeps across the circle of light, enlarging hugely these minor body shifts, and in so doing reveals the emotions that provoked them.

It is a while before I recognise the shadow-butting, in which the dancer tenses its neck and nods, its shadow nodding back, more expansively and somewhat out of kilter because of the irregularities of the rock-face. And so the creature and its shadow lunge towards each other with stolid grace, pull away, locked in an old pattern of not quite making contact, not quite leaving go. Which is the servant, which the master I can't tell. The courtesy and deference seem mutual.

The shadows want to be seen. They don't possess the shyness of the heavy creatures, of whom I have only fragments of a picture: and because of their diffidence I'm reluctant to portray even those. I'll say only that they're large by human standards, their shapes are ever-shifting and their great age has not jaundiced them.

I could watch the heavy creatures dance for hours. Yet in no way am I a passive spectator. My whole body is drawn into the gentle, graceful, awkward, funny poignancy of their dancing. It resonates to the drums. The air is flecked with spice and sulphur. I'm in a giant chamber of which only one small yellow patch is visible – a beating heart. I am a small part of that chamber.

I could never, by myself, join in the dancing. But Alex senses what I cannot.

She grips my shoulder, whispers to me, fiercely.

Come, Zack. It's time to dance.

No. We can't invade them.

But they want us to. They're beckoning us. Can't you see?

I stare at the shadows, bobbing, wheeling, nodding, stupendous shapes cavorting round the rock. I'm not shut out, but nor am I invited.

No.

Have courage, Zack.

As she rises, she takes my hand and tugs it. Her pull is irresistible. She drags me, stumbling, across a sandy floor I cannot see, into the light. Once there she positions me between a pair of heavy creatures, then moves away from me, out of my sight.

I stand for a while, uncertain how to move, the shadows now towering above me, stretching to my left and right, linked to each other in some palpable way too subtle to define, linked now to an extra one, smaller than the others, more skeletal, wraithlike, her sense of involvement and innate joy apparent in every move she makes.

Four heavy creatures, Alex and myself. Yet there are only five shadows on the wall. Mine is missing.

Dance, Zack. Dance!

The voice is Alex's, but the whispered words come from within me. It would not have been right to call across the cavern, whose essence is silence, where it is better even for whispers to be mute.

Dance and find your shadow.

So I do.

Uncertainly at first, self-consciously, but the rhythms are compelling, they draw me in, I close my eyes, spread into the dance, and when I blink open my shadow is before me, huge and wild, clear as the others.

I feel a surge of happiness, close my eyes again.

**

He's taken it away. I want it.

I want that beaker of sweet sticky stuff Mummy calls blackcurrant. I want to shake it, pry its top off, tip it over the edge of this high chair onto the floor.

Give it back to me! I want to make a bigger mess. I want to throw everything in the whole world onto the floor.

Don't smile at me and shake your head. I'll scratch your face, stick my tongue out at you.

I'm strong. Why don't you worry when I scream at you. I'm going to tear your smile to pieces, throw it all away, forever.

When I'm big I'm going to squeeze you in this chair so you can't move at all, and I'll pour blackcurrant in your eyes.

There. That's the biggest scream in all the world. Why don't you cry? Give me the beaker. Why don't you hold me? No, leave me alone. I'll scratch you.

Leave me alone. Don't pick me up. See my fingernails. I'll spit into your whiskers. Put me down! I'll kick you right over the house.

I don't want you to hug me. Let me down. Don't stroke me.

I'm not crying because I'm sorry.

I'm sorry. Hold me.

This deep *thump thump*. I want to be inside this deep *thump thump*. I want to be inside it again.

**

When I open my eyes the heavy creatures have disappeared. Alex is behind me, her shadow larger than mine, enveloping me.

She's moving slowly. Her shadow is stroking mine, without touching. Her hands are moving over all parts of my body. I feel purged, eased, in total harmony.

I want to turn to her, to reciprocate the massage, but I know she won't allow it. This is her gift to me and I should accept it, fully, abandon myself to it.

I try to, then I don't need to try. I'm swept up by her stroking, engorged by it. Not sexual at all, though the atmosphere is so inflammable the tiniest of sparks could make it so. I give myself up to the experience, close my eyes again.

When I open them, I find I'm still dancing. But my shadow has gone and so has Alex. All the drums are quiet except the Earth's heartbeat. The sweep of light is gone, just a faint illumination, a kind of phosphorescence, that shows the last few rungs of my rope ladder, swaying slightly as it dangles from impenetrable dark. I feel a little chilled but happy.

It is time to leave. Before I start climbing I stand on the bottom rung, lean back and swirl around. I see nothing to remind me of the heavy creatures or Alex's shadow-hands stroking me. I don't mind.

I'm only a few rungs into my long journey back when I realise how exhausted I am. I'll have to climb with great economy of effort. My body feels so relaxed I know I can do it.

Jerfal.

The word is whispered, from far above me. I sense that all she wants is to let me know I'm not alone. She's no wish to play our word game. Nor have I.

I breathe my reply, feel it swell into the large air of the cavern.

Yatterfail.

We climb in silence.

**

I'm standing on Nellie Preece's tall thin stool, looking sharply down from the lowest panes of a tall thin window, into the disappearing street below.

The deep red sheen of the moulded Accrington brick from which the outside window-sill is formed is pitted and stained with two hundred years of pigeon-shit and increasingly potent acid rain, bringing down into the town the particles and poisons that have swirled out of the chimneys of thirty thousand huddled houses burning low-grade coal.

I wonder if this window has ever been opened. Certainly it could not be now, its iron catches so rounded with rust the gorgeous colour of Nancy Cornes's hair there is nothing for finger and thumb to grip.

As I glance down into the street, a gust of wind surprises old Mr Perkins, blows his evening paper inside out, covering his face, making him totter off the pavement into the cobbled road, just missing the swishing tail of the rag-and-bone man's horse.

I stick two fingers in my mouth and whistle. But I know no-one will hear me. I'm trapped, the only person in this school condemned to die. Its doors have slammed, keys have turned on every exit, the weekend looms, and as dusk, thickened by smoke, falls over the town, the school thins, grows taller, pinioning me inside a damp blanket subduing my struggles, carrying me away.

A tug on the canal blows its foghorn. Always the loneliest sound in the world, calling out not for help but for companionship, spreading out, reaching out in all directions, turning thin and blue, never giving up hope, never having any hope, while I shiver in my bed, the village in blackout so the German planes won't see us, not a light in the house as far as I can tell, the bed so big I feel forgotten, I'll never be found, wind rustling the curtains I cannot see, Hitler, knife in teeth, wriggling down the chimney upside-down, saliva swarming down his cheeks into his bloodshot eyes, my sheets starched and cold, my only friend the foghorn on the Mersey.

What is it about Nellie that so frightens me? Terrifies me, in fact, so much so that when she swept in late to supervise our punishment, two hours detention after school, I couldn't race to my desk from my hiding-place, as all the other children did. I stayed in this dark cupboard smelling of mould and dried-up sweat, watched detention through the keyhole.

Though her tongue is vicious, and those sudden swipes across the face with her heavily ringed fingers can sting, I can handle that – after all, old Bamberger is crueler and more violent. No, I think she scares me because she's old and ugly, because anyone so corsetted, varicosed and wrinkled must be close to dying, so when she spits out droplets as she shouts at me, she's showering me with death-seeds I might inhale if I don't hold my breath, and if so they'll sprout inside me.

I'm afraid of Nellie because she's a woman, she's ugly and she's dying. My mother's young and beautiful, and she's not dying. She's always open to me, she always will be. But last week, on the lawn, clothes-pegs in her mouth, bending to the washing basket, she looked misshapen, just like Nellie, and I knew then that one day she'd grow old.

I'm afraid of the wart on Nellie's chin. Great black whiskers sprouting from it, it wobbles when she shouts, it's made of something that's not human, it's been through fire, it's a cinder that hates children. Dead people grow them in their coffins, Hitler's tongue is covered with them.

It can't be killed. Like when Johnnie cut the worm in sixteen little pieces, and one had wriggled away when we came back after playtime.

I think Nellie cut her wart off after Johnnie slipped the note into her handbag:

Old Wartychops. Ugliest woman in the world.

I'm sure she'd sliced it off under the plaster. But back it came after a week or two, purple now, hating us all, bigger and more horrible than ever.

And then I remember we've broken up today. Two weeks holiday, two weeks trapped in this classroom. I've no chance. Maybe rain will trickle in through small cracks in the window, I could stand on Nellie's stool and tongue it in. But if it tasted of pigeon-shit could I bring myself to swallow? Hadn't I read somewhere that it's poisonous, skin peeling away, flesh dropping off the bones? And anyway, even if the water isn't contaminated, I'd starve. I ferret through my pockets: half a packet of Wrigley's spearmint chewing-gum, an aniseed ball and a fragment of a crisp, covered in fluff, which I brush carefully away. I must conserve everything. Perhaps even the fluff would be nutritious. I look for it, but it has gone.

**

This black is green. It is a colour I have not yet seen.

A tide is rising. It will sweep me away.

Why do they think I want to surf the wave inevitably coming, be flung out into a place that makes me clench my muscles, writhe sleeping time away, wrack my body so that the darkness all around me pounds?

**

seven

I said before that ditch-crawling has no rules, just aesthetic principles. On reflection, I should have added it has rituals. These I have learned with no teacher but the ditch itself, and I am happy to abide with them.

The essence of the interactions between creatures of the ditch is collaboration and tolerance, executed quietly, anonymously. If blackberries are in profusion over one stretch of the ditch, eat your fill, collect a further supply, and carry them to another stretch where blackberries are rare. Place them, one by one, gently in the mud, at roughly constant spacing, over the entire length of the deprived region. Hope that creatures less mobile than you will find them. Move on without looking back.

There are, of course, cruelties and killings in the ditch. But these are rare in comparison with the world outside, and are usually prompted by need. The relative peacefulness is due, I think, to our consciousness that we are dwelling below the surface of the earth. We are in close contact with our unsorted substructures, our deep and imperfect interiors. We sympathise with each other's struggles, and we tread softly as a consequence. We know that interactions between us will not mute our essential loneliness, so we help each other from afar. We rarely meet each other, and our only actions are ritualistic ones.

Not all ditch-rituals are designed to help others. My favourite one celebrates play and intuition.

Anyone who has been crawling more than a few times is likely to have encountered, in quiet regions on deep shelves fashioned from dried mud, a cairn of stones, mostly but not entirely white. Sometimes cairns look virtually finished, tall, thin, tapering to two or three single stones, delicately balanced on top of each other. Sometimes their construction is scarcely started. Cairns are always surrounded by additional, unused stones. They are usually located close to nodes.

If you encounter such a structure and feel inclined toward the ritual, sit beside it for a while, absorbing the silence, the spirit of the game, which is to place on the cairn another stone. Not any stone, but the one which will add most harmony.

Before making your selection you must examine all the stones. Treat each one with respect, even if you feel sure that you'll reject it. Cup it in your hands, breathe its dust away, feel how it balances, pulls towards the cairn. If you wish, lower it into place, but don't leave go of it, unless it is the chosen one.

All shapes and sizes are allowed. Don't be afraid to place a jagged one low down. The tower will touch you most when it is close to toppling. Better still, be afraid but hold your breath and place it even so.

When you've laid your stone and the cairn is still not finished, move quietly away. Your job is done. If, however, your stone completes the cairn, sit with it and watch, throughout the afternoon, how filtered sunlight slides across its modesties.

You'll know when it's time. Then, reach up into the grasses that overlook the ditch, pluck one and hold it against that part of the cairn which seems to be calling for its touch. You won't need to push, and you'll scarcely hear it as it topples to the ground.

Leave the stones for the next crawler, and move on.

**

She puts down the phone, continues shelling the peas I've just picked from her garden.

What did they say?

She folds an emptied shell inside-out, runs it between her teeth to collect that sharp, green juice which has one of the freshest tastes I know.

He's weaker. Sleeping. They don't think it will be long.

I walk over to her, rest my hand on her shoulder. She continues to shell peas.

I'll be happy to come with you.

I don't want to go. I'd rather just walk into the wind.

Gales have been rampaging for several hours now, filling the air with leaves in crazy-dance, making the cottage rafters groan.

This is the third time you've been told he's deteriorating. I think you might be sorry if you don't see him again.

She pauses, tosses her knife dextrously into the sink.

Alright. Though I doubt if it'll do any good. But then we hike. OK?

**

The nurse was obviously right. He's changed considerably over the last twenty-four hours. His face has slackened and now has a yellowish pallor. He no longer looks beautiful.

He's in restless sleep, but when Alex takes his hand he mumbles incomprehensibly then opens his eyes. His eyes light up when he sees her.

Alexandra!

His voice is strong. She shudders when she hears it. He closes his eyes again, though I'm sure he's not asleep.

I feel intrusive, but she's made me promise not to leave her alone with him.

When he speaks again, he sounds further away.

Alexandra. Will you pray for me?

Gently she withdraws her hand from his.

I can't, father. I don't like your God.

He struggles to find the strength to speak.

You don't have to like him. Just ask him. Ask him to give me peace.

She hesitates, biting her lip, but her response is clear and firm.

I can't. That's not what I want for you.

Pain ripples across his face.

So be it.

No sound comes from him as he speaks those three short words: I lip-read them.

She stands up quietly, turns and leaves the room. I follow. We don't speak until we're on the grass outside the hospital.

I told you it wouldn't do any good.

It won't, as long as you don't try.

She blazes at me.

You don't understand. So why don't you keep quiet?

She's not far from losing control.

You're quite right. I don't understand.

She smiles at me, somewhat ruefully.

He hasn't called me Alexandra since I was little.
I noticed you shudder.
Yes. Now Zack, can we leap into the wind?
Hike or leap?
Both. In that order.
She strides off. I run to catch up with her, squeeze her shoulder. She smiles at me and takes my hand:
I want to take you to the Edge.

**

I retreat from the bedroom to the kitchen, lean against the door-jamb, heart pounding. I shouldn't have done it, I should have gone away when she asked me to, not kept on quizzing her, invading her, intensifying her fury, my frustration. Tony is so obviously right:

Be realistic, Zack. You know Elinor. It doesn't matter a fuck whether your questions are reasonable or not. As she's feeling at the moment she won't answer them, so it's pointless asking.

Why can't I understand that? Now there'll be another day of the withdrawal and ostracism that churns me up so much – and I'm due to go away tomorrow.

What an amazing tantrum it was, sitting up in bed, spitting at me, her legs flailing underneath the comforter, her eyes blazing hatred.

I enjoyed it, I have to confess. Not so much the spectacle, dramatic though that was, as the violence of her outburst. I'd touched her, broken through, provoked a real reaction, far more palatable than the cold withdrawals and dismissiveness that have driven me to distraction over the past few days.

Now, however, I feel fearful and exhausted. How can I avoid a perpetuation of this stress that knots my stomach? I must be calm, low-key, ask no questions, swallow hard words without retaliation. If I can do so, her confidence may begin to grow again, we could come closer.

She's moving around the bedroom, coming through into the kitchen. Keep cool, Zack. Smile. For God's sake, smile!

She walks in, not looking at me, clearly intending to go past me into the living room.

Coffee?

She ignores me, starts to sweep past. I flip, stick out my arm to halt her. She recoils.

Don't you dare touch me.

Why can't you be civil?

She hisses at me.

If you make one more move towards me I'm going. For good.

Her hair is in disarray, her eyes on fire, her face suffused with passion. She's a wild animal.

God, you look beautiful.

Her cry of anger, anguish, is simultaneous with the crack of the flat of her hand against my cheek. I feel tears jolt into my eyes. I start to laugh.

She crouches a little, begins to bob and weave in front of me, her fists jabbing towards my face, not quite touching me. She's wanting me to flinch, show fear.

I'm fascinated, exhilarated and in despair. I feel like laughing again, but hold back. She looks ludicrous, world spider-weight champion, but there's something magnificent about her passion.

Her fists clench more tightly, her knuckles whiten further. They are now halting only a skin's-width from my face. She's panting.

You don't think I'll hit you, do you?

And then I want her to. I crouch a little, thrust my chin towards her.

Go on, then. Hit me.

She continues to jab at me, but less powerfully. I thrust my chin further forwards, willing her to strike it. I raise my voice.

Here I am. Hit me. Here.

She withdraws a little more. I kneel in front of her, upturn my face.

Hit me. Like this.

My fist surges upwards, crashes into my chin. I taste blood as my teeth bite my lower lip.

You can do it. It's easy.

I thump myself again. And then again, several times. I know exactly what I'm doing, but I can't stop myself. I don't look at her, but I know she's aghast. I'm replacing all the insidious hurt, the nagging stomach-aches and niggling pains of the past few weeks, with real, honest-to-goodness physical pain. And it feels good.

Stop it, you fool!

I uppercut myself with all my power, know I'm close to losing consciousness. I hit myself again and slump onto the floor, head resting on my arm, giggling feebly.

I have the fleeting impression that she's bending down to put her arms round me, but instead I hear her walk away.

You've done it now, I mutter to myself.

But in a strange way I feel contented. I want to sleep, here on the kitchen floor. My mouth is swelling, my chin beginning to ache.

**

The wind is even stronger, which makes the hike utterly exhilarating. Sometimes we hold hands, swing round, sometimes we let the fierce gusts swirl us.

We have to shout to be heard, and the nonsense words we come out with are whipped away as soon as they are uttered.

Nackerfarks.

Truthcomb.

Ridally.

Nettlegripe.

All my past, all my problems disappear, and I feel sure that's true for Alex, too. I'm entirely in the present. Nothing I feel is digested or assessed, qualified or conditional. It is simply and wholly what it is.

Gribbets.

Nanglejar.

Rumalinga.

Chope.

**

The Edge is a small outcrop of rock, no more than twelve feet long, at the summit of the hill. Beyond and below it is a fissure whose appreciable depth is partially obscured by the profusion of ferns growing inside it. Beyond the fissure is a grass-covered slope, up which the wind is shrieking, straight into our faces.

Alex tugs me back a step or two, makes me lie down with her so that we're in the lee of the summit, in an oasis of silence so profound we're able to speak in whispers.

I want to teach you how to fly.

Her excitement is contagious.

I might fly away.

I'll risk it.

But you'll have to show me first.

She unfastens her rucksack, takes out an oil-skin cape which she puts on, not fastening the buttons down the front.

We struggle back against the wind to the summit of the hill. She stands on the Edge and as she opens her cape she leans further and further forward until she's almost horizontal, supported by the flow of air.

She looks like some giant bird. She screams like one. Her wings are full of air. She could easily take off.

Waiah!

As she shouts she dips her head, thrusts forwards. She glides, rides on the wind, her limbs perfectly still, her journey so slow I feel I'm dreaming. Yet I also know I'm not, she's flying, she'll cross the fissure, which must be at least ten feet wide. She's no longer human, she's an untamed creature relishing its element; disconnected from the earth, from me.

She succeeds, drawing up her knees to land neatly, turning a swift somersault out of pure delight, whipping round to me, opening her arms in triumph. I fist the air in celebration.

She makes her way back to me, hands me the cape. I put it on swiftly, climb with her to the place from which she launched herself.

I spread my arms, sink into the buffeting, close my eyes.

I'm weightless, levitated, with a wonderful sense of freedom. I could lie on the wind, ride its bluster and pummelling for hours. I'm perfectly happy and safe.

Alex is smacking my leg. I open my eyes, look back at her.

Fly! she gesticulates.

She looks wild and wonderful.

I turn towards the fissure and am aghast at its width. If I fall into its depths I'll be badly hurt, perhaps killed.

I can't do it.

Of course you can.

I lean into the wind again. This time I feel no

pleasure in my weightlessness. The fissure has grown wider and deeper. I turn back and shake my head. I'm paralysed. I daren't leap and I daren't withdraw. I close my eyes and pray that the wind will drop.

Suddenly I'm flying. She's pushed me. The fissure looms and shrinks, I land safely on the other side.

Waieeeh!

I look back at her. She's dancing a jig on the summit.

I scramble up the slope, skirting the fissure. She's waiting for me, holding out her hand for the cape. I shake my head.

No chance! This is my party.

She laughs as I push past her, open my wings, thrust off, glide once again across the crevasse. It's so easy to fly.

I make four crossings before I concede the cape to her. We have a few more flights each before the wind drops, suddenly and completely.

**

After an easy, dreamy period of crawling along a benign stretch of the ditch, I arrive at a place where fern-fronds are woven into a semi-circular arch blanketing what might be simply a section of a wall, but is in fact an entrance to a dry and airy region which I'm not able to resist exploring.

The light is low, I'm deep into my dreaming, so I don't identify the point at which the floor my hands and knees touch changes from springy softness into wood.

Floorboards, and as I continue I enter regions where dry-rot has crumbled them away, I peer nervously over nibbled edges, see nothing below except blackness swimming with even darker motes.

More insidious are places where the floor looks firm, but as I lower my weight onto my foremost hand, it gives way, my arm plunges through, I find myself lying flat, my head and shoulder half-through the hole, dust in my eyes and a sour smell teasing as I scrabble backwards towards safety.

I'm in the attic of an underground house which is not only very tall, but grows continually taller as my journey progresses, though it never rises to the surface of the earth. I suspect that in some way I can't fathom, it's linked to the corridor and galleries where my gathering is in full swing.

Mrs Campion is always there, in a cobwebbed region under the eaves. The webs are hung with coloured beads, feathers, butterflies, and when the oil-lamp gutters its light invades the surrounding darkness, revealing more treasures, of similar spirit. Old rugs and cushions are piled in the most private space, where the slates, fastened to battens whose nails have thinned by rust to drunken needles, angle down to reach the floor. A small fire, set on a marble slab and ringed by stones, is perpetually burning, fed by the huge supply of rotten boards. Their smell, as they burn, mixes with that of cloves and cinnamon in the cauldron suspended from an iron chain, a few inches above the lazy flames. The overall aroma is sweet and full of comfort.

She is always there, sometimes knitting, her gold-rimmed spectacles, defying gravity, bobbing on the end of her nose. Sometimes she's rolling dough, fiercely, the board flat on her lap. She is wearing many skirts, and her hugeness is the most effective antidote to terror that I know. Her parrot rarely speaks now, usually sitting on the roof of its cage, sometimes hanging sideways from the rust-thick chain, dipping its beak into the cauldron.

Whenever I enter, she sweeps out a space for me

with her brawny, bangled arm, I sink into the cushions next to her, she passes me a tin with an embossed picture of Queen Victoria on her diamond jubilee, and my nose gathers itself for the smell of fresh-baked scones. She ladles spice-tea into a chipped enamel mug and passes it to me.

All this before we speak, always the same words.

Thas been comin' a long time, lad.

Best scones in the world, Mrs Campion.

**

She reaches back into the shadows, wheels into the candlelight her harp, covered with a thick black overcoat, which she removes, folds carefully, places at her feet.

She nods, to see if I'm ready. I smile, nod back. She begins to play.

Sometimes I watch her fingers to hear better. Old, arthritic, they are in no hurry. They are at the same time assured and tentative, assured because the link between the music in her soul and her fingers' communion with the strings is strong, tentative because she knows the shifting qualities of dreams.

Now, for some reason, the melody transports m e to a London street, long ago, to the top of stone steps leading down into Piccadilly tube station. The man with no nose is standing there, in his tattered mack, with a bundle of *Evening Standard*s under his arm. For years I've been both terrified and fascinated by those huge dark passages drilling back into his head. But today, as I see his face in neon light, uplifted to fierce rain battering him, he looks brave and beautiful.

I walk gently to him, feeling somehow that because he has no nose he can't see me. He's smaller than I thought. Water is cascading down his yellow oilskin cape. I bend down and kiss him on the forehead.

He looks up at me. There are droplets hanging on the fierce hairs guarding the entrance to those caves. I can sense crimson just out of my view.

His voice is melodious, broad Yorkshire, with no hint of reproach.

Now thas got that out tha way at last, perhaps tha'll stop staring at me and let me get on with sellin' ma papers.

I'm sorry.

And perhaps tha won't have nightmares any more.

But truly... I didn't...

He shakes the rain off his head, and as he turns I can see that there's something wrong with his foot. His eyes follow mine.

Aye. That's much more of a nuisance than my face.

He hesitates. I want to leave, but something holds me back.

I were one of the lucky ones, believe it or not. At least I came back.

I slip my hand into the rear pocket of my trousers, close my fingers round a five-pound note, withdraw it stealthily.

He must have seen me. His face turns pale then livid. It isn't beautiful now. He pushes me ferociously in the chest, causing me to slip over, finish up sitting on a step next to his twisted foot. Before I can recover from the shock his eyes are level with mine, and full of hate.

Fuck off, pal. Now, before I kick your face in, make it look like mine.

I stagger down the steps, not daring to look back. I never used that tube-station again.

Even so, when I lie in bed and his ravaged face,

upturned to the rain, floats back to me, I'm always moved by its beauty.

And in the same way, those stiff and swollen-jointed fingers, moving fluidly between the strands of wool that serve as strings on Mrs Campion's harp, are beautiful. So too is the music, the more so because it's silent.

I look at her. She is making sound, of course. It's just that it couldn't be detected by a microphone, however sensitive. It couldn't be detected either by anyone who couldn't see her fingers, either in the flesh or in the mind's eye. I can do both, and the music that flows from them across the attic space washes over me, sooths my eyelids, sore for weeks now, makes me feel I'm with her and totally alone. I embrace that feeling because I know it to be true.

It is the wool's silence that gives power to the music, opens it to all possibilities. Gut or nylon would be much more constrained, because the sounds they made would stifle the listener's imagination.

I look at her. Her face is craggy, tough. It holds nothing feminine. It is simply the face, male or female, of unbeaten age.

I reconstruct that afternoon, all those years ago, when I hated her. How wrong I'd been.

**

It's summer, and in my memory the air is thick with white butterflies; a scattering of speckled red ones too, that now seem to have disappeared forever.

I'm outside, playing in the garden at the rear of my house, shaping figures out of Cheshire clay, spreading them out over the grass, to dry in the hot sun. I hear laughing and strange shouting from Hillside Road, so I wander down the drive to see what's happening.

As I reach the pavement I'm assailed by the wonderful smell of tar, a smell I feel I've known since before I was born. The council workmen have sprayed the road with it, spread chippings on top, and now the steam-roller is flattening the surface.

It has halted just opposite my house. Mr Campion, the driver, in dark blue overalls, is joking with his mate, a tall thin man called Jed. They've just returned from the Bull's Head, and are staggering a little as they thump each other's shoulders, laugh and argue. I see Mrs Campion, at the front door of her house just two doors down, shake her head, wipe her hands on her apron, go back inside.

Like fallin' off a bike, Jed shouts: *Dead easy.*

Mr Campion shakes his head.

Takes skill. An' you've not bloody got it.

Betcha ten bob.

Like takin' milk from a babby. You're on.

The two men shake hands with exaggerated heartiness. Someone slips a much smaller hand, warm and sticky, into mine. I look to the side. It is Ernest. We stand together to watch what happens.

Mr Campion stands in the road, arms akimbo, looking up with a big grin on his face as Jed's foot twice slips off the step before he swings into the driver's seat of the steam-roller.

You haven't an icicle's chance in hell, Mr Campion calls.

Big Jed leans through the side panel, and at the same time turns on the ignition. The engine roars into life. He yells over its thudding.

Fifty yards up the road without hitting the pavement. That what you said?

That's right.

Piece o' cake, Charlie. I'm on my way.

Quick as a flash Mr Campion lies down in the

road, on his side, feet against the steam-roller, blocking
its path.

Jed waves at him in an exasperated fashion.

Get out the bloody way!

Mr Campion waves to him mockingly.

No.

It's not fair.

Mr Campion waves again.

Not against the rules, Jed. Ten bob you owe me.

Get up you fool.

This time it's Mrs Campion, shouting from her
doorway.

Shut up, woman. Can't you see I'm tired.

Mr Campion places his hands together, as if he
were praying, turns on his side and rests his face on
them.

Jed revs the engine loudly.

Up you get, Charlie! I'm coming.

Mr Campion turns on to his back, stretches as if
awakening from sleep. One side of his face is spotted
with fresh tar.

Wake me up in half an hour.

Once more he feigns sleep.

Jed revs again, threateningly.

Get up you idiot, yells Mrs Campion.

Mr Campion blows her a kiss out of his sleep,
sends a second one to Jed.

The steam-roller surges forward.

**

What has caused the ditch to sink, I can't fathom.
Perhaps it isn't truly sunken, but simply that its upper
edges have somehow been rounded, perhaps by a
shovel or a scythe. What I am sure of is that the ditch is
old, and deeper than any others I've crawled along. It is

narrow, too, and hugely overgrown, and on a dull day little light could percolate through the brambles, ferns and ivy to the floor. But today the sunlight is brilliant, and the mud we crawl through is laced with shadows.

We'd planned a brief excursion, but the ditch is providing us with so many treasures that we've been crawling roughly south for several hours. We've just passed through a region where in several places the ditch gradually opens out, to perhaps twice its normal width, then just as gradually slims down to normal. It is as if it has varicose veins.

The chambers, as we call these wider sections, all have special features, none of which are the same.

The first one we come to is filled with whirling leaves, brown ones from last year which have somehow been protected from winter rains. At floor-level the eddies are smooth and silent, moving in great circles, with no overtaking, and seemingly no loss of energy. In contrast, at higher levels, the motions are chaotic, violent, and the air is filled with cracklings, rustlings, seethings. The Turmoil Chamber, Alex calls it. Elsewhere in the ditch the air is virtually still.

The walls of the next chamber are covered, utterly, with moss. So too are some boulders and thin stretches of the floor where water doesn't gather. What astonishes me is the infinite number of shades of green, and the moss's hairiness, which can readily be seen in the flecked sunlight. It feels safe to touch the moss, though only gently. Its texture is deep velvet and when I take my hand away, indentations from my fingers persist on its surface for some minutes before fading. She names it The Emerald Chamber.

Other regions are characterised by ferns, fungi and bramble-hoops. The final one is festooned with cobwebs, in some of which acorns and dead leaves are quietly trampolining. Others are intertwined into amazing shapes, like a village of drunken playing cards.

I'm feeling somewhat sated with all these riches as I follow Alex round a gentle curve. She halts so suddenly I collide with her, but before I can speak she reaches behind her, finds my arm, tugs me alongside her, and kneels, quivering, in dappled light.

Directly ahead of us the ditch has lost its angularity. Always, in my experience, even when foliage has bridged the gap, blocked out the sky, the walls of the ditch are vertical. Their cross-sections may be complicated by hanging ferns or brambles, but they remain, essentially, rectangular.

But this section of ditch is different. It is shallower and roughly semi-circular, like a railway tunnel, several feet long. Even more striking is the tunnel's structure, illuminated by narrow shafts of sunlight which puncture the roof in several places. It is ribbed along its length with a multitude of delicate, arched supports, roughly equally spaced, made of some white material which clearly is not metal, darkened here and there with grey.

We crawl up to the tunnel, halt and peer inside. We see, to our astonishment, that the material is bone. The supports are ribs. All flesh has disappeared. The tunnel seems too large to have come from a horse, but no other explanation comes to mind.

The floor is carpeted with years of bracken. We crawl inside, turn onto our backs, lying close together, and look up.

All colours are there, all shapes I can imagine and more besides. A loop of ivy dangles deep into the tunnel. Behind it is a splash of red I think is a wild rose. Petals from some other flower breathe on a cobweb stretched between three ribs, a giant spider motionless beside them. Something glitters in a tiny clump of heather: a shard of glass perhaps. I glance down at

Alex. A rainbow is dancing on her wrist's pale skin.

To me, this ribbed roof just above our heads is more magnificent than any I've seen in a cathedral. That may be, in part, because of its proximity, but mainly, I think, it is because it is natural, and changing even as we look at it. No drawings or pre-ordained dimensions, no tools or scaffolding: it lives.

Slowly all colours in the tunnel turn to grey, presumably because the sun has disappeared behind a cloud. The bones stand out more strikingly, look sturdier than before.

Alex clutches my arm, looks deeply into me:

Our heads are where its heart was.

I know she's right. We lie together, quietly, eyes closed, and when, after a while, I pick out a faint *Thump, Thump,* I'm sure she hears it, too.

I think I must have dozed. When I open my eyes she's kneeling by my side. She unzips a pocket of her backpack, withdraws a stub of candle and a match. The light has faded further, so the flame is brilliant. Since its illumination is from within the tunnel, it exposes features we couldn't see before: wisps of dead grass coiled around the ribs, water dripping from the base of a white stone, a thistle standing to attention, a birds-nest balanced on an arc of bone, so subtly blending with turf-roots to which it's fastened that it's virtually invisible. A slight movement suggests the nest is occupied.

Alex has seen it, too. She glances at the candle. I nod. She blows it out.

The clouds must have shifted and sunlight is filtering wanly though the roof. We lie in our cathedral and watch shadows gravely play. The heartbeat maintains its steady rhythm.

**

Someone screams. I can hear it now, but I still can't tell who it was.

The steam-roller is still thudding. Jed is staring down in horror at Mr Campion, whose eyes are closed, his neck arched, his lower legs out of sight under the huge iron cylinder. His cap has fallen off and I notice he's starting to go bald. Perhaps I've never seen him before without a cap. Ernest's face is white, his nails digging into my palm. The smell of tar is overwhelming.

Nothing is moving except for Mr Campion's head, which keeps jerking, as if he's trying to sit up.

Put it in reverse, you fool!

Mrs Campion is screaming at Jed, and at the same time is kneeling by her husband, trying to tug him free. His eyes are still closed, his face grotesquely twisted.

The engine sound changes, then the roller jerks forward, covering a little more of Mr Campion's legs.

Reverse! Mrs Campion screams.

The engine cuts dead, Jed scrambles down, stands head bowed in front of Mrs Campion. His voice, in the sudden silence, seems incredibly loud.

I can't find reverse, Nell.

Something vaguely like a smile flicks across Mr Campion's ashen face. I think I lip-read rather than hear his words.

Doesn't matter now, you silly bugger.

Mrs Campion grabs her husband by the shoulders and shakes him hard. She glares down at him.

It matters, alright. Don't you dare give up.

Suddenly Ernest and I are swept up by Mrs Wharton from next-door-but-one. We're whisked into her kitchen, out of sight of the road.

Now sit down, both of you. Here's some lemonade. Stay here. I've got to go outside.

She rushes out. Ernest is sick all over the lino.

**

That night, as I lie in bed, Mr Campion – still, I imagine, with that twisted grin on his face – cooling slowly in Mr Claybrook's Chapel of Rest, I decide I hate Mrs Campion more than anyone I've ever met. Not only had she shaken her husband fiercely when he was dying, but she'd slammed the door on Jed when he'd come to apologise. Jed was crying, a man was crying and she'd slammed the door on him.

Somehow, being cruel to Jed was worse than shaking Mr Campion: and both were somehow worse than Mr Campion's death. It was simply an accident, why couldn't she see that? Jed had thought Mr Campion was joking, that he'd roll away, out of danger as soon as the steam-roller started to move. How could Jed have known it would leap forward like that – he'd never driven a steam-roller before? How could Jed have known that Mr Campion didn't think Jed would make it move? Women didn't understand about dares and jokes. Or at least, Mrs Campion didn't.

In the nightmare that followed, Mr Campion was sitting on the roadside with no legs. His ears were blowing tar bubbles. He was smiling his crooked smile but was at the same time sad because Mrs Campion had his legs and wouldn't give them back to him, however much he pleaded. She was boiling them in a cauldron in the middle of the road. They weren't flat anymore, they were round and hairy. She'd put them in upside-down, so his boots were sticking up in the air. They had iron studs on the soles – the kind that made sparks when you scuffed them on cobbles in the dark.

I'd liked Mr Campion. I forgot that I'd liked her, that she'd always been kind to me. I turned my face away from her when I saw her in the street. I wouldn't answer when she called to me. Once I peed in her flower garden, and when I saw her watching me from her bedroom window I didn't care.

She's waiting for me, one afternoon after school, as I'm strolling dreamily home dismembering a fresh-baked loaf my mother had asked me to pick up from Rhaney's; rolling the bread into tight balls, enjoying the taste of every morsel, enjoying the dark crust even more.

She grabs my arm as I walk past her gate, and before I've time to think she's yanked me roughly up her drive, into her kitchen, thrust me down into a chair. I feel shaken, frightened, and at the same time guilty.

Ginger beer, Zack?

I shake my head.

Carrot cake?

I shake my head again.

She pours a large glass of her home-made ginger beer, cuts a thick slice of cake, thrusts them in front of me.

Get 'em down yer.

She says it so fiercely I feel compelled to, and once I've savoured their familiar, wonderful tastes I take more. But I'm determined not to forgive her.

It is a while before she speaks.

You hate me, don't you lad?

I can't look her in the eye. Her voice becomes gentler.

Don't worry. I won't eat yer. You do hate me, don't you?

I nod.

Because I was rough with Charlie, wasn't it.

I burst into tears. All my hatred spills out of me, dissolves onto the floor.

How could you? And how could you turn Jed away when... when he was crying?

She reaches out to me, folds me into her enormous breasts. She smells of hens.

After I've sobbed my grief away she steers me gently back into my chair, gives me more ginger beer and cake.

I don't know if this'll make sense, lad, but I shook Charlie because I loved him so much. I could see him slipping away. He'd given up. He'd reconciled himself to dyin'.

I didn't want him to go. I wanted him to fight.

She sweeps her arm around the room. The mantelpiece is full of photographs of him, and her, and their daughter Melanie who people say is simple, who walks along the streets all day pushing an empty pram.

Not just the photos, lad. He made these cupboards, built these shelves, tiled the floor, painted the ceiling. He did all this for us, and I wanted him to stay. To enjoy it. To enjoy us.

She's quiet for a while, blinking back tears.

That's why I shook him. D'you understand?

I nod.

As for Jed, p'raps I were wrong to shut him out. But I've known him all my life. We were in the same class at school.

She smiles.

We were sweet on each other once. But he's so feckless.

I must have looked puzzled.

I mean, he's bright, but he never bothered with lessons at school. He never learned anything. He just liked to play and joke and drink himself silly. That's why he couldn't find reverse when it mattered.

Dad said it wouldn't have made any difference.

Mrs Campion shakes her head.

He's probably right. I shouldn't have slammed the door on him. The bloody fool.

I'm sorry, Mrs Campion.

You've nothing to be sorry for. You hated me

because you cared. And that's good, lad. That's why I want you for a friend. OK?

OK.

**

How could I have thought she didn't care for him. I remember now one summer evening, a year or so before the accident, when my mother asked me to nip to Mrs Campion's to borrow a screw of tea. She called me into her living-room.

Help yourself, love, I'm all greasy.

The fire is banked half-way up the chimney. The heat is ferocious. Mr Campion sits in front of it, as close as possible, naked apart from shorts I can faintly discern beneath some shining blubber, with which he's coated, head to toe. It is dripping from his knees onto the floor, where chickens are scuttling round. From behind this mask he seems to give a shame-faced smile. Mrs Campion, enormous, sleeves rolled up, dips her hands into a bowl, kneels ponderously, and massages the thick white fat into his chest with slow circular movements, fingers stretched back so the ball of her hand makes the contact. It is a picture from the Bible, but I can't place it. She's humming softly, and as she massages him he delicately plucks a feather from her hair.

Goose-grease, she explains. *Always does the trick when Charlie's chest is bad.*

At Mrs Campion's wake, years later, Mrs Turner told me how she'd nearly had a row with her.

We'd lived next door t'each other for nigh on fifty years, and never a cross word. She looked after all my babbies as though they were her own. But when she put those bloody chickens in her bedroom, and I could hear 'em through the wall, thrutchin' and squigglin' long before the light, I decided I had to say summat. But before I could, she brought me her first dozen eggs. I got used to the squawkin' little sods after a while.

**

A fierce winter day of lashing rain. It is one of those times when, for both of us, crawling is more important than company. We don't have to be alone but we each need sufficient space to have untrammelled communion with the ditch. So though we remain within earshot we are usually out of sight of each other.

Alex takes the lead and we're soon off the main track, slithering through thick mud down a side-ditch almost wholly overgrown.

I've not seen her for some time when I finally battle through a clump of vicious brambles, and find her sitting in the ditch, on a narrow shelf, on which she's left room for me. I join her.

As she turns to me, her eyes are shining with what seems like mischief. Raindrops captured by her hair become dislodged from time to time, and slide slowly down her cheek. She tongues them in and swallows.

My breathlessness soon disappears and I feel calm. When I look up I see ragged cumuli, and rainshafts slanting down. But here, in this sheltered region of the ditch, all is quiet – not just an absence of sound, but freedom from disturbance of any kind. I close my eyes and float. I begin to suspect we're sitting at a node.

She touches my shoulder. I blink awake. She's standing next to me.

I'm off now, she whispers: *Good luck.*

Before I can respond she's crawling back the way we came.

I'm a little surprised, regretful too, but these feelings are swiftly expunged by a peace that deepens all the time. It dawns on me, with gathering astonishment, that for the first time in many years the continual hissing in my head has disappeared. I'm experiencing total silence.

I treasure this moment. I know it won't last. But at least I know it's possible.

I crawl back slowly. I don't want to catch up with her. I need to be alone. I'm asking myself how Alex could have known. She's not been in this ditch before, and I've never told her about my tinnitus. I can't answer my question, but it doesn't matter. The more I'm battered by rain turning to hail, the more joyful I become. The hissing is back again, but I don't care.

**

Yes, the bottle's still here, in the spare closet, behind the fur-lined winter boots I bought from the Salvation Army. At first I think it's empty, but when I shake it, it rattles, and I remember the beautiful grey creature wobbling across the kitchen floor to try to drink from the dog's bowl, remember the lack of fear in its eyes as we stared at each other, its terrible thirst its only emotion. Remember its passivity as I picked it up by the tail, dropped it into a plastic bag. Remember its dangling weight, my plea for forgiveness. Remember the violence, fuelled by terror, with which I tied the neck of the bag, the neck of the second one to make it double-wrapped, the third to make escape impossible. Remember finding, some hours later, a thread of blood across the water-bowl's rim. I recollect exactly the words of the promise I made to a dead rat, never to use poison again.

But now I'm planning to violate this promise.

I recollect the pellets being bluish-green, but I hadn't realised they were phosphorescent, frighteningly hideous. Rats were either colour-blind or more stupid than I've always thought they were.

Can be fatal if swallowed. Keep out of the reach of children and animals.

I'm already nervous, I don't need this injunction.

How can I gauge the dose correctly? I need sufficient to produce some effect, a headache perhaps, at most mild vomiting: but not enough to do real harm. I try to calculate the ratio of Elinor's body-weight to that of the rat, come out with an estimate of fifty. I slide the packet around so I can count the pellets without touching them. Twenty-two or thereabouts. And at least three-quarters of the packet has gone. So it seems safe to give her one pellet.

I try to tip just one out of the packet, but three fall out, so I steer two back with a screwdriver. I ease the chosen one onto a tissue, fold the paper round it, pinch the paper so that the pellet's cylinder is a mild mound in the tissue, tap it firmly with the handle of the screwdriver until I feel sure it's fully ground to powder.

I unwrap the tissue, fold it into a chute, slide the powder gently into the mug of chai.

Flecks of lurid green-blue poison wink at me from the surface of the liquid. I prod one with the screwdriver but it doesn't want to sink. There's no way she wouldn't notice, so I spend ages drowning them one by one, feeling squalid, feeling that I'm wasting time, exhorting myself to halt this persecution, tip the stuff away, knowing all the time that my choice has been made, that I'll give her rat-poison tonight. I add some liquid shit, vintage yesterday, for good measure.

I feel suddenly lustful, go to bed, conjure her, have wild and sensual sex, masturbate until I come into an empty pesto bottle. I get dressed, tilt the jar over the mug. My semen slithers into the chai, sinks without protest, without trace.

She's in fine form tonight, animated, voluble. In this mood she's more wonderfully alive than anyone I've known.

The dog lies between us in the bay as she raises the mug and takes a large sip.

Best brew ever!

She smiles at me, raises her mug.

I try to gloat, feel pleasure in my control of her. She's drinking my semen, tasting rat poison and thanking me for it. I try to feel amused. I try to feel justified. But I feel none of these. I simply feel terribly sad. I love her and I've lost her. She's someone exceptional in this world. She's given me her trust again, and I'm trying to harm her, to corrode, contaminate her.

When I look at her I recognise that it's right for her to be free, there's something about her that should never be stifled, something so wonderful that it probably won't last, so is even more precious for that.

So what I feel most of all is shame, shame deepened by the knowledge that I'm hooked into this pattern, and if the poison doesn't trouble her I'll give her a double-dose tomorrow.

**

eight

You taught me to fly. Now I'm going to show you how to build a secret room. OK?

I'd like that, she smiles.

She tosses her apple-core high above the roof of the shippon, catches it one-handed and flicks it over the hedge.

We're in a farmyard at the far end of the forest. We'd approached slowly, not wanting to share our time together with anyone else, but curious to investigate this place on the edge of nowhere. The closer we came the clearer it was that no-one was around, the only sign of life being a fat, black cat, asleep on a hay-bale in the late afternoon sun.

It was the hay-barn that had attracted my attention, bringing to mind a game I'd last played more than forty years ago, on my Uncle Bill's farm in Shropshire, where bales of hay were stacked in a tall open barn, consisting basically of a sloping corrugated iron roof supported by four huge pillars. The stacking was terraced, so that despite the steepness of the rick, it was possible to use the bales as gigantic steps to climb up to the top. The game I'm remembering was to move the bales around to create a secret space, invisible from the ground, in which plots were hatched, eternal friendships forged, the rules of our gang written down.

The hay-barn this afternoon is similar, and Alex and I climb to its top, to stake our claim to it. It's not easy because some of the steps are two bales high and – stable though they look – the bales tend to move when we pull against them.

We rest for a while, panting. The bales are stacked virtually to the roof of the barn, with only just enough space for our bodies above them. So though we can see out in all directions, it is only through horizontal slits, which give the impression of being in a fortress.

Zack. Look!

She's pointing down into a hollow where a bale is missing. In it is another black cat, with six kittens, clearly new-born, still blind. The mother is washing them, one by one. When she sees us she arches her back and hisses, but when Alex speaks soothingly to her, she turns her attention again to the kittens, though she maintains a watchful eye on us.

We move out of her view, I explain the game to Alex and we crawl around until we find what looks like a good spot to make our secret room, about three-quarters the way up the rick, where there's a flat region on which we can build.

We construct the room by intuition and improvisation rather than a plan. We tug bales out of the structure of the wall, slide or heave them into position, wrest out two others to serve as a roof while we're standing in the room. It lists somewhat, feels rather precarious, but on the other hand the warmth, simplicity and friendly bulk of the bales creates a benign atmosphere.

We finish building and sit opposite each other in our tiny space, in which not only are the walls, roof and ceiling golden, but the light also, percolating to us through a gap we've left between the two bales that form the roof. We are alone, and no-one in the world can find us.

Alex reaches into her shoulder-bag, draws out a joint, which she lights.

Don't drop the match. We're sitting in a bomb.

She laughs, inhales and, rather hesitantly, passes the joint to me. I feel under the influence after a single breath.

Our words grow slow and dreamlike, punctuated by long silences.

It was in one of these rooms that my cousin Norman and I became blood-brothers.

How?

We nicked our wrists with a penknife and rubbed the blood together.

Let's do it.

She rummages in her bag. Her nearest approximation to a knife is a nail-file, and we make several unsuccessful attempts to draw blood before she drops it irretrievably down a crack between two bales. We peer down at it, a glint of silver lost in the deep gold, and find the picture so funny we laugh until we ache. I'm quite stoned, and Alex is far gone.

I'm going to Russian dance, she announces. *You clap.*

She squats down, starts to dance, kicking out her legs prodigiously, while I try to clap to her rhythm. Her exuberance is enormous and infectious. She goes faster and faster, whooping from time to time. I'm clapping as hard as I can, cheering her on. She reaches some kind of crescendo and crashes, laughing, into the wall.

Our house collapses.

Not only does the roof cave in but a number of bales from higher in the stack, which had been undermined by our construction, fall down on top of us. I hear Alex scream, feel a sharp pain in my wrist and then we are plunged into darkness.

I think I must have been knocked out for a moment, and when I come to I can't move. Something heavy is pressing on my chest, the air is musty, I feel hot, my wrist hurts.

I try with my good arm to push the bale away, but it won't budge. I start to panic, but I know I'm lost if I lose control, so I force myself into some kind of calmness. I find I can turn onto one side, which eases the pressure, enabling me to wriggle forwards, away from the weight of the bale into a space in which nothing is pressing on me.

Alex, I call.

There is no answer. Once again I panic, and I have to fight hard to keep calm.

I use my good arm to estimate the dimensions of the air-space which is allowing me to breathe.

I can't climb towards the roof, the clefts are too narrow. There is virtually no space to each side. Behind me is the bale which was squashing me, but ahead there is more space to wriggle into.

I follow that route. The space opens slowly out, and soon I'm in a cavity large enough to sit up in, and to my delight there is a small amount of light, though I can't spot the source of it. The journey I've just made has seemed interminable, but I doubt whether, in reality, I've covered more than two yards.

Alex! I shout, as loudly as I can.

Again there is no answer.

I need to start searching for her, but it seems best to take a moment to compose myself, take stock.

My throat is hurting, and I find I've several scratches dipping down below the collar of my shirt. I follow them with my good hand and to my horror it closes round something sticky and warm. I pull it out, find I'm clutching the remains of a blind kitten, crushed to pulp by the great bale or my wriggling.

I'm sorry, I say into the dark.

I wipe my hands as best I can on the hay, and discover that I'm shaking. I'm sure I can escape, but I'm equally certain that Alex is dead, squeezed into oblivion just like the kitten. Even so, I call again, with all my might, and this time, as I strain into the dark, I hear a sound – not a reply, but a sound made by some living creature.

I call again and listen.

**

I'm running, running through a tall wood, wet leaves on the ground, moisture filling the air with brown and yellow smells, I'm running fast, not towards something but away from it, though I'm not sure what it is, I'm not even sure I'm frightened, I just need to get away from those little suction pads on slender tentacles, blindly searching for me, though why I do not know.

I run faster, faster. All my body's dross is sloughed away, I feel myself transformed into an athlete made of sinew, muscle, gristle, my reservoir of energy unlimited. I learn to dodge the hanging branches, I drink giant raindrops tumbling through the shade. I am – for this afternoon – immortal.

**

The sound is still there, not far from me. It doesn't seem human, though I can't be sure. It's unearthly, somewhere between bubbling and a continuous moan. I stretch into a black cleft from which it appears to be coming, and my fingers touch hair and then the warm skin of a face, from which the sound is emerging. Thank God!

I wriggle as far forward as I can, which brings our faces opposite each other. When I reach beyond her shoulders I find she's trapped underneath a hay-bale. I touch her face lightly.

Are you hurt?

The moaning and bubbling continue. I move my good hand carefully all over her face, head and throat. Everything feels alright, there's no sign of blood, she's breathing normally.

Alex. It's me. I'm going to get you out of here.

She quietens for a while then starts up again. I stroke her head, whisper into her ear.

You're safe now. I'll soon have you home.

Her moaning continues.

I decide to try to find a way out, with the hope that Alex will come to while I do so. My left hand is useless, painful too, but in compensation my eyes have adapted well to the dark, making exploration easier. I find a place where I feel a breeze slipping between the bales, and by leaning back and using the strength of my legs I manage to force it forwards and eventually topple it into space. My cave is suffused with evening light.

I crawl to the edge, look down. The first part of the descent will be tricky, especially with one hand, but it's navigable, and the rest will be easy. Now I need to release Alex.

As I'm crawling back towards her the moaning ceases, and she cries out.

Please don't love me any more.

The anguish in her voice is overwhelming.

When I reach her she's trembling, shaking her head violently from side to side. I stroke her forehead, her face. She recoils, tries to arch away from me.

I don't want any treasures. Please!

I reach down the side of her body, find her hand, and as gently as I can steer her arm up, over her stomach and breasts, until it's free.

She's weeping now, and I hope that's a good sign.

I do the same with her other arm, by which time I'm confident I can haul her free. But first I need to try to calm her.

I take her hand in mine but she wrenches it free.

I'm not hungry any more.

I lie next to her without contact, and as she weeps I make soothing noises, sometimes tunes, sometimes strings of nonsense words. I take one hand, then the other and she doesn't pull away. Her weeping subsides, she seems to sink into sleep, but when I try to disengage my hand she clutches it tight, then throws her arms around me. Her grip is suffocatingly tight.

Don't leave me, Daddy. Don't leave me.

My violence is calculated. I slap her face, hard. She blinks open, sees me. Her voice is heavily slurred.

Where are we?

We're in the hay-barn. Our secret room collapsed. But we're safe and I'm going to take you home.

Oh, I've had such terrible dreams.

I know. Now, are you hurt at all?

I don't think so. I'm just a bit stuck.

I'll pull you out. We need to be quick. It's almost dark, and we've got to climb down yet.

It is dark by the time we reach the farmyard floor, and the slow walk home, with Alex navigating, is mostly in silence. We're almost back when I give her a brief account of what happened. She halts and turns to me.

Did you slap me when I was in such a state?

Yes. Out of love.

I'm glad.

At her cottage she flicks on the light and spots my hand. The middle finger is dislocated and is lying flat along the back of my wrist.

She takes my hand gingerly.

God, that must hurt.

I nod. The pain is fierce, and now the major trauma is over I'm feeling quite faint.

Before I know what she's doing she's taken my finger and yanked it back into position. After the first sudden spear of pain, which brings me out into a sweat, it feels fine.

Sit down, Zack.

She steers me into an armchair, then recoils when she sees the scratches on my throat. I tell her about the kitten. She pulls a face.

She pours me a glass of brandy, makes me knock it back, pours me another one.

How come you've sustained all these injuries, while I'm unscathed?

I look at her, beautiful and fragile.

I wouldn't put it quite like that, Alex.

She sits on the floor, squeezes into the space between my legs, rests her chin on my thigh, looks up at me.

Thank you for saving me.

Just making us quits. You saved me from drowning.

Is drowning worse than madness?

I stroke her hair.

We don't need to decide that question.

We're quiet for a long time, listening to the crackling of logs on the fire, watching the traffic of the flames. She's biting her lip. I think I know what she's wrestling with, and I'm nervous.

She looks into my eyes and whispers to me.

Would you like to make love? I think it would work tonight.

I look at her, and what I feel is happiness, not desire. All I want is to fold her in my arms and go to sleep.

Tonight I love you too much for love-making.

She touches me gently on the cheek.

That's the most beautiful thing you've ever said to me.

**

Who was the strong one, Mum? Who was in control in our relationship?

Each time I'd drive to visit you, during those last two weeks in hospital, I'd feel full of love for you, think of the comfort you'd given me throughout my life.

Once there, however, after no more than half an hour, I'd be bored, I'd want to leave, I'd want you to go back to sleep.

There was nothing to discuss. Tony had persuaded me that we should conspire with you in not acknowledging that you were dying.

If she thought we knew, she'd be worried sick about our being upset.

I knew he was right. You had no enemies, no affairs to settle. And you'd always shied away from intimate conversation.

When I visited you I'd sit fumbling for words. You'd have little to say. When we spoke it would usually be simultaneously, we'd defer to each other, our sentences would dry up.

Eventually you'd close your eyes, though I feel sure the sleep was feigned. Or you'd say *I think I'll sleep now*, and though we both knew you wouldn't, I'd been given licence to leave. Which I did.

Apart from those last two days, when you were mostly in coma and so ravaged by cancer you looked scarcely human, more like breathing, insentient meat, you looked generally better than you had in the preceding weeks at home, causing Tony to think you might recover.

I never thought you would, and I wanted you to die swiftly. Part of that, of course, was that I didn't want you to suffer, but that wasn't the whole story. In fact, you didn't seem to be in much pain. No, the issue was so agonising to me I wanted it to end. I didn't want the worry and inconvenience, the inevitable wrestling with my conscience that would have occurred if you'd lived on and needed to be looked after. The only way I could get rid of those feelings was for you to die.

Did you know I wanted you to die? Did you decide to die? If you knew what I wanted, did you still love me. I'm sure you did. If you knew what I wanted, did it hurt? I'm sure it did.

Who was in control, the man who willed his mother to die, or the woman who decided out of love to do so? You were, of course. I'm now inclined to think that underneath that skin of complaisance and helplessness was iron discipline. True strength.

If only that had been matched by self-regard.

**

She shudders, grasps my arm.

What's that horrible noise? she whispers.

It's called the death rattle.

I know it too well. First with my father, then my mother: gurgling sounds as thick, dark fluid hauls itself up the windpipe, slithers back with each breath; climbs up the ladder again, slips down, the pattern all the more horrific for its implacable patience.

We've just arrived at the hospital. It's the middle

of the night. The nurse had phoned to say he was sinking.

We creep through the wards leading to his room. Apart from one old man sitting upright in bed, his huge eyes following our passage, everyone is sleeping, and I think how sleep is a great leveller.

He's been propped up on two thick pillows, but has slipped to the side, and the angle of his body makes him look as though he's trying to get out of bed. There is no flesh on the arms protruding from his pyjama sleeves or, it seems, behind the appallingly white triangle of skin defined by the top of his pyjama bottoms and the unbuttoned lower part of his top.

They've taken his feeding tube away, she whispers.

I move a chair up to the bed, and she sits on it, taking his hand. I sit a few feet away, preparing for a long haul.

For a while we sit without speaking, absorbing the death-rattle into our consciousnesses, knowing it will cease only with his extinction.

I had forgotten the power of the silences between each rattle, each one stretching beyond the point at which it seems too late for another breath. And I remember the imperceptible transition, as the hours passed by, when each of my parents was dying, between panicking at the thought that he or she was dead; and willing each silence to stretch on forever.

His sleep is restless. He fidgets a lot, plucks at the sheets, and a couple of times stretches in an erratic, disjointed way.

After some time she half-stands and puts her mouth to his ear.

Dad!

He makes no response. She repeats the call two or three times, each one louder than its predecessor. He gives no sign of having heard her. Despite the restlessness, the coma must be deep. I feel we're both free to talk, without fear of being heard.

What d'you want to say to him?

I don't know. I suppose I simply want to know if it's possible to talk.

From time to time viscous liquid, somewhere between dark green and black in colour, oozes from the corner of his mouth. She wipes it away with a paper towel, not tenderly, more as if he's a nuisance she's obliged to attend to. He doesn't respond to her words, and the remorseless music, over the next two or three hours, like gargling in slow motion, tells us he's inching towards drowning.

Wake up! Stop pretending!

She's shouting at him, and at the same time she takes hold of his shoulders and shakes him. He topples to the side, hangs over the edge of the bed. I have an impulse to call out to her but something in her face restrains me. She needs to do this, whatever it is, and it's Alex I care about, not him.

His death-rattle continues. A gob of fluid stretches from his mouth, thins onto the floor. She yanks him roughly back to an upright position, sits on the bed facing him.

She shakes him again.

Open your eyes, damn you!

This time his head falls onto his chest, where it hangs, seemingly supported only by two pencil-thin bones. He's bald at the back, where his skin is stamped with scarlet ferns.

She grasps his hair, though not fiercely, eases his head back onto the pillow. She stares at him for a while, panting, then sits back in her chair, takes his hand again.

I'm going to talk to you, Dad, even though you're pretending not to hear me, like you always did. I'm holding your hand and you can't escape me. So listen.

She wipes away some fluid trickling from his mouth.

You're dying, Dad. In an hour or two you'll be as dead as Julius Caesar. Your life doesn't matter any more.

Mine does, don't you see that? I might have another twenty, thirty, fifty years. And you, in these last few dregs of breath you'll ever take, have the power to help me.

You have control over me, as you've always had. I don't want that to continue after you're dead.

I want you to release me. You can't take me with you. All I ask is that you set me free. You owe me that.

In case you want to know, I've loved and hated you more than anyone else in the world. I don't want that to be true after you're dead. I want you and what you did to me to slip into my history. Into extinction.

This is your last chance, father. It's mine, too. Please open your eyes and let me go.

She halts, and I notice that she's clutching his hand with both hers, kneading his fingers, squeezing them.

Please open your eyes!

His body is fluttering. Then the agitation slips away and I see strain develop within him. He's mustering every scrap of energy still contained in his ravaged body.

I love you, Dad.

His head strains forward and slowly, first the left eye, then the right one opens. Both are totally milked over. He has gone blind.

The urgency in her voice is replaced by gentleness.

You can go now.

His straining subsides as slowly as it came. He lies

back on the pillow, and once again there is something beautiful in his face.

The room feels amazingly peaceful. I realise the death-rattle has ceased.

**

Legger died in the autumn, suddenly, of an attack of asthma, to which he'd always been prone.

I felt devastated. My concept of death was totally changed. When Billy Bickerstaff's father had been killed, or when – despite Ernest's conviction – I concluded that his father was dead, I invested the events with a romantic aura, a glamour. I think I enjoyed them. After all, they were soldiers. I expected soldiers to be killed. And as for Wendy Eva, whose name haunted my sleep, I'd never known her in her life, so death was her natural condition.

This was different. There was no romance attached to it, just fear and disbelief. I spent hours hidden in the rhododendron bushes at the side of the track leading to his cottage, willing him to reappear. I closed my eyes and pictured him bouncing a tennis-ball as he walked to school. I could remember every detail perfectly, not just the way he looked, but the way his fingers must have felt as he spun the ball, or as it thwacked back into his palm.

I composed obituaries to him. I felt riddled with guilt because I'd played unfair tricks on him. Most of all I thought about him when I was in bed, in that hazy time just before sleep. I felt a kind of obligation to perpetuate him by remembering everything about him, and recording it in my old ledger.

**

Early in the war, no-one seemed to notice Legger's hare-lip, perhaps because he wore his Mickey Mouse gasmask as often as possible. Later on, however, we started taunting him. So each morning, in the school washroom, he'd mask it with black shoe-polish, which he'd spend ages removing at the end of the day. His moustache was sparse, jet-black, and its crooked line curled upwards on the left side when he smiled, giving him a cruel, sardonic air. When he was angry, or more frequently, upset, it curled the other way, and with his popping eyes and gasping words he seemed an absolute buffoon.

His only close friend was Ernest. They always sat together at the back of the class, and in every test Ernest was bottom, with Legger immediately above him. I'd often see them walking together on the hill.

He was obsessed with saving conkers, which he hung – each individually strung – inside his gang-hut, an abandoned pigsty at the bottom of his father's garden. There was no gang – none of us, except Ernest, would deign to join – but there was a list of rules, which he showed me. The first was that all meetings should take place in the dark, in whispers.

In return for conkers, for which I made increasingly great claims – Roman ones, or champions hardened in cow-dung for a hundred years – he gave me miniature sports cars that were tucked, as inducements to buy, inside the largest cornflake packets. Each day he came to school with more, and when I ran out of conkers to swap for them, I stole replacements from his hut.

One evening Mrs Letherton brought him to our house. Both appeared to have been crying. My mother made a pot of tea. Mrs Letherton smiled at me.

You've always been a grand scholar, Zack. Your Mum and Dad must be very proud of you.

She paused. I knew what was coming.

Didn't you realise our Leslie's been stealing money to buy cornflakes? To get those cars for you?

I shook my head. In fact, I'd had my suspicions, but I'd preferred not to think about them.

When they'd gone, his mother not quite able to refuse six duck-eggs from mine, she asked if I realised they hadn't any money. Again I shook my head. All I knew was that his father's job was to clean the lavatories after school; and that Dirk had accidentally pissed on his head while proving he could clear the wall between the boys side and the girls.

The next day Legger told me he wasn't allowed to play with me again. But after school he took me to the overgrown field by Pardy's house. The bomb crater behind the old mortar mixer contained a great heap of cornflakes. Legger smiled his crooked smile. It hadn't rained for weeks, and they cracked and splintered as we waded through them, kicking and dancing. Then he plunged, breast-stroking, and all I could see was his patched bottom forging through a golden pool. We had to strip to remove the cornflakes from our clothes, and his attack of asthma was so fierce it was dark before he could go home.

His cousin's uncle was a slow, left-arm bowler for Worcestershire and England. This was our closest link to fame, so for a few weeks in the summer Legger achieved dignity. He'd open the bowling in our impromptu matches between Churchfields and Overton, and each time he panted in a weird, crab-wise lope up to the wicket, he'd gasp a litany whose words I felt sure he didn't understand:

Roly Garfitt, from the members' end, ambles past the umpire, tosses the ball into the sun.

And as Yonner crashed it to the fence, or scattered chickens in Mr Ditchfield's yard, Legger would continue, hands against his knees:

Beautifully flighted, it beats his groping bat and flicks the offside bail.

Yonner's lack of reverence appalled me, and I played every ball that Legger bowled with huge respect, admiring the subtlety I couldn't see.

Mrs Letherton told my mother that on the night he died he was mumbling about cricket.

**

On the morning Old Shelley breaks the news to us, in prayers, Ernest looks utterly forlorn, prompting Johnnie to ask him in a gentle voice:

Do you think he'll be the only angel with a hare-lip?

Ernest takes the question seriously. It is some time before he replies.

I think it will be smoothed away, because everybody's happy in Heaven.

Even Johnnie looks ashamed.

Later that day, after the final bell, I notice Ernest, at the back of the classroom, sitting in the desk he used to share with Legger. He's hunched, engrossed in something. I wait until everyone else has left the room, tiptoe down the aisle towards him. He's holding a figure he's just made from plasticine, and is turning it round to view it from all sides.

He feels my shadow and cups his hands around it.

C'mon, Ernest. Let me see.

Reluctantly, he opens his hands.

Legger is delivering his googlie. His left arm is outstretched, angled slightly upwards. The ball is lying in the palm of his right hand, extended behind him, twisted to the sky. His lips are moving. His face isn't wounded at all.

I want to hug Ernest, but I wheel round, scurry from the room.

**

We sit in hard chairs in the corridor outside his room, waiting for a couple of nurses to do something unspecified with his body. Another nurse has brought us cups of strong, sweet tea.

Alex looks pale but composed. She smiles at me, rather wanly.

We're both orphans now.

Welcome to the club.

The nurses emerge from his room, signal that we can go back in. I ask Alex if she wants to be alone with him, but she shakes her head.

He's shrunk and looks quite boyish. They've cleaned him up, there's no sign of the struggle he's been waging against cancer, or perhaps against life's reluctance to let go of him. He could easily be peacefully asleep.

That's how he looked when I was little, she whispers.

She ruffles his hair.

Our conversation takes place in low tones, the only possible antidote to the hours of viscous rattling and dreadful silence from his throat.

I'm going to dance him away, dance him out of this world, away to wherever he goes now.

Where d'you think that is?

Oblivion.

She slips out of her jacket, and then – to my surprise – out of the rest of her clothes, which she drapes over the bed-rail.

She sits on the side of the bed, looking down at him.

I'm going to dance for you, Father, as so many times before. But this is the first time I've chosen to. I hated dancing to your tune.

I'm going to dance you away, out of this world, out of that place in my life where you've been too long, too strong. I'm going to dance you out of my life into my memory.

When I've finished the dance I'll kiss you goodbye and go away. I won't come to see you, stiff and powdered in your coffin. I don't want your ashes, and if they bury you instead I won't visit your grave. You're over, Father. I need you to be.

I want you to know that despite your vileness I always thought you were beautiful.

She slips off the bed and starts to dance. I close my eyes to expunge all extraneous visual sensations, and when I think they might have gone I open them again, so I can look freshly at the scene.

In the background everything is clinical. White walls without a blemish, an aluminium rack draped with transparent plastic tubes, in which liquid resides without moving. A monitor sits on a metal table, its screen blank.

In the bed lies a dead man, just one hand and his face visible. He is on his side, face turned towards a naked woman dancing, and though his eyes are closed he looks responsive.

She's let her hair down. Her movements are sinuous, languorous. Sometimes she stretches up or out. Sometimes she squats or lies on the floor, but she is never still. Sometimes her eyes are closed, sometimes open but not focused on anything in the room. At times she makes wordless sounds, and though I don't want to invade her, I keen too, just for a second, she hears me, beckons me to continue, in concert with her.

Yes, she is dancing him away. When I look at him

he is no less substantial than before she started, but when I look at her I can see him leaving, gathered, swept up by her movements, eased away, out of this room, out of her world.

The door opens and the nurse who'd brought us tea looks in. She stares wide-eyed at Alex, who doesn't spot her. I raise my finger to my lips, and the nurse nods, absently. She swallows, watches for a further few seconds then withdraws. I have the strong feeling that she regards what she saw as sacred, and will never tell anyone about it.

Alex dances more and more slowly, as if she's reluctant to complete her father's obliteration, and then stops. She's breathing hard as she sits beside him on the bed, leans over him, lowers her head to rest against his. Her left nipple appears to be touching his mouth. It lingers there, then moves along the thin line of his lips.

She says something to him so quietly I can't catch it, then she dresses quickly and we leave.

It's scarcely light, and the air is cool and fresh as we walk out of the hospital driveway into the country lanes.

Did the dancing do what you wanted?
She nods.
I thought so. I felt privileged to watch.

She smiles, but obviously wants silence, so we don't speak again until we've climbed to the edge of the forest. She halts and turns to me.

I want to go to the Edge. Will you come with me?
Of course.

As we start along the trail I feel impelled to ask her a question.

Can you tell me what you said to him as you left?
She's quiet for a moment.

I said: My parting gift to you, Dad. See how much

warmer I can be when you don't force me.

I hate him, Alex.

I don't hate him any longer. I don't love him, either. It feels wonderful to be free.

**

Elinor has just phoned, bright and friendly, saying she's enjoying our friendship much more than our partnership as lovers, looking forward to seeing me soon. She's feeling well, her apartment's spruce and attractive, she's sailing.

I'm still re-living the last few weeks, still amazed at the strength of a six-inch turd as I spoon it from the water, slip it into a jar, intact except for a thin stain on the porcelain.

In a practical sense I've been lucky. I've committed acts which, if I were found out, could send me to prison. I'm not under suspicion, as far as I know, and my relationship with her has improved.

In an emotional sense, however, I've got what I deserved. I've not had a good night's sleep since I started the campaign. I have terrifying nightmares, tend to wake up shaking, covered in sweat. I detest myself, I detest the pleasure I've found in the squalid, furtive acts I've committed. It's Elinor who, in a literal sense, has eaten shit. But in terms of damage, I'm the one who's done so, and I've no-one to blame but myself.

Added to all that is the fear that I'm addicted, and if I don't stop now something calamitous will happen, to her, to me, to my relationships with others.

I have to break out of this pattern. I have to do so now. I mustn't try to find those heavy-duty tablets I've kept from years ago when I had the attack of facial shingles. So strong they blotted out the most excruciating pain, but at the same time most of my consciousness. If they did that to me, what impact would they have on someone as sensitive and finely-tuned as Elinor?

I have those tablets somewhere. Perhaps it's better to find them now and destroy them while I'm resolved, than to leave them where they are, stumble on them later and be tempted.

I begin the search, grow increasingly frustrated as I turn out drawer after drawer and fail to find them.

At last they surface. Four small bottles, one opened, the others sealed. I'll flush the tablets away, that will be safe. On the other hand, perhaps I should retain some in case those pains start up again.

Yes, it would be silly to throw them away.

**

nine

The lid of the box, tucked away behind two larger ones, seems firmly shut, but after wrestling with it for a while it opens to a simple finger-touch. It must be pivoted or sprung with some hidden mechanism. The air trapped inside, perhaps for half a century, is in no hurry to lose its identity; and I, kneeling, hidden from all view, am in no rush to establish who or what is inside. There is no draught, just a gentle percolation, a slow intermingling with the atmosphere outside. I open the lid a little further, tilt the box onto its side. Nothing happens for a moment and then a marble rolls out, drops a couple of inches onto the granite floor, bounces twice, and gathering speed, disappears from view.

I close the lid slowly, heave the box into its old position, check that it's hidden as well as before, and slip back to the centre of the corridor.

No other box-lids have slid open for quite some time, and I feel sure that everyone has finally arrived. I move around the corridor, galleries and alcoves, but I'm either unrecognised or invisible, because no-one greets or even acknowledges me. So, despite the fact that my anonymity allows me to spy and overhear – which always gives me satisfaction – I feel somewhat piqued. It is, after all, my unsorted sub-structure in which these people have been dwelling. This group would never be together if it weren't for me. I sit quietly on a box and watch with increasingly riveted attention:

Wendy Eva, just a name released each morning, reluctantly from Miss Hutton's pursed lips, a name I've carried with me for more than fifty years, a name that can still make me weep into the sheets, the *Eva* always conjuring sad words like fever, never, leave, grieve – Wendy, faceless, incorporeal, who died before she lived, a ghost expunged by *Jesus loves me*, the only tears in the whole school sliding slowly down the cheeks of Ernest Moon. Ernest who had never known his father, reported missing in the first month of the war, and who spent hours sitting alone on the top of the hill, staring out over the canal, hoping to see him, somewhere in Germany.

Ernest and Wendy have both come today. He's kneeling by her stool, offering her a plate of sausage rolls, and her mouth that isn't there is smiling thanks. They're so tender with each other I feel jealous.

One side of the largest crate has been pried away with an iron crowbar which now lies beside it on the corridor floor. My father reaches into the opening and, puffing hard, tugs out a wheelbarrow.

It's a strong one, painted red, with a pneumatic tyre and thick rubber grips around the handles, the kind he used for mixing concrete when he laid our driveway; three parts of sand to two of gravel to one of cement, which puffed into the air when he sliced the bag with his spade, rather like the ashes from my mother's urn fifty years later, when the vicar emptied them into Mr Claybrook's fresh-dug hole.

But the wheelbarrow is dwarfed by Mr Trolley, sprawled into its well, eyes closed, though I don't think he's sleeping. Folds of obscene fat overspill from his trousers, the width of which diverges amazingly from the lumpinesses in the region of his crotch, of which Ernest lay in terror, night after night, terror so acute that when his bedroom door sneaked open and Mr Trolley appeared in stockinged feet, Ernest's first reaction was to feel relief that the agony of waiting was over. Though it wasn't long before he wished it back again with all his breaking heart.

Each time, in the morning, he woke to find a sixpence on the table by his bed, the amount unchanged whether his sheets were bloodied or not. He stored them in a jam-jar which was almost full when Mr Trolley was finally exposed, by Johnnie, who volunteered to take the contaminated sixpences and drop them in the quicksands in the forbidden part of Hobay Wood. And nobody cared – least of all Ernest – how Johnnie had got the money to buy his flashy yellow bike with the silver bell that played a jingly tune.

I think back to that day, the Sunday-school parade in which we marched in pairs behind the dignitaries, single-file, grim-faced with banners. *Jesus, Lord; Jesus loves us; We are sinners; Teach us the holy way.* And at the end of the procession Mr Trolley, the preacher, the message on his banner changed by Johnnie from the classic he'd borne in previous years to: *I bugger little children who come unto me.* And he strode steadily down Five Crosses Lane, up Manley Road past Mr Maddock's field, unknowing, nodding gravely to right and left of him, blessing the unenlightened: and all those who read the message knew it was true, knew they'd always known, but hadn't wanted to accept it, so they hated Mr Trolley not only for his crime but also for making them acknowledge they were wrong, and so they confiscated his belongings, mutilated him, threw him on a non-stop train to Crewe.

Now he's at my gathering, fleshy as ever, lolling in the wheelbarrow, crotch brazen to the sky, wearing the pin-striped suit they stripped from him, stuffed with straw to make a Guy Fawkes for the bonfire, and burned to the sounds of ribald taunts and chanting. Here, breathing easily in his feigned slumber, there is no sign of the carrot, huge and warty, that they stuffed up his arse just as the porter blew his whistle, stuffed it in so far that all that could be seen was a wisp of green sunk deep into bruised purple.

No-one cried for him, except Ernest. And Ernest cries for Hitler, for Wendy, for everyone in pain.

Further down the corridor, Mr Maddock, Keeper of the Keys, 96 years old, custodian of the Methodist Chapel in Five Crosses Road, is kneeling, transplanting lettuces in a patch of well-manured soil he's spread over the stone flags. I've always known he was God, and that God must therefore be a gardener.

From time to time he rises, leans on his fork, takes a swig of buttermilk from a brown stone jar. He doffs his cap each time Nellie passes, pinches his long beard to squeeze out the liquid he's spilled. He fumbles in his pocket, draws out his leather pouch, unzips it, slides his pipe inside, tamps the tobacco with his enormous thumb, takes several matches, sucking hard, to light it.

I'm delighted God had time to come to my gathering. It seems right to me that he's shy, smokes Gold Leaf Medium, has to look at his fob watch to know what time it is, scratches his neck, grinds spent matches deep into the soil, gives all his attention to a puny seedling of a lettuce. He's the real God, not the airy-fairy one who lives above the clouds, who hasn't any feet, and doesn't wear boots with iron studs you can strike a match to light your pipe on.

Johnnie is in conversation with Mrs Campion and Emil Zatopek, the great long-distance runner, all sitting on boxes turned onto their side. His cool wit makes them smile or laugh from time to time. But he's not involved, he doesn't listen when they speak, his eyes keep skating along the corridor. From time to time he winds the chain of his watch around his finger. I think he's looking for me. I wave, but his gaze moves seamlessly by. He looks tense, excited, as always when he's hatching a plot.

Legger has tied a skipping rope to one of Lionel's toes, which the creeping flames have not yet reached. He stands on a box and swings it round. Aunt Lil and the noseless man duck under the rope and begin to skip, with surprising nimbleness. Legger swirls faster and faster, but they still skip faultlessly. Perspiration is pouring down them; onto Aunt Lil's breasts, which have bounced free of her blouse; and also into the noseless man's dark tunnels. From time to time he snorts, squirting two jets of sweat high over her head, but neither of them break their rhythm. She winks at him suggestively. He blows her a delicate kiss.

My mother, pockets stuffed with clothes-pegs, has left Alex's lap and is moving around the corridor carrying our huge brown teapot with the chipped spout that always, in pouring, sends a subsidiary twisting stream outside the range of acceptance of the cup held below it. When this happens she says *Oh dear, never mind*, kneels down, dries the trousers or the small pool on the floor with the corner of her apron. She nods and smiles to everyone, doesn't register anything they say, even Mr Maddock's gruff *Much obliged* as she dries his soggy beard, fans it into shape.

All the time she's looking for the babies she's now not quite sure she once had. She doesn't want to wake them, just to breathe the air that they exhale, catch an echo of the *pop-pop-pop* their lips make when they dream of milk. When she thinks no-one can see her she looks for them under piles of rags on shelves, in drawers that slide open very smoothly, in sooty cavities in chimney breasts, in deep pockets smelling of tobacco. She doesn't find them, but she's never quite sure that they aren't there. So each time she pats the rags back, eases shut the drawer, she lowers her mouth to where they might be, whispers *Toodle-oo-pom-pom,* pulls slightly away, repeating it more quietly, several times, until she's sure they are asleep. And I'm lying in my bed again at Hillside Road, eyes closed, straining the dark, knowing she's climbing backwards down the stairs, halting at every second step, sending towards me yet another *Toodle-oo-pom-pom,* knowing I'll be asleep before she reaches the ground floor.

Of all the things I need, as I crawl through mire, decaying leaves, half-buried barbed wire, the ditch deepening, its walls pressing down on me; of all the things I need, the most is dreamless sleep, which can only be engendered by the fading voice I've always known, that would forever whisper *Toodle-oo-pom-pom* into the dark.

**

They keep telling me I must be angry with you, mother, and when I say *No* they say I'm in denial. When I argue that with your huge cross you couldn't have done better, so how could I be angry with someone who always did her best, they say anger isn't rational, it's not to do with blame, and I won't be healthy until I shed my sentimentality, my dishonesty, and recognise that I'm furious with you.

They're doing to me what you did, not allowing me my feelings. I'm angry with them because they should know better. I'm not angry with you, because there's no way you could have known.

But it was worse for me because I couldn't hate you. The fury was there but I didn't have a legitimate target. So I hit out, almost at random, when the pressure grew too great. All it needed was some slight, some perceived discourtesy or confinement of my power, and I unleashed my venom, sometimes screaming aloud but more often in secret, so that the victim saw only my loving smile, and never the bitter curl of my lips behind it.

I'd feel a moment of elation, then settle back into despising myself. I was in control again.

As for your anger, which I never saw until you lay in your coffin in Madelaine's Chapel of Rest, I think you carried it, fierce and cold, throughout the eighty-two years for which all people who knew you thought you were a gentle, almost saintly figure. But I can't be sure about it, I've yet to find a route to knowing you, a route you always blocked while you were living.

When you were alive and always available I'd no wish to know you better. I thought you were good, too transparently and unquestioningly good to be of interest to me. Now I suspect you fooled me, conditioned me to feel there would be nothing to find if I probed deep.

**

The floor-to-ceiling curtains on one side of the corridor look black in the half-light, though I think they are actually deep green. They are thick and very old, pimpled with gilt tassels not just at the bottom, but all over. They beckon me. I start to climb.

The corridor grows taller, and when I glance down the people look like dolls. Hitler's head is bowed over a wooden block, waiting for an axe that will keep him in suspense forever. A thin spiral of vapour is coiling upwards from Professor Alam's calmly cogitating brain. Uncle Harry is wondering if the rook he's just captured would hatch if he tucked it in the deep folds of his buttocks that no-one has seen for thirty-seven years, and no-one has fondled for sixty. He has suddenly remembered that when he was little he was desolate to learn he could never give birth to a child. He wonders whether hatching this egg would be an equivalent experience. He decides to find out, and slips it in. He gives a preliminary grunt and cackle which Professor Alam does not notice. Uncle Harry likes the slow pace of the brown-skinned man, wonders if his next move will be made before the chicks are hatched.

**

You're like a blister in old paint, she says.

The door must have been in the ditch for decades.

It is early morning, scarcely light, I wasn't concentrating, and the first I know about it is when my knee breaks through the panelling, oak splinters tearing my trousers, scraping my thigh. I pull myself onto a narrow stretch of grass, apply ointment from the jar I always carry, feel suddenly tired, stretch out and fall asleep.

Everything has shrunk except the silent music from the woollen strings of Mrs Campion's harp. It flows around me, buoys me up, so I would float if I let go of the tassels. I slip my arm into a pocket in the velvet, and my fingers touch warm flesh, the outline of a face. I am not surprised. I duck my head into the slit and wriggle in.

The light is purple. The face is opposite mine but now is covered by a gauze or veil, and it would not be right to touch it.

You've been a long time.
I'm only just learning to fly.
Was it my mother stitched me in the curtain?
I've been a long time.
Even so, you're too early.
I thought I'd never find you.
I think you never will.
Was it my mother stitched you in the curtain?
This is the only safe place in the world.

I wriggle backwards, out through the slit, hang from a tassel, looking down.

Shelley has strapped Ernest to an iron frame, and is force-feeding him with champagne, which he pours into his mouth through a funnel made by rolling Mr Campion up into a scroll. Ernest's feet begin to jig. God, in the bearded shape of Mr Maddock, washes them without inhibiting their movement. Professor Alam moves at last, advancing a pawn. Uncle Harry immediately castles. He has forgotten about the egg he slipped between his buttocks, and wonders why his thighs are sticky.

I am shaking. I think I know who I've just been talking to, but I daren't put the thought into words.

**

An autumn evening, in the meadows near the pond, with Elinor and Sholto, great leaves turning yellow and more so daily; the plants and grasses every shade of yellow, orange, red; a patchwork quilt in which no sharp boundaries exist, the colours of one patch interweaving gently with those of its partners, Elinor not feeling well, not wanting conversation or contact, so though companionable in a way, and beautiful scenically for both of us, it is a lonely hike, contrasting with those times we've walked this way and felt close.

Sholto bounding through the grasses, his tail as high as high can be, chasing little creatures, imaginary and real – never catching any, never wanting to – a jiggety, erratic path responding to the jungle of smells through which he races.

And in the nightmare early this morning, a high bed, Sholto lying on it, the quilt slightly askew, Elinor somewhere close by and my cousin Keith – whom I've never cared about and haven't seen for years – cross because the bedding might be dirtied. Sholto drools a little, then more, then brown-stained water flows sluggishly from him down the bed. Elinor's attempts to sponge it with a scrap of tissue are hopelessly inadequate. I use a white towel which is saturated straight away. And still the brown pool deepens. Elinor is wincing. She can't engage with this.

I look at Sholto standing on the higher reaches of the bed. His entire face is wet and dripping. It is terribly wrong.

Now he's standing on the floor, smaller, shrinking. Elinor says something that means this can't happen. But we both know it is happening and that it's hopeless. She is paralysed. He's now tiny, still standing, with strange-shaped legs as if they were carved and had to fit on rockers. He's lonely because we're big and far away. Soon he will be gone entirely.

I kneel to him, try to find words with which to tell him a story.

**

Throughout the duration of my gathering I've been half-aware of an alcove in the wall containing something or someone protected from view by a mote-speckled haze of yellow light. I'd known it was premature to enter it, but that sooner or later the time would come.

It has.

As I advance, slow-swimming, through the aura, the sounds of animation die away. If I concentrate I can still hear them in the corridor – Ernest being tickled, squealing with laughter on the edge of agony; Uncle Harry, sucking contentedly on his silver moustache, pleased to have outfoxed Professor Alam; the trickle-swirl of tea spiraling from my mother's giant teapot into Nellie's primly proffered cup; Mrs Campion's harp music, lacing everyone and everything together without touching. But I allow the yellow haze to sponge away these sounds, and the silence that results is deeper than in a noise-free region.

She is slender, naked, beautifully proportioned. Her hair is fainter than the aura, which feeds it, makes it glow from her pillow, the straw on which she's lying; a supple, accommodating bed.

She is not breathing, but neither is she cold. Her skin has a sheen of dampness, a scattering of droplets nestle in her first few pubic hairs. I glance down at the stone tiles on the floor. And yes, below her, are several small pools of water which have dripped from her. They must have carried her directly from the pond.

I've never seen her before, but I've known her almost all my life. I've conjured her in darkness, in my bed, but she's always been just outside my reach and vision. I've known she's just as lonely as I am, that if we could ever meet we'd have little to say, but even so would find comfort in each other's presence.

She's the golden girl who drowned in Profitt's Pond.

**

It is a summer afternoon in the long school holidays. I am six, with my mother visiting Auntie Doris in her house that smells of soap. I always feel nervous there. It is too posh to relax into. The taps in her kitchen have rubber spouts on them, red and shiny, so water eases out of them in a smooth, expansive flow. It doesn't hiccup and spatter like in the sink at home. Her armchairs are covered with crocheted mats, so our coats and trousers won't soil them. But most disturbing of all, in contrast with our battered tin which smells of years of currants, she has a glass cake-stand with three tiers. It swivels at a finger-touch, and allows me to look at the scones and cakes from underneath. It fascinates me. It seems stupendously aristocratic.

So I'm fidgeting, uneasy, when the door flies open and Auntie Marney from three doors down staggers in, flops into a chair, bursts into tears.

It takes several gulps of tea before the words she keeps choking on congeal into a sentence I can understand.

The golden girl, she blurts:

The golden girl has drowned in Profitt's Pond.

I know now that her name was Alice Goulden, and if I'd known that then I doubt if she'd have come to me, night after night, for more than fifty years: and she wouldn't be here now, with all these other people from my past.

But she is here, drying slowly on a bed of fresh straw. She's the sister I wanted and never had. She's the other side of me that I've occasionally glimpsed in a dark cupboard. She's the only person with whom I shared my childhood loneliness. She's the golden girl who drowned in Profitt's Pond. She's my golden girl, my shining spirit, my unavailing hope.

She was four years old when the bulrushes parted and she fell through into the water. So those wisps of pubic hair that make me want to cry as I gaze down at her must have grown long after she died.

I know that if I touch her hand it will feel warm, that if I slide my finger along her palm hers will close around it, and I'll have found something I've I wanted all my life.

But I can't do it. Not yet. Perhaps not ever.

I step back through the yellow light to the sound of Ernest's squealing, and Alex scratching on the floor.

**

Oh, these times of restlessness and nightmare, hatching of evil plots that keep becoming reality because I dwell on them so much, revel in their details as I smirk into my pillow.

**

The bottle is nearly full, the tablets smaller than I remember. The label is stained brown and its typing has faded, though I can still pick out my name and the words *Not more than 3 to be taken daily. May induce severe drowsiness.* I wonder if, over the ten years since they were prescribed for me, they've lost their potency.

I didn't consciously make the decision to go ahead with this extension to my plan, but there's no question of not doing so. Perhaps it's easier to proceed because, as before, I've no wish to hurt, just to unsettle, inconvenience a little, exercise control in secret.

Elinor will be coming round soon to pick up the dog, and will almost certainly accept my offer of a drink.

I tip a few tablets onto the counter, select one and put the others back in the bottle. But one will probably have no effect at all, though I'm scared of trying two. So I take a second one, cleave it across its diameter with a carving knife, return one half to the bottle and place the other with the whole one on a paper tissue which I carefully fold over them.

I take my small metal hammer from the drawer, tap the tablets a few times through the tissue. The paper is embossed with a moon and a half-moon, but when I unfold it the tablets are still intact. I hit harder and soon they are reduced to powder.

I pour chai to half-fill the mug and carefully tip the powder into the liquid. A little remains on the paper and I stroke it into the chai with my finger.

It doesn't sink, at least not all of it, so I sprinkle cinnamon onto the surface, which masks the powder's whiteness pretty effectively. I don't want to add milk now because she may decline the drink, and though the chai will keep, the milk will not.

The only emotion I feel as I move through these procedures is satisfaction, a quiet pleasure in performing a job well. I don't think of Elinor at all.

I place the mug of doctored chai in the fridge, the hammer back in the drawer. The tissue, with its indentations, could give me away, and for a moment I panic, uncertain how to destroy it. In the end I decide to throw it to the winds when I'm well away from home, so I stuff it deep into my pocket.

She arrives, animated and beautiful, and I'm engulfed by a wave of longing and despair.

She'd love some chai, so I add milk, warm it up, sprinkle some more cinnamon which dusts the surface a gorgeous rust colour, warm it in the microwave, serve it to her in the bay. She sips it slowly, chatting all the time, and when she's finished it she gives me a hug and leaves.

I tip away the residue, hoping all the powder

hasn't sunk to the bottom, scour the mug thoroughly, put it away.

I wake in the night, heart pounding, remembering now what a zombie I felt after taking a single tablet, how effective it was at expunging the horrendous pain around my eyes.

I'm almost twice her weight and only half as sensitive. In addition to which I've given her an extra half-tablet.

I picture her, lifting out of sleep into semi-consciousness, knowing that something is badly wrong, that she needs immediate help but is too fuddled and exhausted to get out of bed.

I imagine her heartbeat growing stronger and stronger, until her body is in danger of bursting open. Her mouth is completely dry, issuing no sound as she tries to call out.

Her face hovers in front of me, bright, vivacious, full of love. I've no wish to hurt her, I just want to hold her in my arms.

I wake early, convinced she's dead or in a coma. The time drags interminably, and although we have agreed that I should never call her before 9 o'clock, I dial her number at 7.30 am. Her phone rings for a while, and my suspicions seem increasingly likely to be confirmed.

She answers, not unpleasant but brusque.

What's up? Something important?

I'm totally flustered, more disappointed than pleased.

No. Nothing of consequence. I thought it was much later. Sorry.

Huh. Be more careful. If it happens again I'll know you're checking up on me. Now, let me get back to sleep.

She hangs up. I'm in a fury. I take the bottle of

pills from where I've hidden it and take out three.

No. I must be careful. Perhaps the effects are cumulative. I put one back, fold a tissue round the other two.

**

Alex is hissing at me and I'm afraid of losing her.

I don't trust you when you rail against the sky's elusiveness. I know this ditch is deep, its sides slippery, its footholds poor. But you could clamber out if you really wanted to. The problem isn't that the route is difficult, but that you welcome the clay's suction. You don't want to leave. Your story is a lie – you didn't find this ditch just weeks ago, you've been here all your life. This is your home.

I know you've scrambled out from time to time, entered the world above, cut quite a figure there, legitimately, because you brought with you the flavours of the ditch, its scents and sensualities, its subtle shades of brown. You brought a texture, a dark tapestry that were grasped at by people who all their lives have blinked into the sunlight, furnished their rooms in white, missed the chance to wallow, savour. They enjoyed it, grasped at you, too.

Your sediments enriched them, and you freshened in their cool, clear air. You revelled in the long-range views from mountain-tops, they grew tipsy in the darkness of the tomb you steered them to.

But Shropshire clay is patient, implacable. Its elasticity made sport with you, played you out, almost to the horizon, but it never quite let go. It drew you in, stealthily, with remission intervals, but would always land you, back in the familiar comfort of the ditch.

And there you were, hands sticky with mud, exerting your own suction on me, your friend. You'd suck me in, I'd feel trapped, be stifled by the stench of stagnant water. The damp would penetrate my bones, chill me as I tried to struggle free.

The ditch has been good to me, Zack. So have you. I needed it. I needed you. It's been a necessary place, a place of healing. Those poultices you made for me from ferns and coloured mud, they saved me, sucked my bitterness away. The filtered light eased the pressure on my eyeballs, the seepages of water washed my dreams.

But it's time, now I've grown well, to say goodbye to this dark hospital, to crawl out of the sediment, re-enter the sharp world.

I had thought we'd leave together, share a journey in the upper world, for a while, at least. But if you can't come with me, I'll go alone. My time has come. I'll not linger in this ditch. I tell you, I will not.

She's hissing at me, and though now I realise it's only in my dream, and the words she spoke were in my vocabulary, not hers, I'm still afraid of losing her.

**

ten

If you're not careful, lad, you might find your life has slipped away like ice-cream.

Ice-cream?

Aye. Ice-cream spilt on sand.

There is now great hubbub and conviviality at my gathering, with incense shadowing and distorting everything, but I'm in an oasis of quietness and fresh country air. Just me and him. My father.

He's dressed, as almost always in the years before he died, in an old blue suit with matching waistcoat, with a tie which looks confining on someone so squat and muscular. I'd hardly noticed him earlier, nor had I missed him, which seems strange to me now, as we'd always been close and I'd been devastated when his heart finally gave out.

What we'd never shared was words. The brief exchange we'd just had was about as intimate as any in the fifty or so years we knew each other. When he was dying I'd wanted very much to talk, mostly because though we never had, I'd often felt he wanted to, but our relationship was so entrenched I couldn't initiate it myself. So we didn't. Perhaps now we will.

He sits down in a stiff chair, next to the cushion on which I'm lolling.

Life slips away anyway, Dad. And ice-cream through sand is slower than a stone through water.

He runs his forefinger around the collar of his shirt. He's not skilled in imagery and abstractions. All his life he's dealt in specifics, tangible things: screwdrivers, fuse-wire, soil, boot-polish, spades, tobacco; and despite his opening sentence I suspect that's not changed much since his death. In the past I might have let him flounder for a while, but not now. I'm pleased to see him, I appreciate his trying to talk my language, and I'm remembering how he struggled, night after night after a long day's work, sitting in his blue overalls at the kitchen table, learning algebra in order to teach me, when I was doing badly at school. *What is this bloody X?* I heard him groan to himself one night, when he thought I was asleep and I came downstairs in pyjamas for a glass of water.

Good to see you, Dad. I thought we'd burned the suit along with the rest of you.

His smile is somewhat strained, his voice gruff.

You always 'ad a funny sense of humour.

I'm sorry.

Forget it. That's not what I want to talk about. It's this.

He draws his chair a little closer.

It makes my 'eart bleed to see how you've been living recently.

Makes my heart bleed. Those words sear me, because I've heard him say them before, twenty years ago, only then his heart was bleeding not for me but for my brother, whose business dealings – into which, little by little, he'd sunk all his savings – were a succession of unadulterated calamities. The irony for me is that even so long ago his heart was wrecked, it was bleeding in reality, and his incessant worrying about Tony's ventures had surely done nothing to staunch the flow.

But I'm feeling defensive, ashamed. I've no wish to acknowledge anything I don't have to.

D'you mean things you think I've been doing recently?

Not think, lad. Know. And not just things you've done, but ones you've attempted, ones you're contemplating.

My mouth goes dry. It's true that sometimes in the course of what I now recognise has been a persecution campaign against Elinor I've reined back somewhat after asking myself what he or my mother would have thought. But it's only now that I feel a strong sense of shame. Their deaths gave me licence to behave more squalidly, but it has taken my father's resurrection for me to understand that.

You mean Elinor?

There isn't a single word to describe the expression in his face. It holds sternness, disapproval, perhaps an edge of contempt, but at the same time there's compassion, concern and love. There's also something that feels rather like amusement, which I'm irritated by.

That's a large part of it. There's such a massive difference between what she did to you, and the way you've hit back.

I start to interject but he sweeps my words aside.

What she did that hurt you so much was 'ealthy, lad. I mean, she was just following her impulses. She's so much younger than you. I know she cheated and lied, but she didn't set out to 'urt you, and there's no way she could have known how deep your pain would be.

I know he's right, but I can still feel anger simmering inside me.

Whereas what you've done to 'er has been wicked, downright malignant. You've set out to systematically unsettle her, make her feel out of sorts, uncertain, needy. You've tried to make her want you, and the reality is that you don't want her at all. You're manipulating her. You're sniggerin' at her behind your sweet, warm smile. You've been squalid, and I'm sorry for you.

Bugger your sorrow! I don't need it.

Don't you realise, son, that the person who's most 'urt by your obscenities is you? You've lost all self-respect, you're out of control. You might fool yourself that it's in the past, but if you don't change your attitude it'll keep on.

If you don't make yourself stop now, you'll meet disaster. And you couldn't 'andle it, however much your melodramatic mind kids itself you want it.

Every word he speaks turns the knife in me because, in his ponderous way, he's telling me what I know and keep dodging.

I turn my festering, seething anger against him.

If you'd shown me affection when I was little, instead of stifling it, worrying about whether you'd fathered a sissy, I'd have made a better job of dealing with this stuff.

You're right, son. And I'm sorry.

The simplicity and completeness of his apology floors me for a second. But I hang on to my anger, fuel its flames. His words have humiliated me, and I want to hit back harder.

Words are cheap, Dad. Don't hide behind them. Face the fact that you failed as a father. You didn't understand me. You never tried to. Everything you did as a parent was ham-fisted and destructive.

I can feel his hurt. But it isn't enough. I need another weapon.

And she was just as bad. Neither of you knew how to love.

I've never seen a dead man cry. I never saw him cry in the fifty years we shared on Earth. But now tears are trickling down his face. He doesn't try to stop them, he's not worried about seeming a sissy, he just lets them come, falling slow onto the trousers of his suit.

I want to comfort him, put my arms round him, but I'm held back just as fifty years ago, when he'd wake me very early, we'd tiptoe downstairs, listen on our crackly old radio to commentaries on world heavyweight boxing championship matches from Madison Square Garden, Joe Louis versus Billy Conn or Tami Mauriello, me sitting at his foot, wanting to rest my head against his knee, not doing so because he'd stiffen and feel embarrassed, though he wouldn't have prevented me.

Now, though, he'd welcome the contact, and I'm the one who doesn't want it, not because he's dead but because it's too late to change our pattern. On the other hand, he's crying because of my cruelty, and I don't want him to feel hurt. It shouldn't be difficult for me just to touch him. He speaks as I'm agonising over this dilemma.

Don't worry, son. Wantin' to touch is good enough for me.

He smiles, ruefully.

But then, it always was.

He's composed again, but he's not finished speaking. I can see him struggling to find the right words.

You're right in thinkin' your Mum and I didn't do a very good job. You're wrong in thinking we didn't love you.

I know that, Dad.

I think we felt that loving someone is doing things for them, not telling 'em about it. The love is in the actions.

Yes, it is. But if you'd hugged me from time to time – if she had, too – I wouldn't have been so afraid of touching others.

I know. We got that wrong. All I can say is that we'd have done better if our own mothers had been around when we were growing up.

I'm puzzled by his statement, at first. I'm aware, of course, that my mother's mother was shipped off, in disgrace, to America in the first week of my mother's life, but I'd forgotten his mother had died of throat cancer when he was small. I want to hug him now, but I still can't do it.

**

He's wearing his bell-bottomed blue overalls, and he's bursting with energy. He's racing to the chalked bowling mark in the middle of Hillside Road, hurling the ball towards our improvised wickets. He's pushing incredibly heavy barrow-loads of wet concrete over thick planks that sag beneath the weight, hour after hour, shovelling, kneeling, tamping until our new driveway is laid. He's striding jauntily down Silver Pin, a huge sack of fresh-dug leaf-mould on each shoulder, his body dappled with the shadows cast by oak-leaves in the setting sun, me walking behind him, carrying the spade, feeling proud of his superhuman vigour.

**

I'm kneeling on the swivel-chair at Barber Corker's. The chin-rest has been wound too high, so my neck is stretched and painful, but I don't know how to say so.

Something hard and cold is nibbling the back of my head, behind my ears. It bites me each time it starts to go away. The fingers that twist my head from side to side are also hard and cold. I keep my eyes closed, but if I peep I can see my mother kneeling below me. She's pulling silly faces, smiling, blowing kisses. This makes me cry harder. My cheeks grow damp and my chin starts sticking to the leather.

It was better when I'd grown and sat facing forwards in the chair. I felt less vulnerable when my throat wasn't pressed against the chin-rest. Even so, I'd feel disturbed as my curls fell to the floor and mingled with the ones already there. If I went late in the day the pile of hair was almost ankle-deep, and though my hair wasn't merged by the time he'd finished with me, I could tell by the way the rest of it was mixed that mine would soon lose its identity and so – in some way I didn't understand – would I.

When I looked at this soft rug lying on the floor, black and yellow tinged with red and grey, I thought of the open jam-jar Johnnie had left on the wall in his backyard, one summer evening. It was not quite empty, and when we came back later, after playing cricket in Fletcher's field, it was almost full of insects flecked with many colours. They were suffocating, drowning. There was no way out. A dirge came from the jar as new arrivals circled the it, then hurtled into the seething pack.

I felt sorry for them. They had so much life, and even sang as they were dying. I could understand their feelings, empathise with them. They were utterly different from the huge flies, black and bloated, that clung in vast numbers to the bleeding hunks of meat hanging hugely in the window of Mr Gregory's butcher's shop. I could see them growing fatter by the minute. Their stillness terrified me.

I thought also of the sodden mound of clothes on the rag-and-bone man's cart, pulled slowly by his ancient horse along our road each week. Sleeves, shoes, arms, legs splayed in all directions, inextricably jumbled, forever.

One day I plucked up the courage to ask Barber Corker what happened to the waste hair.

I feed it to my chickens to make them grow more feathers, he snapped.

Though it didn't seem likely, he looked so severe that I believed him.

I lay in bed that night, thinking how the hairs would tickle the chickens' throats, and wondering why I'd never seen a chicken with grey feathers. I hugged the pillow to me. I could have lain there forever, dreaming, thinking, mingling the two, until I couldn't tell which of the millions of hairs round Barber Corker's feet, rippling and shifting each time the door opened, were mine.

**

Now, at my gathering, my father is in his overalls instead of his blue suit. He's vital and strong, I can feel his muscles rippling, sap surging through his thick black hair. But at the same time he's vulnerable and small, his overalls could be a baby's jump-suit, his body is quivering for arms to take him, fold him in. I still can't do it, so I try to make a cradle with my voice.

Who did you think of most when you were dying?

He bows his head, reflecting for a while.

Your mother, of course. When I was conscious.

And when you were dreaming? In coma?

My mother.

Did you talk with her?

I tried to. But she couldn't remember me. She was absorbed in stretching back.

What d'you mean?

It's 'ard to put it into words. Seems to me that whereas life is forwards, its flow moving down the generations, death is backwards. Someone who's dyin' always strives to return to where they started.

To the womb?

I suppose so. Yes.

We're quiet for a while, he with his mother, me with mine.

You know, Dad, I so much wanted to talk to you before you died.

I'm glad you didn't have the courage.

I feel hurt.

Why?

Because I wouldn't have trusted your concern. I'd have felt like a specimen. At times like that, when the chips are really down, it seems to me you're a watcher. What's it called? A voyeur.

I know he's right. That though I seek intimacy, my capacity for it is limited, so that as it grows I step back, and only an effigy of me continues to move forwards. I watch what develops from the sidelines.

This pattern has occurred now, in this longest conversation I've ever had with him. But I don't want to observe it any more. I'm tired of it. There's nothing to be gained by talking to a dead man.

Goodbye, Dad.

He holds up his hand.

'Old on. I came to see you because there's summat I want to say to you.

Haven't you said enough already?

No. What I want to say is that you've two routes

to avoid disaster. You can come out of that bloody ditch entirely or you can embrace it, warts and stinkin' mud and all. What you can't do is be only half there, fragmented and disconnected. If you continue to do that you'll lose your identity, you'll be dangerous, you'll kill someone, perhaps yourself, or Elinor. Perhaps Alex.

Alex, where are you? What he says is right. But I can't embrace the ditch by myself. Nor can I get out of it alone. You're the only person I can journey with.

What d'you think, Dad? Shall I try to escape it, or plunge in fully?

Safer to get out, Son. Most people die unfulfilled. But you won't, you're too intrigued by life. So plunge in. Don't even try to swim.

And Alex?

Don't drag her down with you. You can breathe under water, under slime. She can't.

He rests his hand on my knee and squeezes it. I resist at first, then I place my hand on top of his. He puts his other one on mine, and without thinking I put my other one on top of the heap. He slides out his lower one, slaps it down on my upper. I tug mine from the bottom of the heap, plonk it swiftly on top of the pile. And so on, faster and faster. It's crazy! This is the game we'd play every evening, fifty years ago, after I'd had my cup of cocoa, before I went to bed. So it's not true he wouldn't let me touch him.

I halt, panting, feeling happy and bewildered. He's grinning at me, his eyes full of love.

You might have the weirdest imagination in the Northern Union, but you've got a lousy memory, lad.

As I smile back at him, I remember another intimacy we used to share.

I hold up my hands, palms facing him. Somewhat hesitantly he does the same, towards me.

As we pat our hands against each other's, gently, regularly, I start to chant.

Pat-a-cake, pat-a-cake, baker's man.

He's trying to join in, but he seems to have forgotten the words. I mouth them to him.

Bake me a cake as fast as you can.

We stumble through it, our eyes engaged more deeply and for longer than at any time we'd shared during his life.

When we stop he grins at me.

Pat-a-cake was your Mum's game with you, not mine.

He puts his finger to his lips.

Can you hear her voice?

I can. We sit quietly for a while, in our own worlds, listening to her Cheshire brogue, its cadences. When her voice dies away, we breathe out at the same time.

This has been our valediction. Now we can part.

Goodbye Dad.

His face stiffens, grows grave again.

I meant what I said about Alex. She can't handle the ditch. Don't try to make her.

I know. Now bugger off, you pompous old fart!

Goodbye, Son.

He's gone and I'm shaking, close to tears. The incense is thick and billowing. I blow on it and a small region thins. I blow again, and now I see him, in football outfit, his shirt blue-striped, white shorts baggy, playing outside-left for the local football team. He feints one way then the other, accelerates round the bemused full-back, skids into the corner-flag as he floats the ball across the penalty area, its flight perfect for Uncle Alan's header; the net and me dancing for joy.

That's my Dad, I say proudly to someone

standing next to me, who turns out to be a woman of about my mother's age. I point to him as he lies sprawled round the corner-flag, panting, legs splayed.

He's got a nice pair of thighs, Ducky, she says.

**

The sun has just risen by the time we reach the Edge, and the sky in front of us as we squat on the summit is every shade of red.

There is a mild breeze, but nothing visible is moving. The air is fresh and there is no sound. I wonder if I've felt such peace since the morning of my father's death, when I sat alone, deep in ferns, on Windy Rock.

Knees drawn up to chin, she's in her favourite position, looking out over the fields below, though I doubt if they are what she's seeing. I'm waiting for her to speak. She's been silent since we started the uphill trudge. I'm nervous.

She opens and closes her mouth a couple of times before the first words come. She doesn't look at me.

I'm frightened.

I move to her, put my hand on her shoulder. She lets it rest there, but she's tense, clearly doesn't want it. I ease it away.

I'll look after you, Alex.

That might be what I'm frightened of.

I feel hurt. And why won't she look at me?

I don't understand.

She turns to me, eyes blazing.

Stop pressurising me.

I move away without speaking. I'm angry, try to tell myself she's in shock.

On the far side of the fissure is a large rock I've not seen before. It's shaped like a saddle and a young woman in a long dress is sitting on it. Her auburn hair is glinting in the sun. It's my mother from before I was born.

She's looking my way but I have to wave before she sees me. She waves back and mouths a silent message across the crevasse:

Be careful, love. Mind you don't hurt yourself.

I'm fine, I signal back. *It's safe here. I can fly.*

I can't tell if she's picked up my response. As I look at her she vanishes slowly from the feet up, until all that's left is her face, and then just her lips spelling out the same words:

Be careful, love. Mind you don't hurt yourself.

She disappears entirely, and now I feel nervous, wonder if I'm safe.

You see, Zack...

As Alex speaks she drops her hand onto my knee. I'd not seen her move to me, and for a moment I'm not sure who's speaking.

...I've waited so long for the release that came this morning. All my life, more-or-less. And I don't want to fritter it away.

By being with me, you mean?

Don't be so egotistical! If I tell you I've a problem you always assume it's to do with you. I do have a life apart from you, you know.

I don't respond. My anger has returned, but I don't want to show it. I think she's being unfair, but I also know there's some truth in what she says.

Look, Zack. I don't want to sound pathetic, but I feel in danger. I've come out of the dark and I'm blinded by the light. I don't know where I am, which way to turn.

It's not that I've lost my father. I'm glad he's

gone. It's that I don't know how to handle what I've found now I've closed his eyes.

Even as I speak I realise I'm being cruel, but I don't stop myself.

Did you notice that when he opened his eyes just before he died he was blind?

Of course. But he was looking at me, even so.

Something only Ernest might have said. I feel ashamed.

Tell me how to help you, Alex.

She smiles, but still looks sad.

I think we'll have to do it by feel. I need some space, not from you particularly, but from everything. On the other hand, I want you to be around. I need you.

Are you sure? Perhaps I should go away for a while.

I make this suggestion casually, but the more I examine it the more I like it. I need a break from the intensity of the past few days.

Alex, however, is distraught.

No. That's not what I want. Don't abandon me.

I won't.

I feel forced into making the promise, feel a surge of irritation. It's she who's pressurising me.

We walk slowly down the trail. The birds are awake now. The sun is catching the uppermost leaves of the oaks. Butterflies are dancing round the lower branches. She takes my hand.

As we reach the road she gasps and points to something on the verge. I move to it quickly. It's a sparrow, fluttering, injured. It must have flown into the telephone wires. Its beak is gaping, but emitting no sound. I kneel to it. It doesn't struggle as I pick it up.

Alex comes to me, strokes it with her finger.

It's alright, little one. We'll make you better.

I shake my head, point to my fingers, through which red and yellow liquid is slithering. The sparrow's head is almost severed.

She strokes it again. I stroke it, too. Its beak has halted in mid-gape, but its chest is still fluttering. I look at Alex.

She nods.

I lower it back onto the grass, stand up. It looks so small. Alex is watching, riveted, terrified.

I measure the distance, leap in the air, and before I come down hard I close my eyes.

On landing I step back and open them again. I'd not missed the bird, but it still seems to be breathing.

I jump again, and again. The floodgates are opened and I stamp on the bird until I'm exhausted. I step back, open my eyes, wipe my feet on the grass. There is no sign of the sparrow.

That was horrible, Alex says.

Yes.

I mean, you were horrible. You enjoyed it. How could you be so cruel?

She starts to cry, and the tears she hadn't shed over her dead father flood out over this speck of life that has just been extinguished.

I want to hold her, ease her pain. But I'm furious and I want to run away. I'd felt nothing but pity for that bird, I'd tried to help it, I'd ended its suffering. I didn't deserve her contempt.

Yet I know what provoked her reaction. It was my stamping well beyond the time that the sparrow was dead. I'd felt compelled to do it, I had to separate myself from the slime and stickiness that threatened to suck out of me something I daren't lose. But I was stamping out of fear, not from the wish to hurt.

I force myself to relive the episode, and at the same time ask myself if I derived any pleasure at all from stamping this creature into oblivion. The pity pours back, so does my terror, but on top of that there's something that makes me bite my lip – it's not exactly pleasure, more perhaps the enjoyment of a sense of total power over life and death. Whatever it is, I hate myself for it.

Alex is still in distress, almost hysterical. I take her in my arms, hold her tight and let her sob herself into quietness.

Let me take you home.

I'm sorry for what I said. I didn't mean it.

It doesn't matter at all.

But it does. I want to get away. For a few days at least, if not forever. I can't handle what she's shown me about myself. I want to go away and lick my wounds.

When we reach her gate, I tell her I need to take a walk by myself. She looks frightened.

You'll be back soon, won't you?

I remember Alex saying she couldn't stand being lied to. I hesitate.

Yes.

She's not satisfied.

You won't abandon me, will you?

Of course not. Now in you go. A warm, deep bath will do you good.

I kiss her gently. She tastes so sweet. Tears are trickling down her cheeks.

Let's make love, Zack. I want to.

This isn't the right time. You know that.

I'm close to tears myself as I smile at her and turn away.

I walk down the lane, knowing she's watching me and waving. But I don't turn. I daren't.

At the phone-box in the village I rummage in my pocket, find some coins, open the heavy door of the telephone booth, dial Elinor's number. She's at home.

**

eleven

The trial is about to begin. Mr Maddock, presiding in the Judge's chair, thumps his gavel on the teak. Silence falls, and all eyes turn to Ernest in the witness-box, handcuffed to a huge drum which every so often Hitler taps on with his cane. Ernest's head is bowed. He looks bewildered. He looks as if he's trying to be brave.

Mr Campion is a scroll on which the charges against Ernest have been written in large, black copperplate. Nellie Preece unrolls him and reads them out.

1. That he wastes time looking for his dead father, especially from the top of Frodsham Hill.

2. That he smiled when Johnnie Greenway made a farting noise while the school was singing Jesus wants me for a sunbeam.

Objection in the face of all the law, shouts Hitler, saliva spewing.

Objection underlined, says Uncle Harry quietly.

He has stepped away from his chess-game while Professor Abdul Alam is cogitating, and is painting a crimson gallows on the wall.

D'you take sugar, Mr Hitler?

My mother hands him a cup of tea. He takes it,

mutters his thanks, sits down and stares morosely into it.

Nellie unrolls Mr Campion a little further.

3. That he gave ginger beer to a person whose mouth has disappeared.

4. That he broke his ankle trying to reach the sky.

Nellie smirks flirtatiously at Mr Maddock, allows Mr Campion to curl up tight again, and sits down, wart nodding.

Skin the bugger alive, screams my Aunt Lil, who's just arrived in a ghastly purple hat laden with onions and cherries: *He's worse than Adolph Hitler.*

He's not. I'm the worst in human history, yells Hitler, in a fury, beating on his chest.

Which charge shall we commence with? asks Mr Maddock, calmly.

Attention focuses on Emil Zatopek, who is loping the long corridor, red shirt oozing sweat, tortured face uplifted to the ceiling.

Number three, he calls out, his Czech accent delicate against the Cheshire burrs from all around him.

He picks up speed and disappears.

Mr Maddock turns to the accused.

Ernest, he says kindly:

You are charged that you gave ginger beer to a person whose mouth has disappeared. How do you plead?

Ernest's handcuffs rattle as he speaks.

I don't know how to plead, Almighty. But I think Mr Shelbourne would be able to tell you.

Shelley rushes up to the witness box, cuffs Ernest round the ears, turns to Mr Maddock.

Shall I whip him, your Honour?

No need for violence, Mr Shelbourne. Sit down, please. Now, Ernest, tell me the truth. Did you give ginger beer to Wendy Eva?

Oh yes. A whole bottle.

There are gasps and mutters from all round the courtroom. Johnnie sneaks up to the drum and plays a few bars from a death march. Mr Maddock holds up his hand for silence.

Did you know that Wendy's mouth had disappeared?

Ernest nods. He smiles towards Wendy on the exhibit stand, sitting demurely on a milking-stool, her fingers as always making labyrinths for tadpoles.

Yes. But that doesn't stop her feeling thirsty.

How could you tell she was thirsty?

Her face was crying through the ash.

What ash, Ernest? I don't want any lies.

Mr Maddock looks severe, now, like the God in the Old Testament, his beard no longer soft, his great hands reaching for a pair of thunderbolts.

D'you take sugar, Mr Maddock?

She's done it again, and this time I'm glad. She tips a couple of heaped teaspoons into his cup, stirs it for him, backs away. He takes a sip and speaks, his voice gentler now, rumbling like coal.

What ash, Ernest?

The ash from Lionel's burning.

Attention switches for a moment to Lionel, still quietly aflame beyond a scattering of boxes, his shadow gaunt and flickering. He is smiling in his sleep.

Who put Lionel's ash on Wendy's face

Johnnie did, Almighty. I think he was trying to keep her warm. But I knew she wasn't cold. She was just thirsty. So I poured ginger beer onto her face.

Did it quench her thirst?

I don't know. But she smiled.

How could she smile, lad? She hasn't got a mouth.

You don't need a mouth to smile, Almighty.

As guilty as the day that he was born, screeches Nellie.

A growling and muttering of approval reverberates around the corridor. I can't tell where it's coming from.

Which charge next? calls Mr Maddock.

Zatopek, reeling in from the opposite direction, is too exhausted to speak. He lifts a finger.

One, he breathes, before he staggers out of view.

Mr Maddock bangs his gavel on the teak. The hubbub dies away leaving just the harp music, lyrical and lovely, so that I wish God would never speak again.

Ernest. It is charged that you wasted time looking for your dead father, especially from the top of Frodsham Hill. Is this correct?

Ernest shakes his head.

You lying little sod, screams Aunt Lil.

He's lying, he's lying, several voices add.

Ernest shakes his head again.

People have seen you, says Mr Maddock fiercely.

Ernest bites his lip.

But I wasn't wasting time, Almighty.

Why not? You didn't see him, thundered God.

I did! I saw him when I closed my eyes.

Mr Maddock seems frustrated.

Did he speak to you?

No.

Did he look at you?

No.

Ernest is crying now.

Did he know you were there?

No, Almighty. That's how I knew he was dead.

Ernest buries his face in his arm. In the silence, Uncle Harry adds a crimson cross-piece to the scaffold.

Mr Maddock again brings down his gavel, this time quietly and sadly, so that its sound rises slowly, uncertainly, sinuously coiling around the plangent notes of Mrs Campion's harp. All else is silence, except for Aunt Lil's stifled hiccups and occasional spurts of flame from the soil-rich crevices between Lionel's knobbly toes.

The Court will regress for an hour and sixteen minutes.

Mr Maddock rises, picks up his garden fork, and starts to loosen manure, steaming quietly in the alcove behind the chess-game, where Professor Abdul Alam, after a thousand mental pages of calculation, has worked out a twelve-move sequence into which honour and ambiguity are so subtly insinuated that Uncle Harry couldn't possibly realise he was being tricked into winning.

Professor Alam smiles to himself, moves his white bishop – which to him is simply a white bishop, and has lost all resemblance to an egg – three spaces diagonally forward. He is completely riveted, but his brain is tired, he looks forward to the respite which will follow his move. He becomes conscious for the first time of the harp music and wants to glide and loop with it.

Uncle Harry, however, returned from the scaffold, wastes no time. He's spent too much of his life waiting for paint to dry to be bored with the slowness of his opponent's moves, but he wants to help the professor understand that chess isn't as hard as he seems to think it is. He picks up the egg Professor Alam has just laid down and tucks it into his tobacco pouch. He spits onto the floor, grins across the board.

Thought that'd fool yer.

The professor sighs to himself, closes his eyes, takes one last swoop over the rooftops of the village huts in Pakistan, where he grew up, sees no-one that he knows or knew, but catches the aroma of fresh-crushed cardamom rising from an iron pot over a wood fire. He breathes it in and fills his lungs with it, and as it percolates his blood-stream, flows around his body, he finds the strength again to address the mathematics that have fascinated and bullied him all his life. He smiles at Uncle Harry.

That was a most audacious move.

Although he doesn't understand the meaning of the word, Uncle Harry feels its spirit and is pleased.

Aye. You have to be audacious if you spend your life at the top of a ladder.

Professor Alam nods. He doesn't yet understand Uncle Harry's concept but admires the freedom with which, at his great age, he's so readily able to be unorthodox.

I'm feeling somewhat oppressed. I need a break before the trial resumes. So far I haven't engaged with anyone, and I'm beginning to wonder if that's the truth of my life, that I can't or won't engage, even at my own gathering.

I'll crawl for a while, let the drops of dew and rain that fern-fronds hold for days in the cool shade of the ditch fall onto my forehead, calm it.

I look for Alex, but can't find her. I tie on my kneepads, part the velvet curtain, relish the smell and feel of mud.

**

I need to be alone. What I need is not the serrated, nagging loneliness that has assailed me in the corridor, but the companionable kind offered by the ditch, the warty, snouty, sludgy, leafy loneliness that Alex understands, in which I know I'm surrounded by natural things, organic and inorganic, which have not been contrived or prettified to fit some functional or aesthetic definition, which are what they are, and have perhaps been so for centuries, perhaps just for this moment, their limitations enormous, their integrity total. I need to be naked, too, so I can fully embrace the intimacy of the ditch.

As I crawl my spirits lift, I start to whistle. A patch of sunlight on spidery roots of turf on the wall to my left brings out a colour or a smell – I can't tell which, the senses here are so tightly intertwined – painting a picture of the last time I was happy with Elinor.

**

We are in good shape, or at least a state of truce. We've hiked for an hour or so along a twisting path which grows increasingly steep until it levels out at the summit of Glyder Fawr, which is in cloud that thins and thickens as the wind gusts round us, causing the lunescape, the impossibly listing giant slabs of rock, to move in and out of view. There is no sound. By implicit agreement we sit separately, without talking, each of us the only person in our worlds. I'm still in a trance when she touches me lightly on the shoulder, holds out her hand to me.

I'm glad we're here, she says softly.

I feel moved by her words, and feel no need to respond. We're on borrowed time, I know, our age-gap is too great. It's not wise for her to stay with me. But the prospect of losing her seems unbearable.

We've leashed Sholto and are descending, in cool shadow mostly, punctured from time to time with shafts of golden light that draws richly aromatic fragrance from moist soil, reflects from it and swells, so that it hovers, glowing in caves of shade.

I've tied a length of rough rope to the leash, to give Sholto more scope for romping, and as it bounces around, tightens, slackens to our movements, its shadow dances and twirls. The frayed end is alive with exuberance and joy.

This discarded piece of rope I picked up somewhere long ago, its shadow jerking easily along a mountain track, represents something at the deep and inaccessible centre of me, something I need to wrap my arms around, bring slowly to the surface, continue to embrace if I'm ever to be able to live as I want to.

I try to explain my feelings to Elinor, who listens attentively and when I finish talking kisses me softly on the mouth.

Whoever's around you when it happens will be lucky, she says.

**

I don't know at what point the feeling that I might be being followed congealed into a certainty, but I'm beyond it now, someone is definitely behind me, keeping a discreet distance. I'm happy to have company, I'm glad that whoever-it-is is so unobtrusive, but my need to identify my follower is beginning to build.

So when I spot a small alcove on one side of the ditch I halt, tuck myself into it, and wait.

I see her approaching. It is the golden girl, side-stroking along, right arm extended, left hand and her stretched feet flapping very occasionally, just sufficient to keep her gliding without touching the ditch floor. She is still naked, untouched by the mud and slime, the only evidence of her journeying along the ditch being a couple of wild rose petals lodged in her hair.

Her face is turned away, so she doesn't see me, I

decide to let her pass. I'd rather she remained a dream.

But as she draws level with me she rolls over gracefully, hovers alongside me, her face so close to mine that the smell of the petals almost makes me swoon.

You've been waiting a long time, Zack.

I don't reply. Words can't do justice to this moment.

Her voice is gentle.

Look at me.

I open my eyes.

She's pulled away a little so I can see the whole of her. She's still levitated, and by means of small flicks of her fingers or toes she glides forwards and backwards, so that her hair, her face, her slight breasts, her trusting navel, those wisps of pubic hair on which the droplets still nestle, her slim thighs, her angled feet move slowly past me, return in reverse order, feet, thighs, navel, face and streaming hair, several times until she halts again, her grey eyes opposite mine.

What do you see?

Her voice is not sexual, or even sensual, but it shimmers with an edge that thrills me.

My words have been composed without my knowledge.

I see my wicked sister who went away, instead of playing shuttlecocks with me.

Well, she's back now.

I'm so glad.

I want to say more, but I'm close to tears and don't trust myself to speak.

She smiles at me.

You're a good man, Zack, but you're too solemn.

I know.

I have a present for you.

Her eyes and lips are dancing with mischief.

Why?

Because, in your stolid way, you've kept me alive for fifty years. Now, give me your hand and relax.

She strokes it gently, lowers her mouth to my thumb, sucks it long and tight, tight and very slow, and when at last she pulls away it glistens.

I look down at her. Her face is raised to me. Her eyes are full of so much love I can't stand it. I turn my head away. She digs her nails into my arms so fiercely that I wince.

Look at me, you idiot!

I do. And for the second time in my life, I hold my gaze as I look into the eyes of someone who loves me.

It is searingly painful yet I can stand the pain.

At last, she says.

At last. Thank you, sister.

My tone sounds so earnest and ponderous we both start to laugh, and the laughter releases something old and tight inside me. I close my mouth over my still-glistening thumb and suck it until the taste of her has gone.

I raise my head, look at her challengingly.

She smiles, stretches to me, touches my cheek.

Our first banquet, brother. And our last.

So it has to be. I curl up on the ditch's muddy floor. For a while she's hovering above me, and faintly I can hear Mrs Campion's harp.

As the music swells, the golden girl fades away.

**

It has been a wild reunion.

She met me at the station, drove me round to my place, and ten minutes later, having exchanged scarcely any words, we were in bed together, and I was revelling in the urgency, passion and lack of inhibition she clearly felt just as strongly as I.

Those few days with Alex, extraordinary and haunting as they'd been, had left me terribly frustrated, and now, with Elinor, I could explode. I did, and so did she, a controlled explosion, building over a long time, by far the best sex we'd shared for months, so that after we both came, and we lay together, flushed and panting, our bodies so entangled I wasn't sure which parts were whose, I felt a huge surge of love for her. Despite our difficulties we had something real I wanted to hold on to. Lovely though it had been with Alex at times, it was insubstantial, incomplete, unreal.

She half-lifts her head from my chest, and smiles.

When I didn't hear from you, I decided you'd found a new lover.

You said you didn't want to hear from me.

That's not stopped you phoning in the past.

I don't respond. I want to tell Elinor about Alex, because I'd like to be more honest than I've often been. Also, she might respect me more, not take me so much for granted. On the other hand, the atmosphere between us is now so lovely I don't want to run the risk of jeopardising it.

Well. Did you find a new lover?

Of course not. Did you?

She laughs.

You know I don't like you asking questions like that.

You asked me.

That's different. You don't seem to mind.

I feel the old dissatisfaction, as if I'm being manipulated, as if our relationship is once again out of balance.

But at the moment that's a small price to pay for

the excitement of being with her again. I skate my tongue round her ear. She moistens her thumb and squeezes my nipple. We're on our way again, more languorously than before. It is delicious.

It's dark by the time we roll apart.

I love you, Elinor.

I sometimes lust for you, Zack. Now let's sleep.

She turns away. Again I'm unsettled by her response, but my body is glowing with satiation. We've not eaten, but I'm replete. I drift into sleep.

**

Who the hell is it this time of night?

I don't know if it's Elinor's voice or the phone itself that pulls me out of deep sleep.

Sorry, I say, though I don't know why.

I start to get out of bed but Elinor holds my arm.

Don't bother. It'll be a wrong number.

My answerphone message clicks in and then I hear Alex's voice, clear and troubled.

Zack. Are you there? Please pick up if you are.

Elinor switches on the bedside light. She looks at me with a puzzled face. I feel paralysed.

Are you there, Zack?

Pick up the phone, Elinor says.

I shake my head.

I want you to know that the wind is rising and the moon is beautiful.

She hangs up. My heart is pounding.

Who on earth was that? Elinor asks.

Oh, just some woman I met a few months ago. She's not very stable. She's phoned me once or twice, always at crazy times.

What does she want?

Nothing, as far as I can tell.

Are you involved with her?

My mouth has gone dry. She's looking at me, accusingly.

Of course not.

I don't believe you.

I can't help that. Look, it's 1 o'clock. Let's sleep.

She shakes her head in a puzzled fashion, switches off the light, and soon I hear her breathing deeply. I lie awake, worried about Alex; feeling guilty about both of them.

**

I'm not sure whether I'd been to sleep when the phone rings again. The ghost-fingers on the bedside clock say 2.30am. It seems for a moment as if Elinor will sleep through the noise, but then she stirs and swears just as the answerphone message takes over.

Alex's voice is more troubled than before.

Please pick up, Zack.

Elinor flicks on the light, stares challengingly at me. I shake my head.

Then I will.

She leaps out of bed, but halts as Alex's voice comes through again.

Do you know that if you sit at the bottom of a hole that's deep enough, you can see the stars, even in broad daylight?

She hangs up. Elinor goes over to the phone and lifts it off the hook.

Goodnight crazywoman, she says.

She stalks across the room, gets back into bed. She's furious, but her voice is calm.

Now tell me the truth.

So I tell her about Alex. Not all the story – I omit

our attempts to make love, and her brutality to her father – but most of it. Elinor listens without interruption.

So why didn't you tell me?

I don't know. I suppose I didn't want to spoil our time together.

But what is there in your story that you think I won't like?

I can see how the inquisition will develop, but I don't know how to change its course.

Nothing, really.

Then what you say doesn't make sense.

I shrug, defeatedly.

So you did make love with her. You're a liar.

Suddenly I've had enough of this grilling. I don't think she cares whether Alex and I made love, she just needs to be in control. She's turning the knife, remorselessly, to demonstrate her power.

For Christ's sake, Elinor, get off my back. When I went away last week we were estranged, we'd no commitment to each other.

I don't like being lied to.

You tell lies.

No I don't, she shouts.

I happen to know, Elinor, that when I went to London last Easter you slept with Ken Farnell.

So?

Now it's my turn to be angry.

So you not only violated our agreement, you lied to me.

I didn't lie. If you'd have asked me I'd have told you.

Bullshit! There's no difference between telling untruths and omitting to tell the truth.

There's all the difference in the world.

I think that if I'd stopped at this point we might

have retrieved the situation, but I wasn't prepared to let go. I saw, however dimly, that Elinor and I would never make things work, and this was the time to draw the line. And I was worried about Alex, I wanted to be with her.

In that case, tell the truth. Did you sleep with anyone while I was away this week?

Her voice is icy.

Yes.

Ken?

Yes. Every night.

I'm struggling to keep afloat.

And did you before we had the fight last week. Apart from Easter, I mean?

Yes. As often as I could.

I'm filled with despair.

Why, for God's sake?

She laughs.

Why d'you think? He's good in bed. Damn sight better than you.

I look at the tangled sheets. They smell so wonderfully of our love-making.

That's cruel, Elinor.

It's honest. I'd be lying if I held it back from you.

Then she overflows, her words all the more hurtful because they're so calmly expressed.

Ken's not the only one I've been with since you and I got married. There are three others. Oh, no. Four. I'd forgotten Tony.

Tony! My brother? You're lying.

She smiles. She's enjoying this.

No I'm not. It was that night at the cottage when you walked up Snowdon to see the midnight moon. It didn't take me long to break him down. Then screwed each other rotten. We were so exhausted afterwards we fell asleep, and he was still in our bed when you came back. I had to keep you occupied in the kitchen while he crept away.

I know she's telling the truth. She'd been flushed, flirtatious, and we'd made love on the kitchen table.

In a strange way I feel better, now. For the first time I'm absolutely clear that I don't want Elinor, and it feels right.

Just one last question before you leave. Why did you stay with me so long?

She winces and looks a little frightened when I mention her departure. But then she decides to brazen it out.

You fed me. Took me out. You were a safe haven from which to have affairs. It was good to feel loved. You gave me sex whenever I wanted it. You left me alone when I didn't. You were the first man I've been in a relationship with who didn't beat me up. Can't think of anything else.

You missed something out. You loved me.

She starts to make some contemptuous response, then halts. Her face puckers a little.

Yes. I loved you. I suspect I still do. But you don't excite me. I was never in love with you.

I know this is true.

I need danger, Zack. I hope one day that won't be true. But for now it is, and you're not dangerous in the way that matters to me.

There's nothing else to say. I can't tell her I've been plying her with poison for weeks. I watch while she gets dressed, slips on her coat, picks up her handbag.

I'll let myself out.

The world isn't all a bad place, Elinor.

She blows me a kiss.

Good luck with Alex.

She leaves.

Yes, I want to be with Alex. But I'm utterly whacked. I'll sleep for an hour then go back to her.

When I wake it's five hours later, I've slept through my alarm, and the first thing I see is my phone hanging off the hook.

**

twelve

This time Shelley is the Judge. He bangs his gavel so hard that I fear the teak will splinter. His mouth is tight and cruel. He is straining to sound impartial.

Ernest. You are charged that you broke your ankle trying to reach the sky. Did you commit this act?

Yes, Mr Shelbourne. I mean, no Mr Shelbourne.

You're lying.

No, Mr Shelbourne. I mean... yes, Mr Shelbourne. I mean not really. I'm sorry.

Nellie grasps Ernest's ear with a pair of pliers and tugs hard. It stretches like elastic, but when she lets go it does not retract, but stays extended, quivering, like a tapered flute. Johnnie creeps from behind and drapes his dirty handkerchief over it. People start to laugh.

Silence! roars Shelley.

Cut his balls off, shrieks Aunt Lil.

That's the best way to grow onions, says Mr Maddock, leaning on his fork.

Horse-hair. Nothing better, declares Uncle Harry, who is feeling sticky and unfulfilled.

Did you or did you not fall off a sandstone ledge in the cave, and break your ankle? Shelley thunders.

Ernest nods his head miserably.

Were you trying to reach the sky?

I was trying to reach Jordan. Jordan was on the ceiling.

Cut Jordan's balls off, shrieks Aunt Lil.

They're firmer like that, says Mr Maddock.

No other way of getting into nooks and crannies. Uncle Harry seems very firm on this point.

Who's Jordan? Tell me. Now, says Shelley sternly, stabbing his finger at Ernest.

He's an unhappy spider who wants to find his oranges.

Shelley looks confused. Johnnie is overwhelmed with mirth. He grabs his snotty handkerchief from Ernest's pink antenna and stuffs it in his mouth.

Where's Jordan, now? demands Shelley.

He's in my lunch-box, waiting for the glue to dry.

What glue?

Shelley's voice is threatening.

Durofix.

Shelley is on the verge of losing control.

I mean, what have you done with the glue?

I was trying to stick Jordan's legs on.

Stick his legs on? Shelley roars.

Ernest's voice is reduced to a whisper.

Yes. Stick them on backwards.

Johnnie is rolling on the floor, thumping his stomach to control his laughter. Shelley turns purple and rips Mr Campion in half. He leaps to his feet, towers over Ernest, who is shaking.

Backwards?

He raises his gavel, but before he can strike my mother shuffles between him and Ernest, teapot tilted, dribbling onto his suit.

Nice cup of tea, Mr Shelbourne.

She hands it to him, and he resumes his seat. She pours one for Ernest, stirs three heaped spoons of sugar into it, hands it to him. He smiles his thanks.

Drink that up, love. You're not looking very extra this morning.

She waits while he sips it. Her head is bowed, her eyes downcast, the teapot still dripping. She wants nothing more than to be invisible. Yet once again she's transformed the atmosphere, quietened the commotion, so that the only sounds now are the harp, Lionel's spurts of burning, and the soft click of Professor Alam's queen as he captures one of Uncle Harry's pawns.

Shelley has stepped down. Mr Maddock is once again the Judge.

Tell us your story, lad. All of it. The spider, the missing legs, the oranges. Take your time. Don't leave anything out.

As Ernest speaks, he slowly gains a fluency he's never shown before. His antenna shrinks until by the time he finishes it is an ear again, bruised and bleeding from the savagery of Nellie's pliers, but undoubtedly an ear.

Johnnie taught me about spiders. How they can sing, tell stories, see round corners, how their milk can cure leprosy and earache, how they learned to make boats out of pineapple nuts, and were the first to discover 'merica.

He told me their mothers sent them away too early, so that they always wanted to come back to their oranges. But they couldn't because spiders' legs will only walk forwards. So spiders are unhappy and Jordan, who's the oldest spider of all, is the unhappiest spider in the world.

Johnnie said we could help them walk back to their oranges by pulling off their legs and gluing them on backwards.

He pulled Jordan's off, with tweezers, but he said his eyes were too poor to glue them on again. I had to do it, with Durofix I bought from Alick's with my pocket-money.

His voice falters. He is close to tears.

It was so hard, Almighty. Jordan was patient, he lay very still, but the legs kept flopping, sticking together, and when at last I'd stuck them all on, Johnnie said one was missing and that if I didn't find it Jordan would spin round and round forever.

That's when I climbed onto the ledge, to see if his leg was stuck to the ceiling, near where we found him.

It wasn't. That's when I fell.

Mr Maddock speaks kindly.

Did you ever find the leg?

No. But Johnnie said a hair from a sick unicorn would do instead. He'd got one, from when he went to China, and he swapped it me for three Dinky cars and a packet of aniseed balls.

Is Jordan better now?

I think so. I've glued the unicorn hair on, though I'm not sure it's in the right place.

You see, he's curled into a ball now Johnnie's hibernated him, so it's hard to see where his legs should go.

How did Johnnie hibernate him?

With the candle-flame. To give him enough warmth to last all winter. Johnnie said he'd crackle when he got enough. And he did.

How d'you know he's still alive?

Johnnie can hear his heart beating. A thousand thumps an hour. Johnnie measured it with his watch. And sometimes he can picture Jordan's dreams.

Can you hear his heart beating?

No. But Johnnie says that's because my Dad's heart stopped beating in the war.

Ernest's eyes fill with tears. He looks defiantly round the courtroom.

I won't let Jordan die! He's my best friend, except for Johnnie. And Wendy.

Nellie lashes him across the neck with her cane.

Don't blubber, boy.

Sit down, ma'am, says Mr Maddock quietly.

Nellie thwacks Ernest one more time and slinks back to her chair.

There is a whispering from the dark side of the room and Wendy Eva, recently discharged from the exhibit stand, walks slowly up to Ernest, kneels to him, draws his face down onto her featureless one, and lets him cry.

Case adjourned for fertilisation, declares Mr Maddock.

His gavel descends. He smiles at Ernest and Wendy, climbs down from his stool.

Bite his balls off! screams Aunt Lil.

Someone slips a bucket over her head. I think it was Zatopek but I can't be sure. Her swearing becomes muffled, and as she swallows coal-dust it dies away.

**

Hitler's here, Mr Trolley too. But I can't see Ernest or Alex anywhere.

Shelley stands quivering in front of Mr Trolley, jabs his cane in his eyes until he opens them.

Out! Away! This gathering's not for perverts.

Mr Trolley takes the cane in his huge fist and eats it, inch by inch. He spits out the bulldog tape Shelley had wrapped around the handle for a fiercer grip.

I liked boys. You preferred girls, though if I remember correctly you weren't very fussy. Same difference, it seems to me.

Shelley snorts.

I certainly didn't... I mean...

His voice trails away. Mr Trolley's smile is unadulterated glee.

One hole's the same as another to me. And who cares if it's my prick or your finger.

Shelley slumps, trails away after his voice. Mr Trolley's words catch up with him.

We're both dead, Shelley. Dead and decomposed. You died with pious hypocrites surrounding you. At least I was alone, inside a long, dark tunnel. At least the blood that spattered me was fresh.

His voice rises.

I'm born again, Shelley. I can recommend it.

But he looks sad and exhausted as people filter past the wheelbarrow and either fail to see him or pretend not to.

Nice cup of tea to cheer you up, Mr Trolley.

My mother is standing beside him, leaking tea onto his crotch. He tries to smile and thank her but starts to cry instead.

Oh dear, never mind.

She pulls a rag out of her pinny and bends to him, covering his nose.

Blow hard, that's a good lad.

He trumpets twice, she dries him with the rag and sits on the barrow's handle while he drinks his tea.

Good brew, Missus.

She looks pleased.

It's that extra spot of sugar, always does the trick.

She takes the empty cup and saucer, stuffs them into her capacious pockets.

Now, I'm taking you outside to catch some sun. You're looking a bit peaky this morning.

She plonks the teapot on his chest and starts to wheel him away. He takes the spout in his mouth and sucks it.

She skirts the chess-game. Professor Abdul Alam looks up from the board and bows.

Good morning, Mr Trolley.

Uncle Harry winks at him.

Ow do, you old bugger.

Mr Trolley smiles at them, bites his lip to prevent himself from crying. He fails, though this time the tears are huge and slow. He makes no sound.

Oh dear, never mind.

She halts the barrow, pulls the rag out of her pinny and bends to him again, covering his nose.

**

Distance is much richer in an abandoned ditch than on open ground. Every yard has its own identity, makes its own contribution to the visual feast. There's no need to shake the kaleidoscope. Just breathe on it or tap it with your finger and the picture has changed, subtly and forever. And though I'm almost always lost as I crawl through the deepest parts of Shropshire, I don't feel the loneliness, the alienation and magnificence of standing in fierce wind on a mountain-top. I feel integrated, part of the tangle, the liquidity. It's my place, warts and all, roots, slugs, fallen leaves, wisps of horsehair, rotten wood, shoots of green that defy all odds, brambles, smell of methane, bubbles floating on a stagnant puddle, and once in a while a scrap of cloth from an old jacket. The sky is never blue down here, the air is never fresh, but in some strange way it's home and I don't often lift my head above the parapet.

And, oh the singing!

But I'm not possessive of this world, and I feel pleased when I see him, unkempt and quiet, almost indistinguishable from the grasses and bracken that trellis his face, staring somewhat blankly towards me.

At first I think he's not seen me, but when I halt and smile at him, he smiles back rather shyly. Our eyes touch for a moment and I sense in him a mixture of sweetness and helplessness that makes me want to hug and shake him.

We crawl on towards each other, halting now and then, sizing each other up, though not aggressively.

He's an elderly man, about as old as my father at the time he died. In fact there's something about him that reminds me of my father, possibly the slight tilt of his head as he balances on one hand, perhaps the uniformity of his teeth which I glimpse when he smiles, which in my father's case were false and took me years to get used to.

He looks me again in the eyes, and this time holds my gaze for longer. And now I feel afraid, because there's a yearning in him, almost a beseeching, which is sucking at me and I don't want it. But I do want it, too, I'd embrace it if I wasn't terrified of being swallowed.

It's not even as simple as that. I want to be swallowed, to be taken in, assimilated, calmed. But I can't run the risk of losing my identity. I can't.

It makes it harder that there's something in him of my father. It makes it harder that he's not my father, even so.

I start to turn around, to flee. But that wouldn't work. He'd follow me, his unspoken longing, his attraction to me would yoke me, slow me down. I'd want to escape and yet I'd want him to catch me. Each time I halted he'd halt, too. We'd never be together or apart.

No, I have to pass him. He won't turn round. But I can't pass him if I look once more into his eyes.

So I close mine, lower my head and crawl fast. He won't try to stop me. I wish he would.

The mud sucks at my wrists and knees, but my

panic gives me strength. I'm moving swiftly. I must be almost up to him.

For a moment the crack against my skull makes me weightless, takes me out of my body. I know I'm hurt, but the pain won't come just yet. The mud against my face is warmer now, welcoming. I lie there, in no hurry, gathering.

At last, I raise myself onto one arm, shake my head to clear the dizziness, blink open, see my mud-stained face, see the pockmarked mirror my head has crashed into.

I start to laugh. I lean forward, kiss the lips that move to mine. They're cold but I love them even so.

**

I was enjoying the book, deeply absorbed in it, the slight movement of my rocking chair creating a cradle containing only the story and myself.

But it disappears when Elinor's cool hands close over my eyes, I still can't remember what the book was. I never will.

She holds them there for a moment that smells of lemons, then releases me, squats on the rug in front of me.

Why didn't you invite me to your gathering?

Your wedding-ring hurt my nose.

It hadn't, of course. Not my nose. At least, not particularly my nose. Not the hardness of the ring. Perhaps the glint of gold as her fingers curtained me. More likely though it was the idea of the ring, the resurrection of a long-gone fragrance to which I'd never wanted to say farewell. Whatever it was, it hurts all over, all over again.

She sits still, leaning forward, waiting for my reply.

I didn't invite you because I knew you'd come

anyway. You've been to every gathering I've had since you left me. I knew you were there. I simply didn't seek you out, that's all.

Were you there, Zack?

I know what she means, but I haven't finished with her first question.

You've been on every hike I've had since then. You've sat in every restaurant I've eaten at. You've been round every corner of every path I've followed.

I've not wanted to. You've dragged me there.

That's not true. You've haunted me, whether you wanted to or not.

You like being haunted.

I've found you in every bed I've been in since then. Every climax I've had has been with you. Each name I've shouted out has been in code. Mary, Gerda, Leslie, Hyacinth. All of these were pseudonyms for you, my love. I hope I fooled them, but I don't care very much.

I don't want to be brutal, but you're a fool. When Mary, Gerda, Leslie, Hyacinth shouted out your name, don't you know that sometimes they were reaching out for Steve, or Harry, Winston, Jake?

I don't care about that.

Then how about this. In the months before we finished, the only way I could come with you was to pretend I was with Ken. Does that hurt?

It would have done once. It doesn't now.

I'll try once more. Since I left you, love-making has been wonderful. I've not once thought of you, and I know that if I did I'd find the idea repellent. Does that hurt, Zack?

I can't answer. She slaps me across the face, and this time I feel the wedding ring.

Does it hurt?

Why are you doing this to me?

Because you're on my back and I want you gone.
Because you're a pathetic fool who's wasting his life.

She hesitates, speaks less heatedly.

Because I loved you once.

Don't you still love me?

No.

I don't believe you. Look. Your father's been dead for half your lifetime. You still love him, don't you?

In the silence before she replies, I can feel her pain.

At last she shakes her head.

I don't, Zack. I no longer love him, and I no longer love you. I loved him once, very deeply. You, too, though not as much. But the only love that's healthy is in the now, in the traffic of my present life. Loving you, or my father, is like loving Socrates or Mary Magdalene. It can't be done because there's no exchange between us.

She rises onto her knees, takes my shoulders, makes me look at her. She shakes me slightly as she speaks.

I loved you once. You're part of my story. Isn't that enough?

Come to bed with me.

She laughs. I look into her eyes. Yes, she loves me now. But not enough to sleep with me.

She doesn't kiss me as she leaves, she simply waves from the doorway, gives me a wry grin. But this time I don't feel spurned or slighted. She's hard, she's had to be to survive the chaos of her early life, especially her vicious mother. But despite her deceptions, her wicked tongue, I now realise there's something basically true about her. She has a conception of integrity which she holds to. If she felt something was sordid, she wouldn't do it. If she felt some action was justifiable she'd perform it, whatever the cost.

Dad was right. She doesn't deserve the persecution I've subjected her to. I feel ashamed. And for the first time since my campaign began, I know I can stop it, and that I'll do so now, for her sake, for my parents, and most of all for me.

I need to see her one last time. I race out into the street just as her car is pulling away from the kerb. I sprint in front of it, hold up my hands.

She stops, and when I gesticulate for her to park she pulls into the kerb again. I open the door, get inside. She looks cross and rather nervous.

Well?

I just want to say I'm sorry. For everything.

She turns off the lights, swallows a couple of times before speaking.

You just don't know when to stop, Zack. You've never understood that some things are best not enquired into, not spoken about, that most relationships have not only a limited capacity for intimacy but also a finite lifetime beyond which it's stupid to continue. Those are cruel truths for someone who's terrified of abandonment, but unless you can accept them you won't be able to function in this life.

So I don't want to hear your confession. You carry that burden. I'm moving on. Everything we'll share in this life has already happened. There'll be nothing else. That doesn't diminish what we had one iota.

Now, fuck off out of my life.

I feel relieved. I feel like crying. I know she's right.

I nod to her, get out of the car and am just closing the door when she calls me.

Zack! If I were you I'd retire while you're still at the top.

What d'you mean?

Simply that you make the best chai in the world.

She screeches away before I can respond. I sit on the kerbstone, shaking.

**

Bear down hard, Zack.

But it will hurt. It will hurt all the more because I've been carrying it so long. All the more because I can choose not to give birth.

You're wrong. You don't have that choice, not without a penalty that would crucify you. Your septicaemia has become acute, the pain you fear so much is the only route to your salvation.

You can guarantee me nothing. The route might lead me straight into the pit.

Of course. It probably will, though this time you'll be able to see its slime and decomposing matter. So, bear down, close your eyes and grip the bed-rail hard. Can't you feel it want to move? Can't you feel it coming?

Tell me the colour of salvation.

Green.

**

Uncle Harry always wanted to give birth to a child. That's why, at eighty-eight, he slipped an egg into the dry warmth of his buttocks, forcing him to tilt a little to one side on the stool on which he sits waiting for Professor Abdul Alam to make his next move in their chess-game.

I wanted it, too, when I was a child. But I'm sixty, and the child I might have given birth to would have been almost as old as I am now. In fact, he'd be older, as old as my mother, recently dead, who's carrying her teapot with the broken spout from person to person.

Older than her, perhaps, older than her mother who abandoned her, older than history, as old as the world.

Are you ready for the journey, child-o'-mine? This will be no smooth transition, you'll come out in bits and pieces, in random order, and though the doctors will attempt a patching job, I have little hope of their success.

Or perhaps the log-jam that has piled so high will burst, you'll explode into this world that waits for you.

I know it has to happen. The pressure has been building without remission. It is time.

Mrs Campion is strumming on her harp with woollen strings. Alex is crawling through a nest of bracken. Ernest is on one knee in torrential rain, looking for Germany. Lionel scarcely crackles as he burns.

And as for you, my golden girl, I can't find you in the fog, but from time to time I hear you breathe.

I tape my testicles and penis to my stomach, open my legs, bear down hard.

**

That isn't what it's about. It won't do at all. It's too contrived, it's been edited away. It's stillborn.

Let me try again as snow slants past me, dusts the frozen leaves with white.

The birth that has to happen is wild, chaotic – an eruption of all the enmeshed violences of sixty years, those thoughts that frayed or twisted, those feelings never quite expressed or recognised, actions committed under cover of a smile, those stabs of pain behind the eyes, promises that faded, glances that carried deeper knowledge than any book I've ever read.

I can't see the shape of something not yet born. I've been safe behind a Chinese box of barriers, safe from pain but at the price of not living. What I have to give birth to is myself. My mother was abandoned when she was three days old, and the only way she could deal with a world that had been emptied before it started was to fashion a warm womb back into which she crawled, warm perhaps but terribly alone, on unstable ground, so if she leaned just slightly forwards she would fall, so she lay very still, frightened of the world outside her reach, not learning its language, knowing always that even the lowliest place in the straggling town that grew around her was too exalted for her; collecting twigs and feathers, straw and seed cusps in the winds to make a sanctuary for her children, its walls so high they couldn't look out, so they only saw the world through mirrors.

In the years during which I descended, rung by rung, the ladder she'd not wanted me to see, her silent singing pulled me back, sucked my fluids so I didn't root, and out of terror I collected an arsenal of weapons, used under cover of darkness and a smile. And the perpetrator was the front man, the brittle effigy of me still in the nest, still not born, not wanting to be born, not until now.

I want to be born before I die. It would be easier not to, I'd be less hurt, do less damage. But I no longer want her fate, never to believe that arms would want to hold her. But I can't believe that until I want to hold and rock myself. I must forgive myself, but I can't do that until I recognise my defects, my blindnesses, my crimes.

So out you go, from this womb you've tenanted for sixty years. On your knees or your stomach until you get used to the light, to gravity. Until you slowly learn to stand, propel those arthritic limbs into a sprint that won't stop until you do.

**

thirteen

It is time for Ernest's punishment to begin. He is to be stitched inside the blood-blister on Will Tarporley's lower lip, and I have promised to go with him.

We've had our final meal – my mother's shepherd's pie, with rhubarb crumble and innumerable cups of tea. Ernest has taken a meandering farewell stroll along the corridor with Wendy Eva. Mr Trolley led the singing of *Abide with Me*, unrolling Mr Campion to display the words, for those of the guests who didn't know them. We found that Johnnie had crossed out the *with* and replaced it with *in*. Mr Maddock gave Ernest *a couple of turnips to keep you going*, and Miss Atkins shyly presented him with a mohair pullover she'd knitted for him: *in case it's cold in there, at night.*

There was then a round of weeping, with Shelley at the piano, conducted by the noseless man. The impromptu melodies were quite amazing, as was the quantity of brine that spilled onto the floor. No one except my mother paid attention to me, and I suspect I was still invisible.

I didn't care. I was anxious to get started. So I was relieved when a great bobbin of scarlet cotton was rolled along the corridor, and Nellie – squinting through her inch-thick glasses – threaded the needle with which to seal the blood-blister, after Ernest and I had wriggled in.

**

The entrance is through a curtain of purple flesh on the side of the blister facing the chaos that is Will's mouth, which is why I never spotted it before.

Before we enter I turn round and peer towards his throat's deep well, from which a warm breeze issues, laden with the fragrances of this week's meals. In the foreground is a drunken graveyard, his teeth, mostly listing, many chipped or black, some missing, some sunk so deep only their tops can be discerned, wedged in the pink and scarlet billows that enfold them. Drops fall randomly from his upper molars, flick against the lower ones or are sponged up by his tongue, which seems too large for his mouth, so that its every movement presses against the walls, threatens to block the air-flow to his lungs.

The blood-blister has fascinated and frightened me since the day I met him, my first day at junior school, two weeks into term because I'd been off sick with mumps, and this boy in the playground, giving Joyce Farrington's pale white arm a Chinese burn, ignoring her pleas and then her tears, had this great bruised thing wobbling on his lip, making him look indestructible and merciless, as indeed he was, twisting Joyce's flesh until Shelley rang the bell, leaving her with a crescent shaped weal whose origins she daren't explain when her mother noticed it at bed-time.

I think the emotional impact of the blister was heightened by the single thing I knew about Will before I first saw him. Johnnie had called to see me a day or two before my return to school, and had told me about this boy from the tough part of the village, who had led a group of lads into the Victorian toilets at the edge of the school yard, whose smell I can still conjure up fifty years after their demolition, and for a bet from which he won three packets of chewing-gum and a matchbox full of earwigs, lowered the solid, wooden lavatory seat cover, squatted over it, and shat onto its middle through a hole in his trousers a turd which kept on coming throughout the first half of playtime, rotating his buttocks so that it coiled into a perfect pyramid, glistening, steaming, enormous, green. Every boy in the school came to admire it, Marjorie Bickerstaff, too, but she was sick on Watty Hulse's foot.

We hold hands as we grope our way into the scarlet. Once through the folds of flesh the blood-blister opens out, becomes quite spacious, a basically spherical cavern illuminated with scarlet light, the source of which I can't see, with beautiful stalagmites and slowly dripping stalactites, pulsing diaphragms, pools of foam, wells of black liquid, presumably blood. The ground is sticky to our feet.

The only word to describe what my Aunt Lil is sitting on is a throne, a throne made of weeping flesh. She's large, fatter than before she died, but she's dwarfed by its vast, suppurating pinkness, its billows and declivities, its curves so gentle that its overall effect is innocent, benign. Not so Aunt Lil, her sequin-studded dress too young for her, too short for her, so that as Ernest and I stand in front of the dais on which the throne is mounted our heads are at the level of her knees, which are apart. I feel the draw of that dark region in which all I can perceive are albino thighs, varicosed and flabby, straps connecting her corsets to silk stockings, her knickers' baggy purple, and the shadow of a hungry creature that feeds on little boys and is hiding, waiting to pounce.

Did she know I was watching her, when I was little, secreted away in the safe warmth of the airing cupboard, peering through the slats, while she sat on the stool of my mother's dressing table, turned away from the mirror, towards me, legs apart as now, skirt-line almost to her waist, squeezing a livid pimple on her thigh, crooking her finger underneath the black strap, stretching it then letting go, the smack of the elastic making me shudder, clutch the water-pipes to save me from her suction, she then turning to the mirror, applying thick lipstick, kissing her white handkerchief, spitting on it, making some adjustment to her face, kissing the handkerchief again; and so on until she was ready, she'd stand up, snap her thighs again, smooth her rumpled skirt and go downstairs. I'd sneak out of the cupboard, sick with stomach-ache, and sometime that evening steal the handkerchief from her handbag, take it upstairs with me, count the ghost-kisses she'd pressed onto it, work out the sequence of diminishing age and faintness, remember how the cambric clung to the underbelly of her lips as she pulled it away and I – not wanting to be pulled away – wound my arms tighter round the pipes.

Did you know, Aunt Lil, that I was watching you? That the stomach-ache that came as I peered at you through the slats has recurred throughout my life whenever I've felt the pull of purple places. That as I stand before you, Ernest's hand in mine, in the scarlet light of Will Tarporley's blood-blister, I hate you and at last I'm understanding why.

I was expecting you, our Zack, she says.

Her smile is perhaps meant to be ingratiating, but it looks like a smirk to me. I bridle, feel accused, defensive.

I'm only here to keep Ernest company.

Pah! Don't tell fibs. You've always told fibs. You're here because this is where your home is.

I've never been inside a blood-blister in all my life.

If you were small again I'd pull your trousers down and smack your arse until you told the bloody truth.

What is the bloody truth, Aunt Lil?

The truth you won't face up to is that you've lived your whole life inside a blood-blister you've created yourself.

I hate you, Aunt Lil.

To my surprise a wave of pain washes over her face. She bites her lip, and when she speaks again two of her teeth are covered in lipstick.

I know you do, lad. It makes me sad, both for you and for me, and I want to talk to you about it.

She claps her hands.

But all this is nowt to do with you, Ernest. Be off with you. Take that corridor.

She points to a small cleft in the wall.

Go down there, lad. It's too small to stand or crawl in, you'll have to wriggle on your stomach. But if you keep on past the drunken drums, you'll find him.

My father?

Ernest's face is ecstatic.

Of course. Who else have you been searching for all your life?

I love you, ma'am, says Ernest.

Pah! Now, don't raise your hopes too much. He's not in good shape. And don't look at him too hard or he'll dissolve.

No. I won't. Can I go now?

She nods. Ernest runs towards the tunnel, slips onto his face and his momentum propels him, sliding fast, through the small cleft in the flesh, out of sight.

I bet the silly bugger gets lost, she says.

She says it affectionately, whereas most people tend to sneer at Ernest. I'd already softened towards her when I saw her pain, and now I feel sorry for hurting her.

I don't really hate you, Aunt Lil.

She pulls a rather rueful face.

I know you don't, lad. It's not hatred you feel for me. It's fear. With perhaps a touch of contempt because of my ignorance and uncouthness. Right?

I start to deny it, but she sweeps my words away with an impatient flourish of her arm.

Be honest. There's no point in lying when you're in a blood-blister.

I suppose I do feel something like that.

Good. Now we can start.

She beckons to me.

Climb up here. Sit on my lap.

Nervous though I am, I obey her. Her lap is capacious and comfortable. Her breasts, most of which I can see, are freckled and smell of sweat. Her lipstick is so thick I could scrape it off with a knife to make a healthy sandwich. My legs dangle into the space between her thighs. She slips off my shoes and tosses them onto the floor.

Let's snuggle for a minute before we talk, she says.

I don't want to, but I let it happen.

She folds me in, and I'm drowning in a feast of smells that were faintly present before, but are now pouring from every part of her. I turn my head to find fresh air, but I'm enveloped by her, I'm losing my identity. I try to struggle free, but the weight of her flesh has made me powerless. I start to gasp for air.

Her voice sounds as if it has percolated through a thousand blankets.

Are you frightened, lad?

I manage to nod, and her strong arms lift me out of her lap onto an arm of the throne, where the air is fresh, and I begin to recover.

It's that fear of dark, moist places I want to talk to you about.

Go on.

It's not your fear. It's your mother's. It's not even hers originally. It belonged to her grandparents, who brought her up, who were terrified that she'd turn out bad, like her mother, get pregnant out of wedlock, so they fed her shame and fear of doing wrong, of having anything to do with dark, moist places; and she gave it to you in her milk.

I didn't understand this when I was alive. I thought she was prissy and that you were a little pervert, sitting in that cupboard spying on me, drooling through the slats. I couldn't tell her what you were doing, she'd have been destroyed, and I was damned if I was going to alter my life because of your sweaty palms. So I decided it was your problem, that you'd either grow out of it or you wouldn't.

You need to plunge in, love. Step out of your clothes, out of your skin, step outside yourself, jump off, and I bet you'll find that you can swim.

Oh, Alex! Where are you?

I'll need someone to push me, Aunt Lil.

Nah! Better do it yourself. Just close your eyes and let go. Hold your nose so you won't swallow water.

And if I do?

You'll panic, mebbe drown.

I know she's right. I've spent sixty years trying so hard not to drown, I haven't found the time to learn to breathe.

How do I do it, Aunt Lil?

Don't play games with me, lad. Tha knowst. Get on with it. Let go of the water-pipes.

And so, scared, naked, in scarlet light, in a dripping, sweet-smelling cavern in the blood-blister on Will Tarporley's lower lip, I plunge headfirst into voluminous darkness smelling of sweat and stale perfume, where the air I breathe sends my senses reeling, and I am glad, where the skin of the dead woman I slither over is smooth and coarse and warty, where hair like brambles scuffs my cheek, clogs my mouth, and I am glad, where the ground throbs heartbeats and its moisture sucks on me, where I'm drawn into a torrid space in which I'm sucked away, and there is nothing left. And I am glad.

**

When I wake up Aunt Lil's not there, the throne looming above me as I lie curled on the floor is empty. I wonder if I've been dreaming, but then I see my clothes, neatly folded, by my head.

I dress slowly, not wanting to think, but rather to docket all these experiences for examination when I'm calmer, and not in the middle of an adventure.

I remember Ernest, worry that he's lost, as Aunt Lil predicted. I decide to try to find him. I crawl across the floor to the cleft into which he disappeared. It is roughly vertical, only about a foot high, so I have to lie on my stomach and wriggle in. Once through I find the floor slopes downwards, quite steeply, and since it's also slippery I can slither easily, somewhat like sledging in slow motion.

Like sledging at night, no moon, just a faint glow from the stars which here, deep in Will's blood-blister, is vermilion, its source invisible and far away, as if the light has trickled its way through translucent jelly. It shows me nothing, for there is nothing to see, the flesh I'm sliding through being as featureless as jelly, parting easily at the pressure of my forehead, closing easily over the space my feet have just moved through.

But the light is important, because it signals the existence of some other world outside my body. At one stage it illuminates some growths that look like listing cylinders, and which I take to be the drunken drums. The light enables me to know, in some strange sense at least, where I am travelling.

So I'm filled with fear when the glow disappears, not suddenly but insidiously, so that for a while I can fool myself that its luminosity hasn't diminished; until I have to accept that it has slipped away to zero.

I'm slipping away too, perhaps to zero, nothingness, extinction, perhaps to some new stage of my journey. It helps me curb my panic that there's absolutely nothing I can do. I think the slope has become greater, since I'm sliding readily, there's no way I can stop, let alone go back. I have to ride this flow, go with it wherever it will take me..

Then I realise I'm enjoying myself. I'm quivering. I feel as if all my senses are engaged. Yet I hear nothing, I see nothing, I smell nothing, I taste nothing, and though I'm forging through warm jelly, it's formless, so I'm touching nothing, either. The flesh surrounding me is at body temperature, so there's neither hot nor cold. And so it seems to me that perhaps the most profound experiences come from sensory deprivation, not surfeit. That only when all associations with one's body have been lost can it find that stillness at its centre which enables it to totally embrace itself, its world.

These are my feelings, formulated but at the time wordless, and I revel in them as I glide. This happiness is perfect. I need no-one else in order to achieve it.

But the experience is too profound, too pleasurable for me to bear for long. So I ease out of it, slowly, bringing my conscious mind into action, wondering if anyone, in the whole of history, has ever before found true enlightenment while journeying through a blood-blister. I wonder if Will knows I'm here, if the blister has grown or been excised, if he's dead, if they masked it somehow as he lay in his coffin, to make him look beautiful, which he never did in life; if he remembers – and if so still feels proud of – that prodigious turd that caused Marjorie, who had no soul, to be spontaneously sick on Watty's shoe.

And so I move back to a more accustomed state of mind, in which I feel flawed and comfortable, and am grinning as the sledge levels off, comes to a halt in a small gallery, in which there is light, and I can see Ernest sitting with his father.

**

Alex and I had run swiftly after jumping from the train, but I'm running much faster now. I've stopped trying to fight the panic by telling myself that saving ten minutes will make no difference. I've succumbed to it, and the energy it releases makes me faster.

I bound through her gate to the door of her cottage, rap on the door. There is no response. Remembering, I try the handle, it turns and I race in, run from room to room. She's not there.

I sit at the kitchen table, wondering what to do. Her flute is lying on it, diagonally across a sheet of paper torn from a pad. I lift the flute, read the message written in straggly black letters:

For Zack, to lure me home with.

I stuff the flute in my pocket and set off for the Edge. I feel sure that's where she'll be. If I'm wrong I've no idea where to look.

I'm more composed now and walk briskly rather than run. The weather was gorgeous when I ran across the fields, but now the sky has darkened and is spitting with rain, which intensifies as my climb proceeds.

My hope is that when I break through the trees, enter the clearing at the summit, I'll see her, cape outstretched, poised to fly. But she's not there. The rain is pelting down and the visibility is low as I move to the fissure, look down. There is no sign of her.

I can't tell what comes first, the blinding light, the crack of thunder, the smell of ozone, or the percussion that flings me to the ground. All I know is that I'm still alive and that a yellow ball is floating in both my eyes, whether they are closed or open.

My impulse is to run away. I scramble to my feet and then I find I want to stay, savour this experience I'll never have again. I sit down on the edge of the fissure. The raindrops are smaller now, sweeping into my face, and I'm cold.

I take the flute from my pocket. It's years since I played, and I wasn't proficient then, but I like the way the wind teases my simple tune, holding it then whipping it away, bringing it back.

Zack!

The cry is faint and shifting and I don't believe it. But when I resume my playing it's repeated. It comes from somewhere below me, somewhere in the fissure.

At first I see nothing, but when I move a few yards to the side I see a bare leg, foot uppermost, lying across the scree. The rest of her is hidden in a clump of ferns.

I slip as I start to scramble down, fall about six feet, land heavily but am not hurt.

I make my way over to her.

She's dry. The wind has protected her from the rain. Her face is pale, though she manages a wan smile. I reach down to tug her from the ferns, but she shakes her head and I see that her other leg is jutting out at a strange angle.

You're late, she whispers, and passes out.

**

It's a complicated break, and they decide to keep her in hospital overnight. I sit with her for a few hours, but she's heavily sedated, sleeping, and the Sister forecasts that she'll sleep through the night, so I walk back to her cottage, planning to return to the hospital early the following morning.

The contrast between the sleeping Alex, breathing easily, looking fresh and beautiful, and her father's restlessness and ravaged body just twenty-four hours earlier, is profound and disturbing. So too is the thought that he may still be lying dead just yards away from where her vitality, despite the drugs, shines like a beacon.

I feast at her cottage on goats' cheese, radishes, her home-made bread and camomile tea. Then I put on a tape of some sitar music, curl up in her armchair, tucked into the corner of the living room, up against the bookshelves. I switch on the table-lamp beside me and sit for a while, enjoying the shadows, the contrasts of the light.

A heavily embossed leather-bound book is lying on the back of the chair, partially obscured by the cushion. I flick it open, and the word *Zack* stares out at me. I have only to glance down the page to realise that the book is her journal, and she was writing in it just before she set out for the Edge, last night.

In earlier times I'd have read it without compunction, and I'm strongly tempted to now. But I don't wish to sully my friendship with Alex, who would never dream of spying into someone else's private writing. So I put it down, settle into the music.

The journal, however, nags at me. I begin to think of reasons why it would be good for us if I read it. I'd understand her more fully, be able to help her more, avoid traps that my ignorance of her might lead me into.

My conscience fights back, and in the end I compromise. I won't read anything that pre-dates our first meeting. I flick back through the pages of her spidery writing, interspersed with doodles. There are disappointingly few from after the time we first met.

Flying. I love the flow of air across my cheeks, the slowness and silence of my motion, the outstretched arms of the turf waiting to greet me, cushion my landing, the soft scuff of my knees across the grass, releasing some aromatic vapour that opens my pores, fine-tunes me to the sky and earth, the birdsong.

And now Zack can fly, it's soaked into his bones so deep he'd run back to the launch-rock faster than he'd floated across the fissure. Time and time again. I wish I could feel sure that when I'm not with him he'll take off without a push.

We're so different, Zack and I. Now I'm free, my confidence is limitless, and though I don't want to shackle it I don't want to die either, so I need him to temper it just as he needs me to give him courage.

Tonight, I don't need wind to fly. I could fly to the moon if I felt blue enough. I could swirl around the chimney-pots, dive into old caves, swoop from giant oaks onto the backs of sleeping cows. I need Zack to tell me that wind is crucial to my flight, that the fissure will coffin me unless a gale is blowing.

I need him but he won't come. He's escaping from me, he's perhaps with Elinor, and the Edge is beckoning. I can't refuse it.

There is a line drawn under the writing at this point, and when it resumes it is larger, fiercer, as if she's been clutching her pen as one would a dagger.

He knows I need him to rein in my feeling of omnipotence, but he chooses not to come to me. I'm terrified of doing this alone. I fear the pride that swells inside me, pushes feathers out through every pore, sleeks them down for perfect flight.

Come join me, Zack. We'll glide and soar tonight in a way that's safe and wonderful. I'll teach you how to dip and loop and swerve round corners. You'll teach me how to nest, how to fold my head under my wing.

This time, Zack. The sixth and final time I'll ask you. Stretch out those muscled arms that smell of salt, stretch them out from wherever they are, whoever they're with – and take me in.

No reproach from her, no anger, but I'm filled with guilt and horror. I imagine her dialling my number that sixth and final time, filling with hope, hearing the engaged signal yet again, implacable and merciless; and quietly hanging up, curling up small.

Damn Elinor! Yet I know that's not fair. It's not her fault that I've lost. Lost what? Alex hasn't left me, not as far as I know, yet I feel in mourning. Not for something I've lost, but for something that may not happen now.

I close the journal, put it back exactly as it was.

I stand up, see the table, remember the flute. She left it for me so I could find her. And I did.

I feel light-hearted, snuggle into her side of the bed. I press her pillow to my face and I am flying.

**

fourteen

Ernest's father is horizontal, face down, suspended about four feet from the ground, arms and legs enmeshed in the silk cords of his parachute, which is dangling from something, I presume a tree, out of sight in the darkness above him. He is wearing a khaki battle-dress festooned with medals, all of which are bleeding. His body is swinging gently to and fro. Ernest is sitting directly underneath him on a fallen log, looking up at him, a rapt expression on his face. I sneak up, sit beside him. Ernest acknowledges me without shifting his gaze.

Although his father's eyes are open, they don't appear to register anything, and the conversation between Ernest and myself takes place in whispers, so as not to wake him.

Is this your father?
Oh, yes.
Ernest is biting his lip with joy and excitement.
He doesn't look like the photograph.
That's because he's upside-down.
Has he spoken to you?
Oh, yes.
What did he say?
There weren't any words. Words get in the way

when you're speaking to someone you love who you haven't seen forever.

Ernest is crying now, silently, but the joy in his face is unabated. I feel abashed.

Have you touched him, Ernest?

Ernest nods.

Where?

He let me touch his bullet-hole.

Show me.

I don't think he'd like me to.

I only want to see it. C'mon, Ernest.

Ernest slowly stretches out his arm, points to a black circle just below the soldier's Adam's apple. I feel excited. My first bullet-wound. I have to touch it.

Ernest knows what I am feeling, doesn't try to stop me as I reach upwards, slide my middle finger all the way into the neat hole in his father's throat. It feels dry, almost powdery, and I'm disappointed. I try to slide it out but the hole has contracted, it has locked around my finger and all I achieve as, panic rising, I tug harder and harder, is making him jump up and down on his strings, like a puppet who's in control of me.

I look at his face, but whereas before it had seemed distant, dreamlike, now it is leering at me.

He won't leave go, Ernest!

Tell him you're sorry.

Sorry for what?

Sorry for making him remember.

I'm sorry, Mister, I blurt out.

The grip relaxes. I remove my finger. His face is dream-like again.

It takes me a while to calm down. Then I examine my finger. It looks the same as before. I lick it. It tastes as usual. I hold it to my nose. It smells of gunpowder. It was worth it, after all.

Did he hold on to your finger, Ernest?

I didn't put my finger in his bullet-hole. I touched it with my eyes.

We sit quietly, his father gyrating gently above us, even though there's no wind.

I feel a splash of wetness on my head, then another, then a slow patter of drops. I look up. Ernest's father is dissolving, uniformly, all over his body, so that he grows pale and then transparent but remains recognisable. Drops are now falling steadily on me, but though I feel their wetness when they land, my clothes and skin are still dry.

I look at Ernest. His head is thrown back, unwounded throat exposed to his father above him. His mouth is open and he is drinking drops that fall into it. He is drinking his father.

I can't watch any more. I put my head between my knees, close my eyes.

When I blink open, Ernest's father has disappeared. Just his battle-dress remains, limp, swinging slightly. His medals have stopped bleeding.

Time to go, Ernest says.

He looks light and happy.

He takes my hand as we wander out of the gallery into the next. I lift my other hand to my face, sniff my middle finger. It still smells of gunpowder.

**

I walk down to the hospital early in the morning, and we have a couple of hours alone in her room, she looking frail and beautiful, in an armchair with her leg in plaster, propped up on a stool; me sitting on the edge of the bed.

Hard though it is in places, I tell her everything about my time away. My need to flee, my phone-call to Elinor, reunion with her, the love-making, my dilemma over the phone-calls in the night, the fight with Elinor, my five-hour sleep, the race back to the cottage, up to the Edge, the lightning strike. She asks me to skip nothing significant, however painful it might be for her, and listens quietly for the most part, occasionally asking a quick question.

When I finish she turns to me.

Telling the truth was easier than you thought, wasn't it?

Yes. Was it hard for you to hear?

Here and there. But so much better than feeling fooled.

She smiles at me, but I still feel uneasy. She's seemed somewhat elusive this morning, whereas I want to get close. I need to find out what she's feeling.

Where do we stand now, Alex? I blurt out.

She reaches across to me, strokes my forehead.

We stand at a point where the road diverges, and we're about to take different tracks.

Oh, no!

My despair feels total.

It has to be, Zack.

Why?

I know why, but I can't articulate it. I need her to spell it out. I need to clutch at the possibility that as she does so, she'll change her mind.

It's been a good road we've travelled, Zack. Beautiful, amazing, real, even the dreams. We've supported each other well. You've saved me from suffocation, I've saved you from drowning. You've helped me cope with my release from my father.

I start to interject, but she cuts me off.

Hear me out, Zack. I need to say this. I owe it to you to say it well. And you know my decision is nothing to do with Elinor.

She reaches to me, squeezes my shoulder.

If I stayed with you, you'd become a father to me.

She must have seen me flinch.

I don't mean you'd try to do some of the horrible things he did to me, things I'll never be able to talk about.

But awful though those were, they weren't as damaging as his love, his clinging, suffocating love.

I was pinioned by it, Zack. It wasn't false. I'd have done better if it was. It was real and true, just as genuine as his abominations. Which weren't separate from the love, of course – they're all part of the same story.

I loved him, I hope you could feel that underneath the anger and contempt.

I nod.

He just didn't have the skill to deal with my mother dying and me being born on the same day. I'll never know if there was anger in his love for me. I could understand it if there was.

My wings were clipped at birth. I kept trying to fly. I thought I taught you how to fly – but I realise now that you weren't flying, you were simply gliding.

Zack, I love you but I want to truly fly. To flap my wings and rise and zoom to every tree, every valley, every mountain-top, every continent that takes my fancy.

I'm going to make that trip. I don't think anyone could come with me all the way, or even most of it. I hope I'll find people to travel with for some parts of the journey. But not you, Zack. Not any further.

Because of my clinging, suffocating love?

Don't be pathetic, for God's sake! You'd drag me down, Zack. You're basically a ditch-crawler who likes to come up for air. I'm basically a bird who likes to rest in the luxuriance of the ditches from time to time.

Those periods of overlap have been lovely between us, vignettes that have enriched my life, and I thank you. But there's not enough in common for us to be true to ourselves into the future. Do you understand?

I can't trust myself to speak, so I nod. Her face lightens, though her eyes are glistening.

Thank you, Zack.

I think we both feel it's too painful to continue this meeting. I tell her I'll go back to the cottage, collect my things and be gone by the time the ambulance brings her home this afternoon.

I think that's best, she says.

I wish to hell I'd answered the phone when you were calling for me.

She answers gently.

I'm glad you didn't.

I read your journal.

I guessed you would. Ditch-crawlers need to find out secrets. Swallows fly away from them.

I can't even kiss her. I ruffle her hair, she squeezes my hand and I turn, move towards the door. I'm half-way there when I hear her voice, soft and teasing.

Gribnots.

I answer without looking back.

Yackerfarl.

Collyoak.

Jubberthingers.

Flinstock.

Rumplewarkers.

I'm in the corridor now, ready to break into a sprint outside. Her voice is at the audible threshold, or is perhaps already a dream.

Noke.

**

I don't know if the dancing erupted spontaneously, or whether someone initiated it. I was there but I wasn't watching, and by the time I realised it had started, it had already been happening for some time.

But I feel fairly certain that Wendy Eva instigated it. Wendy all in white, whirling round the room, her featureless face uplifted to the chandeliers, each swirl and pirouette a masterpiece of grace, and I ask Mrs Campion, plucking on her woollen strings, where Wendy, who died so young, could have learned to dance like that.

She keeps her eyes closed as she answers me.

For all that you're a scholar, thes two things you've never learned, lad. First, thes lots of apples don't come from your orchard. And second, those feet have been dancin' for as long as sap's been risin' in the trees.

I don't understand her, but I can't distract her from her harp again.

I'm excited because I'm beginning to be noticed, a few people have nodded or waved to me. I'm realising slowly that this is my party, and the guests are mine, too. They have made journeys, in their packing crates, especially to be here – all the way from the unsorted sub-structure of me. For the first time in my life I'm not on the periphery. I'm an integral part of my own party. What's more, I want to be. I'm not afraid.

A small but growing group is doing the samba, its twisting line cavorting and side-kicking its way around cast-iron pillars and cows that cartwheel in their sleep. It is led by Mr Trolley in the wheelbarrow, nodding his head like an automaton and holding up a banner which says:

Suffer me now and the sky will be green tomorrow.

The wheelbarrow is pushed by ancient Nellie

Preece, her wart bobbing to the music's rhythm, her customary scowl replaced by the smile that so terrifies me, two smiles in fact, because she's missed her lips entirely with her lipstick, and her mouth that isn't purple seems to be desperately seeking the misplaced one that is.

The Almighty himself, Mr Maddock, turnip hands clamped over Nellie's virgin but newly hopeful thighs, great beard scarfing her as she leans back into his body, is crouching a little as he kicks his legs out Russian style, jangling the bunch of brass keys dangling from his belt, and making a flurry of sparks each time his hobnails scuff the granite flags.

A pair of leather straps are fastened to Mr Maddock's shoulders, with an identical pair around the shoulders of the golden girl behind him. The straps support a stretcher linking her with Mr Maddock. It is made of asbestos, and Lionel lies on it, quietly burning, as ever, arms crossed on his chest, calm eyes open. Perhaps because of Mr Maddock's jigging, Lionel blows a smoke-ring from time to time, emerging, as far as I can tell, from his navel, expanding as it rises, sometimes spreading out across the ceiling, sometimes dipping down, giving Wendy a halo, Mr Trolley a noose and Professor Alam – for once waiting on Uncle Harry's move, which is slow in coming, not because he's contemplating, but because he's feeling what he believes are birth-pangs and wants to savour them – a slowly spinning vortex, which hovers in front of him, causing him to ponder for a while the Law of Conservation of Angular Momentum, and picture Isaac Newton whirling a lucky-stone on the end of a long string.

I see no sign of Alex, although twice, faintly, from high rafters, I hear flute music soaring in the global winds. I can't stretch that high, but nothing will stop me wanting to.

The golden girl is naked, still dripping water from the pond in which she drowned. Her movements are supple, her skin is burnished gold, her hair spills over onto Lionel's, but though his black and her gold crackle and splutter in the flames, they are not consumed, they don't singe or burn. She is humming to the music of Mrs Campion's harp. Stamped onto the wall above her head, illuminated by candle-light, is the Chinese burn that Will Tarporley gave Joyce Farrington, on my first day at school, when she refused to give him a suck of her orange. Its edges are much more visible than its interior, and it looks like a pair of lips, happier by far than those old Nellie plasters on her face.

Behind the golden girl is Old Shelley, drooling a little as he finds she makes no resistance as he moves his hand stealthily around her thighs, never quite touching what he dreams of every night as he masturbates himself to puny climax; what he's touched on hundreds of little boys and girls under his charge; what he's never honestly touched on anyone and never will: not even, I realise, on his wife, of whom all I can remember is a smile that smelled of sugar and a handbag that showed purple when she clicked it open. At last I understand what Mr Fawkes meant when he jerked his thumb towards the headmaster and spoke quietly to Mr Lawless, as I was passing on my way to school:-

That old sod has been corked up all his life. First by his mother, and then that besom he married, who kicks her legs up every Thursday night in Macclesfield.

Johnnie, crazy dancing – fob-watch looped around his neck, and whirling – hangs on to the flaps of Shelley's jacket, whips round, pretends to wipe his arse on them, tickles Shelley behind the ear with a feather, knowing he won't grab it because he won't take his hands from the golden girl's thighs, every so often depressing one nostril and firing through the other a gob of bright green snot which clings to Shelley's jacket as he dances. Shelley has no idea that the boy who japes around behind him has an almost infinite capacity for hatred, and has vowed to make Shelley suffer each time he dies.

The music has slowed, become more plangent, more of a threnody. Johnnie has always been too slippery to touch, so although there are figures behind him as the samba continues, none of them, as they shuffle positions, can grasp him, their hands often reaching out for his wraith-like form, but never quite succeeding in making contact.

The light is darker behind Johnnie, so I'm able to see only parts of these dancers, their hats, outflung arms, a ring of skin between the top of their socks and their trousers. Sometimes I recognise them, sometimes I don't. Then, as my eyes attune to the dark, I realise that most of the shadowy dancers behind Johnnie are, in fact, incomplete, reduced in some cases to the slope of a shoulder, the heave of a fat stomach, a blemish on a pale expanse of forehead.

And so I find not my father, but his smile; and though he's so pared down he's every bit as real and whole to me as if all of him were here. His essence has been somehow distilled into this pair of lips, part open, four or five teeth showing faintly between them. And somehow I know that he'd be just as strongly present if what I perceived of him was his calves – which always looked so unhealthily white when he changed into his bathing shorts on our annual seaside holiday – or the buttons of his waistcoat, or his nose, the hairs up which, when I was small, were so frightening and fierce, so impossible to grow that I knew everyone was lying to me: I'd never grow up, boys could never change into men.

Trampolining by some packing crates, bouncing in and out of a faint shaft of illumination, is a roughly spherical crimson object, tufted with black hairs, and about the size of a football. Its movements are sluggish, rising and falling much more slowly than gravity would normally allow. There is something familiar about it, especially when it radiates pulsating light, deeper than the crimson, which seems to emanate from its interior. But it is only when it misses the trampoline, bounces a few times on the corridor floor, and rolls gravely away from me along the flags, that I wonder if it really is Will's blood-blister.

A small hand is stretched out to me, confident that I will take it. And though I scarcely noticed it at the time, fifty years ago, there is something in the trust with which its palm is open to me that tells me it belongs to the small boy wearing a quiver with two arrows, who was standing, looking lost, at the bottom of Manley Road, and when I went over to him took my hand and said *I want you to be my Daddy*.

I feel my party's pull now, more of an invitation than an urgent need, but I'm not quite ready yet.

**

The samba snake has grown longer, though a few guests have dropped out. Hitler is goose-stepping behind Shelley, and at every stride the black tips of his polished boots stab into the headmaster's plump thighs. Tomorrow Shelley will be lame and wonder why, but nothing can distract him now. Wendy can't bear the idea of touching Hitler, so she's clipped a silk scarf to his leather belt and holds on to it as she twirls her umbrella and kicks higher than I've ever seen.

Mr Campion is rolled up again, but now his scroll is fluted, opening out towards the smoke-filled ceiling, narrowing to a point where the cone's tip meets the floor. He is precessing round the corridor in eccentric whorls and spirals, a drunken spinning-top, a dust-devil.

Loping round them all every ten minutes or so is Zatopek, head rolling so dramatically I'm sure it will fall off. But although his face is as tortured as usual, he's enjoying himself and each time he overtakes us he gives the thumbs-up sign to Lionel, who blows a pair of smoke-rings which shimmer as they rise towards the chandeliers.

Mr Trolley is not feeling well. He's slumped deep into his wheelbarrow, legs splayed over the side, clutching his stomach, groaning. It is Johnnie who realises what's wrong. He snips the old man's trousers around his massive crotch, pulls the flannel aside, reaches deep into the purple dark with forceps. He manipulates them delicately while Ernest massages Mr Trolley's chest and my mother trickles tea onto his face.

Bear down! exhorts Johnnie: *Bear down!*

The refrain is taken up by the spectators: *Bear down! Bear down!*

Mr Trolley grunts and looks determined. My mother fetches a towel:

It'll come in handy when his waters break.

Suddenly Johnnie staggers back, holding the forceps high. There is an explosion of cheers which fades away when we see that what they're gripping is a carrot. Not any carrot, but the same one, fierce and warty, that they stuffed up the old man's arse just as his train set off for Crewe. It has grown prodigiously since then, in Mr Trolley's fertile soil, and the silence is broken by gasps of astonishment which ripple away along the corridor.

Johnnie opens his watch and studies it.

Seven pounds, thirteen ounces, he announces, to great applause.

Mr Trolley gives a sigh of infinite relief and falls asleep. Ernest takes off his coat to make a pillow for him. Uncle Harry, who's been watching avidly, but has mislaid his spectacles, inspects the carrot closely, looks bewildered, shakes his head:

I wonder who fathered this red-faced little bugger.

He reaches deep into the recesses of his smock, hoping to retrieve the eggs he was hatching, but all he comes out with are some sticky shards of shell, and a filament of yolk that dangles from his fingers.

My mother takes the carrot, tucks it in her pinny.

A shame to waste it. I'll give it a good rinse and put it in my stew.

Johnnie, convulsed with laughter, is rolling helplessly round the floor, thumping his stomach when the pain becomes acute. He winks at me and grins. I like him again.

**

The dancing is wilder now, heads thrown back, legs high-kicking. The vitality and abandonment is almost irresistible, but still I hold back, not because I'm frightened but because these are the people with whom I've spent my life: these – largely miscellaneous, warts and all – are the most important inhabitants of a substructure I realise now will never be sorted, will always be chaotic, and it doesn't matter at all.

The light grows dimmer and has a texture to it that seems to be rising from the floor, set into motion by the dancers' feet. As I look closer I find that the granite flags are carpeted to a depth of several inches with what looks like fluff or flecks of lint. I scoop up a handful, study it in the light of a nearby candle. I'm holding a mixture, intimately interwoven, of human hair from Barber Corker's salon and insects, mostly flies, from either Johnnie's jam-jar or the hunks of bleeding meat hanging in Mr Gregory's shop. The flies are dead, or dormant. I wonder if Jordan is somewhere in this graveyard that ripples when breezes pass along the corridor.

The kicking is so fierce and the particles so light they fill the air from floor to ceiling, causing crimson haloes around each candle and a gentle crackling in the flames of Lionel's burning. At the edge of my vision is Barber Corker, bald and small, replenishing the supply by snipping furiously at the unkempt grey hair that droops across the shoulders of the noseless man. A filament from Johnnie's tight black whorls settles on my wrist.

Now, the incense that seeps along the corridor, flirts with shadows scudding round the rafters, the girders, sleeping cows, has deepened, become more potent, so everything and everyone can be seen only through a thickening fog, and then just for a moment. There is no respite. Either I recognise each gesture, facial fragment, artefact, in the moment for which it is in view, or it's gone, and though I know it's part of my history I won't ever identify it or see it again.

And so I recognise the lace from my brown shoes unearthed from an old cupboard, its shiny knot so tight I couldn't even unravel it with pliers. Also the white shirt I wore on my first day to school, its short sleeves allowing a delicious breeze to wash my skin as I trembled in the school-yard because Johnnie had told me I'd have to fight Yonner. A screw of paper Maureen tucked into her inkwell, a kiss a girl blew to me from a passing ferry, the scent of mothballs in my grandmother's hat, the chipped old marble I named Wounded Blue, a spider that crept out of a burning log in a Welsh cottage to find it was still surrounded by flame, a grove of bluebells that looked like the beginning of the world.

All those I can place. I know the stories. But there are just as many that though they are an integral part of my history, I can't put in context: a bloodshot eye in the deepest recesses of a cave, a two-hundred-year-old penny, a dead clock breathing, buttercups sprouting from a rotten shoe, a beggar dancing in the street, corns on an old man's foot, a cake that smells of turpentine, chock of leather against willow before I was born, a girl who willed herself to thin to nothingness, an angel with hiccups, a wooden leg with termites, a hosepipe that wouldn't turn off, a laugh warm enough for baking bread, a hole that passes through the centre of the Earth, an ice-cream spilt on thirsty sand; the notes of a flute played under water.

At last, I take the plunge, join the samba behind Wendy, take hold of her waist. She leans back into me, still twirling the umbrella and kicking high. She turns, brushes my cheek with her featureless face, which tastes of salt.

Her shoe flies off. I leap and catch it. She whirls round, panting through her non-existent mouth, but I won't give it back. She lays her head against my chest.

**

We've not found our way out yet, though it's true we've not been trying hard. Ernest has fallen asleep in this tunnel of warm, translucent flesh that smells of promise. As I look at him, thumb in mouth, occasionally sucking, he seems relaxed and happy. He's achieved the goal he's been seeking all his life.

Which is when I realise that I have not, and that although I offered to accompany him into the blood-blister out of friendship – coupled perhaps with guilt and excitement – I also hoped the journey would help me.

So I slither from the tunnel into a nest of galleries, so tall I can walk upright, though the floor is slippery and a shuffling gait is safest.

Since time cannot be measured inside a blood-blister, I don't know how long it is before I hear the singing; *Bluebells over the White Cliffs of Dover*. I move towards it and duck through an arch into a small chamber. She's standing at the centre, her back towards me, lifting steaming washing from her wicker clothes-basket, taking pegs out of the pocket of her pinny, placing them in her mouth, giving each garment a fierce shake and withdrawing the pegs to fasten it on the washing-line. She's almost finished, and I stand quietly watching as she fixes the last item, one of my father's collarless shirts, in place. Her hair is auburn again and she's wearing her dark-blue frock studded with white spots.

Did you have a nice morning at school? she asks.

She always knew where I was, even when I was hiding.

I'm too podgy these days for those little desks, Mum. And I bet the inkwells have dried up.

She laughs.

You're just in time, love. Lunch is ready. A special treat today. Strawberries. From Alick's. He hasn't had any for months.

Are you sure they won't give me scarlet fever?

She opens her hands, gestures round the chamber.

D'you think anyone would notice, if they did?

She's right, of course. Everything I can see is

some shade of red: squat conical stalactites, pink against the ceiling's deep maroon, as if the act of growing had bled some of their strength away; thinner, longer, even more pallid ones, monotonously dripping onto the floor; flesh formations in the shape of an arch, a beehive, an armchair, a sleeping buffalo; a lake of scarlet liquid with a transparent skin that every so often sighs convulsively. I can just pick out the shapes of the small table and the strawberry bowl sitting on it, but the fruit I know to be there is indistinguishable from the all-pervasive pinks, reds, crimsons.

I approach and she ushers me into the hard-backed chair by the table. I'm glad she shows no inclination to hug or even touch. It's more comfortable to adhere to the old pattern. She fusses round me for a while as I eat the strawberries, which she's sprinkled with sugar, brings me a plate of home-made potato cakes, pours us drinks from the teapot with the broken spout. She doesn't eat with me and I know that if I asked her why she'd say she was waiting for my Dad to come home. She sits opposite me, smiling, our eyes not quite touching.

All this is a preamble, though a necessary one, inducing comfort. No words have been spoken since I sat down, and I don't know how to start. Three questions haunt me. Was she, in life, the angry woman in the coffin? Can I help her in any way, now? Can she help me shed this omnipresent terror of abandonment?

I don't speak these questions, but she knows exactly what they are. She takes each one, in turn, and she looks at me intensely, forcing my eyes to engage with hers and hold their gaze, so that I know that what she tells me will be unvarnished truth. Now I feel her power, and although I never felt it when she was alive, I now realise it was there; she just never chose to wield it.

She raises a single finger, just like Zatopek, and slowly shakes her head.

If you'd allowed your heart to examine your question, you'd know the answer already. It is no. I wasn't angry. A bad start, yes, and wounds that didn't heal, but all in all it was a happy life. I chose to circumscribe it, devote what I could offer to one small sphere, and when I look at my grandchildren, their progeny, I feel my choice was good.

What you saw in the coffin was frustration. With myself. Because my eldest son was floundering and dangerous, and I died before I'd found a way to help him.

Her eyes are still boring into mine, and the response I start to compose shrivels away.

A cloud creeps across the chamber, its whiteness dazzling in magenta light. It envelopes, obscures her and slowly dissipates to reveal her now as the frozen, thin-haired woman in Madelaine's Chapel of Rest. And yes, it's true, it's not anger but frustration I see in that stern face.

She raises two fingers. I wait.

Another cloud reaches her, slowly, dissipates, and then another. Now she's a young woman in white, tennis racquet in her hand. Now she's the mother I first knew, head bent over me, hair tenting my face as I lie in my cot, reaching up to jiggle with my coloured wooden beads. Now she's a pig-tailed girl riding a tricycle, ringing its bell at every corner. Finally, she's in school uniform, at her desk in the front row, a silver star for being good pinned not to her blouse but through her lips, clipping them together so she'll continue, forever, to speak no wickedness. She pushes them forwards and her eyes plead with me to unpin them. I reach across the table and her breath warms my fingers as I try to release her. I squeeze and tug as hard as I dare, until her eyes show pain, but the mechanism is stuck. I shake my head.

She leans further towards me, pouting now, imploring. Bubbles nestle at the almost hidden line of intersection of her lips. Constricted as they are, they're telling me quite clearly what to do.

I grasp the star again and, closing my eyes, yank it as hard as I can. I feel agony sweep through her. For a moment I think I've failed, but suddenly I recoil, the star's points piercing my skin. I hurl it away, open my eyes.

She's a young mother again, sitting back, relaxed, smiling at me, though her gaze is as intense as earlier. Beads of blood form slowly on her lower lip, hang for a moment, fall off onto the table, and are then swallowed by the reds. The tension I'd not noticed has disappeared. She seems at peace.

I feel fulfilled, with nothing more for me to do. We've moved beyond the point at which words have any value. I start to rise but she signals me to halt, and when I'm sitting again she raises three fingers. I close my eyes, count to ten, open them again.

Projected on the cavern wall, distorted by its curvature, is a photo of my mother at the age of three, shopping basket on her arm, at the threshold of a room she doesn't dare to enter. I've known the photo all my life. But as I stare at it, it changes, so subtly each shift is imperceptible, until the figure at the door is transformed into a small boy in a sailor suit. He's looking out from the room into a world he's terrified of going out into. I shiver as I realise that the boy is me. I remember how the roughness of the collar scuffed the skin behind my neck.

She says nothing. Her eyes look tired. I look back at the picture, strive for enlightenment.

Then I'm drowning in the lake and Alex is trying to rescue me.

Swim! she urges, but I clutch her, hold on.

She swipes me across the face, as hard as she can.

Swim for Christ's sake! Only you can do it.

And I do.

I turn to my mother, who is smiling.

It's not so hard, she says.

I nod.

It's almost time to go, but there's one more thing for us to do.

She raises her hands, palms towards me, starts in a gentle voice to chant. I join in.

> *Pat-a-cake, pat-a-cake, baker's man,*
> *Bake me a cake, as fast as you can.*

As we chant, we first clap our hands to the rhythm, then open our palms to each other, clap those together, the touch of her skin against mine delicious.

> *Pat it, prick it, mark it with a B,*
> *Put it in the oven for baby and me.*

I doubt if I was ever happier than at those times, before the rot set in, before I lost the capacity to feel safe. The wallpaper in my bedroom was always warm in those days.

But I can't linger with them now. It is time to leave. We do *Pat-a-cake* once more, her wedding ring glistening, the touch of our hands a little stronger than before.

I look at her this final time. Her lip is still bleeding but the welling of her blood is very slow. She's not just tired, she's exhausted.

I walk away from the table and although I'm tempted to I don't look back. I plunge head-first through a cleft in the chamber wall I hadn't seen before, and I'm gliding through flesh, through viscous mud, which has harboured and constrained me for so long; gliding in the final stages of my life towards my future. At last.

No light, just as before, no touch or smell, but as I slither on I hear the earliest word in my vocabulary, from the oldest voice of all.

Toodle-oo-pom-pom!

I reply to her, and as my speed increases I wait for her response. It does not come. It does not come, and I am glad.

***

Acknowledgements

I am hugely indebted to my editor, Ra Page, for his acuity, energy and insight, leading to many suggestions for change, which undoubtedly improved the novel greatly. Insofar as the work is about anything definable, Ra understands – better than its author – what it is.

The novel has also benefited greatly from the frank and intuitive attentions of my long-time sparring partner, Jennifer Appleseed.

This work could not have been written if a host of people – old friends and enemies, real, fictional or known only in dreams – had not decided to take time away from their lives or deaths, in order to come to my party. I did not invite them – they came of their own volition. In particular, and almost at random, I cite Aunt Lil, Mr Trolley and the noseless man.

Also available from Comma

novels:

Home Is Where
by Heather Beck
(£7.95 ISBN: 1 85754 730 6)

While There Is Light
by Tariq Mehmood
(£7.95 ISBN: 1 857 54729 2)

short stories:

Bracket
a new generation in fiction
Edited by Ra Page
(£9.95 ISBN: 1 85754 685 7)

Hyphen
an anthology of short stories by poets
Edited by Ra Page
(£7.95 ISBN: 1 85754 731 4)

Comma
an anthology
Edited by Ra Page
(£9.95 ISBN: 1 85754 685 7)

Manchester Stories
   parts 1–7
Leeds Stories parts 1–2
Liverpool Stories part 1
Newcastle Stories part 1
Each booklet features 5 to 7 stories each and can be ordered for £1.95 each or 3 titles for £5.

poetry:

Mollusc
by Helen Clare
(£6.95 ISBN 0 9548280 0 3)

All fiction titles available to order from any bookshop, or through Carcanet Press (www.carcanet.co.uk).
Mollusc is available to order from any bookshop, or through Inpress (www.inpressbooks.co.uk).

Find out more about all these books at www.commapress.co.uk